Acknowledgements

Thanks to my husband, Henry, for his unwavering support as a patient listener while the chapters in progress were read aloud to him, and for his helpful comments on the content and the concept of this work.

Thanks also to my daughter, Lynne Green, my painstaking proof-reader, who was invaluable as a stylistic critic to ensure that precise nuances of meaning were achieved.

Thanks to my niece, Carol MacLean, for her enthusiasm for this project, especially when the basic plot line was initially aired.

Thanks to all the people who have bought and enjoyed my previous three historical romances for urging me to write another one.

About the author

Virginia Aitken was born in Preston, but now lives with her husband Henry in Magherafelt, a rural town set in the heart of Northern Ireland.

Having enjoyed a career as a teacher of English and Drama, she is now a freelance educational consultant and writer.

She has written four published novels, three plays performed on the amateur stage, five educational books and two British award-winning short stories.

She is a keen gardener, and when it comes to holidays she and her husband enjoy visiting their grown up family in England, or cruising the French waterways.

Dedicated to

Ian
Lynne
John
Clare

Also by the same author
Oh My Child published in 2002 and 2008
Snowdrops for Ada published in 2004
Red Scar published in 2007

'The Porter Legacy': A Trilogy

Oh My Child is the first in this trilogy, followed by
Snowdrops for Ada and ***Red Scar.***

Set in Ely and Preston and based on actual characters this trilogy traces the changing fortunes and divisions within one family during the nineteenth and early twentieth centuries. Each book can be read separately; they tell independent stories.

When a fortune-teller sees an unusual curve on six-year-old Richard Porter's palm, she predicts that his life will be troubled by family divisions...

Born into a wealthy family in 1816, Richard will one day inherit his father's brewery. His siblings' and cousins' lives are similarly mapped out to run the family estates. But as the years pass, family rifts bring heartache in business and in love. In his twilight years sadly deprived of everything he treasured most – except his small daughter Ada – he realises the gypsy had been right when she saw "a full circle".

An Engaging story spanning 70 years, set in the heart of the Cambridgeshire Fenlands, Virginia Aitken cleverly captures the very essence of life in the nineteenth century. 'The must-read' prequel to *Snowdrops for Ada.*

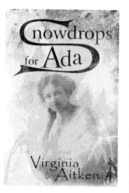

Snowdrops for Ada

Virginia Aitken

In the early morning on the first day of spring, in the year of 1893, Ada was a shivering bundle of excitement. This was the day she had been looking forward to. She was tired of wearing her black taffeta mourning dress with its little detachable and detestable, prickly lace collar. She longed to wear her pink brocade dress again with its long white sash and its twenty-two shiny, satin buttons down the front of the trim bodice. She was only five years old, after all.

It was ever so cold in her bedroom, and the bedclothes were ever so cosy, but neither of these would deter her from getting out of bed and tiptoeing to the curtained sash window. She pulled back the mint-green, velvet drapes to look down on to the walled garden below, her very own secret garden, with its fragile and fading memories. But where she expected to see a host of yellow and purple crocuses under the beech tree, she saw instead an impenetrable blanket of snow, a bleak and hostile white landscape.

Even yet, almost one hundred years on, under the old copper beech tree, and half obscured among dense undergrowth in a long forgotten corner, their wooden garden seat is still here. This is where they once sat together in the moonlight, dreamily looking out across the silvery camomile lawn to a life full of promise.

The once sweeping carriageway to *Red Scar* mansion is now overgrown, and fragments of the sandstone gateposts lie in a tangle of bindweed and ageing brambles at the further end of the estate. There is another gateway today, signposted, directing visitors to follow one-way traffic routes through rows of regimented trees, metallic benches and marble slabs. On one of the cold, vandal-proof benches you can just make out a memorial inscription on a blackening brass plate: "In Memory of Harry and Ada who loved this place".

This is their story.

Preface

Mary Bennet's Chance is a sequel to *Pride and Prejudice* by Jane Austen.

Without compromising Jane Austen's original intentions, characterisation or literary style, this novel traces the story of Mary Bennet, three years after the conclusion of *Pride and Prejudice*.

The year is 1816, the "year without a summer", the year of the Littleport riots, and the year that war-ravaged Europe was recovering after Napoleon's defeat at the Battle of Waterloo.

Twenty-one year old Mary Bennet, the middle of five sisters, is an educated and forward-thinking young woman of her day, but she has resigned herself to a stifling future in the little village of Meryton, looking after her ageing parents. There is no likelihood of finding true love or even finding a husband

On a visit to her aunt and uncle in Cambridgeshire, Mary's world is turned upside down when she meets Charles Tremayne and Fitzroy Sinclair. These two men are to have a lasting effect on her.

CHAPTER I

THE LETTER

Mrs Bennet impatiently waited for the footman to leave the morning room so that she could read the letter he had just delivered to her.

"Oh, my dear Mr Bennet. Do you know who this is from?"

"Indeed, madam, I am neither a clairvoyant nor do I possess superhuman powers to enable me to read a closed letter," he replied, with a sideways glance at his daughter, Mary, to see if she might appreciate this burst of sardonic wit.

"But look at the handwriting!" Mrs Bennet cried, wafting the folded paper in his general direction.

"A hurried missive, with decidedly unruly formation of letters."

"Exactly so! Now do you know who it is from?"

Mary decided to put a stop to her parents' silly conversation which brought no pleasure to either participant. "It is from Lydia," she simply stated.

Mrs Bennet pursed her lips. "Now you have ruined the surprise. To be sure, Mary, you have a talent for spoiling things."

Mr Bennet felt the unfairness of this remark; he was indeed indebted to Mary for keeping Mrs Bennet out of his hearing and sight for most of each day, tending to her incessant emotional ups and downs, as well as her frequent

1

attacks of "nerves". Another glance at Mary showed him that her mother's slight had not gone unnoticed.

"The letter, my dear. Have you forgotten who it is from?"

"Of course not! How can you be so tiresome?" Mrs Bennet broke the seal and unfolded the paper with trembling fingers. There were five lines scrawled in poorly-formed script across the page. "It is from my dear Lydia, my dear Mrs George Wickham," she enthused.

"Then may I suggest you put us all out of our misery and read it? Out loud, if you please, with no embellishments, no gasps, no sighs and no palpitations. It would not do for your favourite daughter to bring on an attack of the vapours."

"*Dearest Mama*, she writes. Oh, how I miss her! Such fun we always had, and now she is gone to Newcastle, she may as well be on the other side of the world."

Here, Mrs Bennet's emotions began to get the better of her and, as she dabbed a tear away with her lace handkerchief, Mr Bennet rose from his chair, ready to quit the room.

"Upon my word, I beg of you, do not leave just yet, Mr Bennet. I have not finished reading the letter."

"Indeed, madam, you have not yet started!"

"My heart is all such a flutter." Dramatically thrusting the page away from her, as if it would do her serious damage should it remain so close to her bosom, she simpered, "Here, Mary, you read it. You spend most of your life reading, so you may as well read this."

Mr Bennet sat down again, fervently hoping that his wife's heart's flutterings would keep her voice at bay until the letter had been read.

Mary began to read, "*July 2nd 1816...*"

"You see, Mrs Bennet, you forgot to read the date," interjected Mr Bennet.

"Pooh! What is in a date?" Mrs Bennet fanned herself, albeit ineffectually, with the limp lace dangling from the cuff of her muslin day dress.

Mr Bennet looked towards the stucco rose in the centre of the ceiling, putting his fingertips together like a man about to pray to a higher authority. "Be so good as to continue, Mary."

"*Dearest Mama, the regiment is to move to Ely. What luck!*"

"Luck?" Mr Bennet muttered under his breath.

Mary barely acknowledged this interruption and continued, "*I shall be going with the regiment, of course, and what larks there will be. So George and I...*"

"Preposterous!" Mr Bennet expostulated.

"My dear?" his wife exclaimed as a half-question with some degree of irritation.

"Why preposterous, Papa?" Mary asked.

"To call her husband 'George'."

Mrs Bennet's patience was threadbare. "Really, Mr Bennet, you are being so irksome. George is your son-in-law's name."

"Lydia should be reminded that he is 'Mr Wickham' to her," Mr Bennet stated firmly.

Mary intervened. She had observed her father's worry that male dominance in the world was under threat, and, as a man with a wife and five daughters, it was understandable that this had been a constant fear in his own life. Mary herself was more progressive in her opinions about the roles of men and women.

"From what I read, it is thought to be more modern to call one's husband by his Christian name," she observed.

"Modern!" Mr Bennet puffed. "Whatever next?"

"Shall I continue?"

"Pray do," Mrs Bennet snapped, but not so much at Mary, who, on the question of Christian names, had sided

3

with her: an occurrence as welcome as it was unusual. She looked in the direction of her obdurate husband.

Mr Bennet nodded his assent, and then shot his wife a quick look of grave forbearance.

"*I shall be going with the regiment, of course, and what larks there will be. So George and I...*" Mary paused momentarily, glancing at her father as he exhaled loudly and noting the contentedly smug expression on her mother's face, "*...will be there on the thirty-first of the month. You and I shall meet up, go to the milliner's, to the tea-shop, have such fun. Father must arrange for you to stay at his sister's in Ely. Your daughter, Lydia.*"

"Must?" Mr Bennet complained.

"Yes, you must," rejoined his wife, now suddenly fully recovered and determined to travel to Ely at the end of the month, there to stay at her brother-in-law John Russell's home, Willow Wood, situated in its own two hundred beautifully maintained acres of drained fenland. With this goal in mind, she began work on her husband straight away. "There is excellent fishing in the lake at Willow Wood... and some of the best shooting rights in Cambridgeshire are on Mr Russell's grounds... and the summer weather is bound to improve, you know... and his library is second to none, should it rain... and it will give my poor heart such pleasure to see Lydia... and there will be soirées and dances... and there may even be some book-learned man there who will marry Mary..."

"My dear!" Mr Bennet interrupted his wife's outpourings. "Marry Mary? The very idea!"

Mary looked down, hurt, folding Lydia's letter over and over until it was barely one inch square.

Mr Bennet continued, "Whatever would you do without her?" Whatever would *he* do without Mary?

Mary loved her mother, as all dutiful girls of twenty-one should do. She saw to her needs and, as daughters go, she was in fact one of the best. All the ladies in the village of

Meryton said so. They also said that Mary was too dull and book-learned to ever marry, and "wasn't that a blessing, as Mrs Bennet would always have someone to look after her, right into her dotage"?

Even though Mrs Bennet might appear to be a woman of mean intelligence, Mary recognised that her mother's heart was in the right place, jumping at every opportunity to ensure that her five daughters were married.

"For what other security could my girls expect when Longbourn has been entailed away to Mr Bennet's cousin?" Mrs Bennet had been often heard to exclaim and explain to any whose attentive ear she secured.

Hence, having listened to her mother's rambling inducements to visit Ely, Mary conceded that her mother was still trying to do what she believed was best for her last remaining unattached daughter.

Three years earlier, Mary had seen how her mother had ridiculously rejoiced in the imprudent match between Mr Wickham, the dashing yet licentious and immoral officer of the —shire regiment, and her youngest and favourite daughter, only just turned sixteen. There had been some unpleasant rumours that George Wickham was a wastrel and a gambler, but Mrs Bennet had insisted that he looked "ever so handsome in his red coat" and she dismissed such rumours as "scurrilous slurs on the family". Mary had held her tongue; she had never trusted the ease with which George Wickham complimented all the sisters for their beauty, including herself, when she knew that she was not noticeably pretty, and unlikely to attract any suitor, unless it be for her musical talents and her knowledge of serious works of literature, historical accounts and scientific treatises. None of the young men of her acquaintance had ever shown a propensity for such academia, despite her mother's efforts to show off such abilities at every social engagement they attended. The ladies of Meryton had even commented within Mary's hearing that she was "the most accomplished young lady in the village and environs".

She had watched her mother work hard with effusive lack of decorum, however well-intended, to secure the affections of rich Mr Bingley for the eldest daughter of the family, the beautiful Jane. It had worked wonders, for Jane was now happily married, with a child expected at Michaelmas.

Mary had understood her mother's disappointment when Mr Bingley had decided to move away from Hertfordshire, taking the beloved Jane with him. Mary suspected that Mr Bingley's two sisters, pretentious and foolishly grandiose by nature, had cast their magic on their brother to ensure that they quit Netherfield Park to be as far away as possible from the undesirable mother-in-law. Visits were therefore less frequent and Mrs Bennet was often thrown into despair, claiming that she was "ill-used, and no one but Jane understood the problems of her nerves".

Mary would have liked to put her arms around her mother to lessen the pain, but her early attempts at affection had been constantly rebuffed by both her mother and her father, so that she now kept her distance and held her tongue. But oh! How she would sometimes like to show her love and be regarded with some kind of affection.

Her father loved her other older sister, Elizabeth, who had married into one of the wealthiest families in the country. She now was the mistress of Pemberley in Berkshire, and at every feasible opportunity Mr Bennet would abandon his study and his books and go to join his dearest Elizabeth and enjoy the fishing in the river which flowed through the grounds of the Pemberley estate. Mary loved to accompany him to the house, so that she could raid the vast library to satisfy her unquenchable thirst for knowledge and book lore, but, as often as not, her mother would refuse to go.

Before the last of these visits, Mr Bennet could be heard comforting his daughter. "Never fear, Mary, my dear, I shall persuade Mr Darcy to lend you two or three weighty tomes for your perusal and digestion, to be returned on my next visit…" he paused for effect, "…when you shall accompany me to Pemberley, if your mother can spare you."

Mrs Bennet had no especial liking for Elizabeth, whom she regarded as headstrong, and she found Mr Fitzwilliam Darcy rather formidable and aloof. She disliked visiting Pemberley.

"I cannot spare her, Mr Bennet, as well you know."

Mrs Bennet would always insist that Mary stay with her at Longbourn for company when Mr Bennet went visiting. However, she sometimes had to give in when confronted by severe looks from her husband and persuasive tactics from Mary.

Kitty was the fourth of the five sisters, and had proved herself to be very impressionable three years earlier under the unruly influence of her younger sister Lydia. Lately, under the sensible guidance of Elizabeth, Mr Darcy and his sister Georgiana, she was much improved, displaying a gentle and easy disposition. A match between her and the newly appointed vicar at Kympton on the Pemberley estate had just been announced. By all accounts, Mr Doorish, the lucky incumbent, was a pleasant and well-meaning sort of man, who was likely to make Kitty "the happiest of women".

Mary was on the point of leaving the morning room with the intention of practising a new piece of music, *Quasi una Fantasia*, Mr Beethoven's *Piano Sonata Number 14 in C sharp minor*, thinking that she would have a few uninterrupted weeks to herself in Longbourn to indulge herself at the pianoforte while her mother and father were away in Ely.

"Now, Mary," Mrs Bennet's tone already sounded insistent, "you are to come with us to Ely. It is settled that your father will spend his time fishing and shooting on the Willow Wood estate."

"Nothing is settled, my dear. My sister knows nothing as yet of your intention to visit and we do not know if it will be convenient."

"Tush! Of course it will be convenient."

Mr Bennet sighed. He was not of a disposition to impose himself and his family on his sister, Ruby, some fifteen years younger than himself.

Mrs Bennet continued her line of thought and addressed Mary once more. "And when Lydia returns to her dear Wickham, as indeed she must from time to time, you know, I shall need you to play and sing for me, for I am sure that your aunt and uncle Russell can have nothing much to offer by way of entertainment."

"My dear," remonstrated Mr Bennet, "you have only met them twice in your life and can hardly be in a position to make such a critical statement. As I recall, my brother-in-law Russell is a sociable sort of fellow, despite some out-dated views on slavery, and my sister was ever courteous."

Mary was intrigued once the topic of slavery had been broached. With the abolition of the slave trade well and truly established throughout the British Empire these past nine years, Mary looked forward to the abolition of slavery itself, and, had she been a man and a member of parliament to boot, she would have been tirelessly campaigning for immediate abolition, along with William Wilberforce and others. She wondered how her uncle was deemed to be out-dated. She was about to ask her father, but her mother was still engaged in her own campaigns.

"With two young daughters taking up all their hours, like all daughters do," (Mrs Bennet was not going to give up on this point), "as you would know if you had spent less time in your study these past twenty-odd years," she added, as a special dig at her husband, "there will be precious little time left for entertaining."

In reality, Mrs Bennet had spent more time in her dressing room with her nerves than he had spent in his study.

Mary felt honour-bound to say, "Indeed, sir, I should be happy to accompany you and Mama." There would have been no advantage anyway to requesting that she stay in Longbourn for the duration, no matter how tempting Mr Beethoven's sonata might be.

"There you are, my dear, your wish has been granted. Mary will be there morning, noon and night to play your favourite ditties and so many Scottish airs that you may dance till midnight, or until your palpitations beg you to stop, for pity's sake!"

CHAPTER II

AN EVENING'S ENTERTAINMENT

As it happened, an entertainment was arranged for that very evening at the Philipses' house in Meryton. Mrs Philips was Mrs Bennet's younger sister. Their father, Mr Gardiner, had been the attorney in Meryton, and Mr Philips had been first his apprentice and then his partner. With the father dead and buried for the past ten years, Mr Philips was now the sole Meryton attorney, a highly respected man of the law. He and his wife lived in a spacious, comfortable town house, a former seventeenth-century hostelry, in the centre of Meryton.

Mr and Mrs Philips were gregarious people who loved nothing better than a get-together to socialise, set the fashion, have fun and meet new friends and old. After dinner, there were to be a few jolly hours of singing, and dancing for those who were energetically inclined, or whist for those who preferred mental exercise of a kind. The weather had been so continuously and strangely dull during the past few months that this kind of entertainment, which was usually a feature of autumn and winter soirées, had been brought forward to this particular July evening.

At seven o'clock, in the light of a copper sunset sky, you may be sure that Mrs Bennet alighted from their carriage with an alacrity which would have done justice to a woman twenty years her junior, and belied her frequent physical ailments. She impatiently fidgeted while the housekeeper attended to her cloak and bonnet. She had barely stepped over the drawing room threshold, blocking her husband's and Mary's entry into the room, before excitedly regaling her sister with the delights of the intended visit to Ely.

"Oh, Sister, Sister! Such news!"

"News, Sister?"

"Yes, it is all settled."

"Settled, Sister?"

"I am to see dear Lydia! Dear Mrs Wickham!"

"Is she to stay with you, Sister?"

"Mr Bennet has sent a letter post-haste to his sister, and we shall be in Ely at the end of the month! Such a treat to see Lydia again! Oh, Sister! I can hardly breathe for all the excitement!"

Mrs Philips knew that she was unlikely to elicit any more detail from her excitable sister about how and why this turn of events had come about. She was already thinking ahead. She would miss her sister's company. They called with one another at least twice a week.

"Shall you be gone long, Sister?"

"Four weeks, for after that, you know, dear Jane and her Mr Bingley are to stay with us for a fortnight on their way to London."

"And is Mary to go too?"

"I am sure Mary can speak for herself," Mrs Bennet said, turning round to where Mary stood behind her, still in the panelled hallway with its old oak beams, for Mrs Bennet had progressed no farther. "Stop hanging back, girl!" she exclaimed, frowning at her daughter.

At this point Mrs Philips guided her sister further into the drawing room, allowing both Mary and Mr Bennet to enter and meet with the other guests, dignitaries and friends from Meryton and beyond, where they were already gathered.

Mrs Philips gently asked Mary whether she would be accompanying her parents to Ely.

"Once it is all settled, I shall be in a position to answer you properly. As yet, it is just a plan, but it will be my pleasure to go with them. They both wish it."

Mrs Philips looked hard at Mary, whose expression gave nothing away, for she was a loyal daughter and would never suggest that she might be in any disagreement with her parents' wishes.

The discerning Mrs Philips had often noticed that beneath her niece's serious expression there was a gentleness in her features, which were far from unattractive. With more care and attention to her wavy chestnut hair as a frame for her soft brown eyes and rose-touched cheeks, along with a lightness of spirit and some gentle outward display of emotion, she could be very pretty indeed. And if Mary spent less time reading and more time sewing, then she could adorn herself with more eye-catching, feminine dresses to show off her well-formed, feminine figure to greater advantage. Perhaps she would suggest a trip to the drapers to buy some silks, and then engage the services of Mrs Snell, her dressmaker.

With no children of her own, Mrs Philips had always done as much as possible to arrange evening entertainments for the young people. Now that only Mary remained at home, all of her energies were directed towards the last of her five nieces who was still to find a husband. However, there were so few suitable young men in the neighbourhood that it was well-nigh impossible to play matchmaker for Mary. Even Mr Philips's apprentice in his attorney business, Mr Bolton, a serious and well-read young man who would have suited Mary admirably as a husband, had unfortunately removed himself from this enviable position by finding himself a rich widow in Bath and was to be married in the autumn.

"I understand that you are to be congratulated, Mr Bolton," Mary said, whilst seated beside the young lawyer at the oval cherry-wood dinner table. She had no inkling that her aunt had had the two of them previously singled out for matrimonial bliss, and so was feeling no sense of pique or disappointment. He was a genial enough man, she thought, and not unattractive, his fair hair shining gold in the candle light, but he was too narrow-minded. She had decided on this opinion a few months earlier at Mr and Mrs Philips's Easter soirée, when she had ventured on to the subject of the ending of the war against France by the victory at the Battle of Waterloo.

"Mr Bolton," she had begun, "now that Napoleon has been defeated, do you think France can ever regain some semblance of normality as a monarchy again?"

Mr Bolton had studied her face a trifle too patronisingly for Mary's liking, then gave voice to a firmly held dictum. "Women should not worry their pretty little heads about such matters," he had said.

Mary had said nothing more on the subject. She had been silenced, not so much by his opinion, but rather because she was not willing to waste her opinion on unwilling ears. She would never again be disposed to discuss any of her thoughts on military victories, past or present, with her uncle's apprentice; nor any other weighty topic, for that matter. She would keep to pleasantries, or listen patiently to the ineffective, jejune topics which he might deem suitable for female minds.

"Ah, yes, Miss Bennet!" Mr Bolton agreed, raising his wine glass as a toast to himself. "I am the luckiest of men. A chance visit to Bath resulted in my meeting with Mrs Maria Tamworth, a recently widowed lady of some fortune, and we fell in with one another and before we knew it we had agreed to be married." Here Mr Bolton took a breath of satisfaction about his luck, before adding, "You will have the pleasure of meeting her when she visits Meryton at the end of the month."

"It may be that I shall be out of the county at that time. I should be very disappointed to miss meeting her."

"After we marry, there will be many opportunities for you to meet. I am sure the two of you will like one another exceedingly well."

Mary nodded her head in acknowledgement of the compliment. "Is she originally from Bath?"

This question set Mr Bolton off in a long explanation of Mrs Maria Tamworth. "Not at all; she moved to Bath when she married. She is the daughter of a clergyman in Bristol. In fact, he has kindly agreed to officiate at our nuptials," and he continued to extol her virtues, her money, her generosity, her family, her sewing, her tapestry work, her reading of gothic novels, and he even rejoiced in the fact that she was tone deaf and unable to sing or play an instrument. He once again insisted that Mary and she would like one another prodigiously. Mary doubted that they would have much in common.

She was quite relieved when dinner was over and the ladies retired to the drawing room, while the gentlemen, including Mr Bolton, remained to enjoy a fine vintage port, specially brought up from Mr Philips's cellar and decanted that very morning. She had heard enough of Mrs Maria Tamworth to last her for some weeks or even months! But it was clear that, as Mrs Bolton, she would be an inevitable addition to the Meryton social whirl, especially at the Philipses' house, and Mary would therefore strive to like her for her aunt and uncle's sake.

When the men finally joined the ladies, two card tables were set up ready for whist. The footman served the ladies with a sweet malmsey wine and the gentlemen with a fine brandy. Mary had barely taken a sip of her post-prandial wine when she found herself addressed by her uncle Philips.

"Come, now, Mary!" he expansively said as he took her by the arm and led her to the pianoforte, "we are all waiting for you to try out our new instrument, sent directly from Hamburg. It promises to be one of the finest of its kind, well suited to your excellent powers."

How could Mary resist? She never needed much encouragement to play for any group of assembled guests, never refused an opportunity to show off her skills at the keys, and the promise of a new instrument was incentive enough in its own right. She had sat down to play, back straight and slender fingers poised ready to begin the adagio movement of Mozart's *Piano Sonata Number 14 in C minor*, which she knew was one of her aunt's favourites, when her mother's voice rose above the general hubbub of chatter.

"I insist you play my favourite Scottish air."

"You have many favourites, Mama," Mary said, smiling at her mother. "Is it one of Mr Thomson's new collection, *The Select Scottish Airs*?"

"You know the one I mean, with the words by that writer."

"You mean the poet Mr Robert Burns, Mama?" Mary replied, politely enough.

"Whoever it may be, Mary, but do get on and play." Mrs Bennet was becoming frustrated. "Anything to liven up the party," she added, pointedly nodding in the direction of Mr Walker, whose brandy glass was balancing at a precarious angle between his finger and thumb, and Mrs Adams, whose lorgnette had already slipped from her hand, coming to rest in her capacious lap. These were the two elderly guests with whom she was to play whist, who looked more as if they were ready to have a cat-nap after the generous dinner portions eaten not above one hour before.

There was precious little inducement for a young lady of one-and-twenty to sit playing whist with those who were one-and-seventy, or indeed with Mr Bolton, even though youth was on his side. So Mary settled for her mother's favourite Scottish air, *Comin Thro' the Rye*. It was undoubtedly one of the liveliest tunes in her repertoire, but, even with her more modernist views, she would not have sung the words of this ballad in public for all the tea in

China. She half wondered what the upright Mr Bolton would think, and whether Mr Walker would open an eye, if she were to sing the story of a man's yearning to kiss *Jenney's a'weet poor body* in the secluded glen.

"Your daughter is a wonder, ma'am," offered Mrs Osmond, whose foot was to be seen tapping beneath her taffeta gown.

"Oh, yes! She takes after me, you know, for her love of music!" answered Mrs Bennet, whose face was alight with the fun and jollity of the air which Mary played.

To a more educated, aesthetic ear, Mary's touch on the keys was accurate and most proficient, but lacking in feeling. But none of the present party, including Mary herself, was aware of this singular deficiency, so she obliviously played on well into the night.

CHAPTER III

THE EXPEDITION

The next day, after breakfast, Mary settled herself down to reading in the parlour, while her mother was occupied entertaining her sister, Mrs Philips, in the morning-room, enjoying one of their regular tête-à-têtes, filled with local village gossip and trivia, tittle-tattle gleaned the evening before. She was looking forward to an hour or two of undisturbed reading at the open window on the inset window seat with its finely-worked floral tapestry cushions.

But the light was so peculiar. Although it was a cloudless sky, the sun appeared diffuse and cast blurred, uncertain shadows as it shone through the south-east facing windows. It was almost as if there were a light mist or fog high up in the air, blocking out the full strength of the summer sun's rays.

Taking her book with her, she ventured outside with the intention of making her way to the shrubbery to sit in the hexagonal gazebo, the one her father now called "Mary's hermitage". She passed the walled vegetable garden where Mr Styles, their ancient retainer who was responsible for growing enough bottling fruit and vegetables to store for the winter, could be heard muttering crossly to himself.

"Good morning, Mr Styles."

"Good morning, Miss Bennet," Mr Styles said, doffing his cloth cap and straightening up his back.

"You do not appear to be your usual cheerful self," Mary observed.

"That I am not, miss. The beans and carrots have almost failed this year, what with this poor summer." He leant on his spade and shook his head. "I doubt there will be enough plums and raspberries for bottling."

"This is indeed worrying." Mary was thinking of the winter months ahead, not only for her own family, but for the other families who depended on the produce from their land.

"The worst crop since the eighties," Mr Styles announced.

"Indeed!"

"I blame that volcano on the other side of the world."

Mary had read Mr Raffles's and Mr Zollinger's published notes on volcanic activity and its effects, and she had come to the conclusion that the present dull weather in England was because of the recent eruptions of Mount Tambora on Sumbawa Island on the other side of the world. But to hear Mr Styles, their gardener, come up with this same opinion was somewhat unexpected.

"Same as 1784," he continued, leaning on his spade handle. "I know the exact year, because that were the year my father died. I remember some volcano in Iceland blew its top."

"That would have been Laki volcano," offered Mary.

"That it were, miss," Mr Styles said, remembering that name from his youth. "Laki! That were it: Laki. Exactly the same problems with the weather and the crops."

"So I believe."

Mary had read Mr Benjamin Franklin's paper on the persistent dry fog caused by the eruption of Laki in Iceland and Mount Asama in Japan, with devastating effects on crops in the northern hemisphere. There had been terrible resultant starvation and widespread disease, not to mention civil unrest and even revolution in France.

"It were a bad year."

Such an understatement, thought Mary.

"Let us hope things will improve, Mr Styles," she said, with genuine worry, as she prepared to walk on.

"I doubt they will." He shook his head sadly. "Not for a year or two."

"Good day to you, Mr Styles."

"Good day to you, miss."

Mary made her way towards the gazebo down the path between the beds of perennials. The lupins, hollyhocks and delphiniums, which Mary marvelled at each year, had this year produced only a few stunted flowers, a disappointment to Mary, who liked to pick garden flowers to deck the house.

She sat in her "hermitage" and opened up a recently acquired book, *A Vindication of the Rights of Woman* by Mary Wollstonecraft, published in 1792. She knew that there was outrage when the book first appeared; the unacceptable notion of female suffrage had reared its ugly head and needed to be shot down! Now, twenty-four years later, the controversy still continued. Mary knew that this book was still regarded as subversive and revolutionary. She was intrigued.

She had already read Miss Wollstonecraft's book *Thoughts on the Education of Girls*, which was based on personal experience as a teacher in the girls' school which she had founded. Such progressive ideas had been deliberately ignored by prelates and educationalists of the day.

Mary was just reading Mary Wollstonecraft's views on her society, a society which expected women to be *docile and attentive to their looks to the exclusion of all else* in a state of *ignorance and slavish dependence*, when she was surprised and a trifle irritated to find herself interrupted by Mrs Hill, the housekeeper, who was out of breath after running down the garden path.

"Oh, Miss Bennet," she gasped, clutching her bosom as if she would expire then and there, "you are needed in the morning room immediately."

"Why, whatever is the matter?" asked Mary, fearing some accident had occurred.

"Your mother and Mrs Philips," Mrs Hill puffed, "they want to speak with you immediately."

Mary gathered her book and her skirts and quickly made her way back to the house, fearing some emergency, Mrs Hill struggling to keep up with her on the gravel path.

When Mary entered the morning room, her mother and Mrs Philips were contentedly seated, drinking tea and indulging in some of Cook's newly baked scones.

"What is the matter, Mama?" asked Mary.

"My dear, you are to go to Summerton tomorrow with your aunt, though how I shall manage without you for the day, I cannot imagine."

"It will have to be two days," announced Mrs Philips. "We shall stay at the Crown Hotel overnight."

"Two whole days!" Mrs Bennet looked as if she might weep.

"Sister, Sister," cried Mrs Philips. "Do not distress yourself!"

"But what am I to do?"

"Have a well-earned rest tomorrow, perhaps a little embroidery, or perhaps Mary will lend you the book she is reading."

Mary wondered with some degree of kindly amusement what her mother would make of such radical writing. In a momentary flash into a possible future, if such things as female suffrage ever came to pass, she doubted that her dear mama would cope in a world where women had more independence and were encouraged to develop their talents in such a way as to be of benefit to others.

Would Mrs Philips fare any better in such a utopian world? Mary thought she would, for she certainly seemed to accept more responsibility for her own actions and the entertainment of others.

"A gentle walk in the shrubbery the following day, Sister," Mrs Philips suggested in commanding tones. "And we shall be back before you know it."

"Two whole days!" Mrs Bennet continued to moan.

"We shall bring you back some delicacy to your liking," Mrs Philips promised, to soothe her distraught and helpless sister. On a more practical note, she added, "You cannot expect us to travel sixteen miles to Summerton and do shopping and visit the dressmaker and make a return journey, all in one day!"

Mrs Bennet saw the truth in all this, and set about eating another buttered scone.

"May I ask the purpose of this visit?" Mary now enquired, abandoning all hope of reading for two days at the very least.

Visits to Summerton were very rare. Indeed, Mary had only been there twice in her life, both times with her father. The first of these visits had been four years earlier to order a new pianoforte which her father insisted she should have, "to entertain your mother", he claimed. They decided upon a Broadwood grand piano, a large and robust iron-framed instrument, and one of the first to be built with six octaves, all of which meant that Mary would now be able to play the new works of Ludwig van Beethoven and Joseph Hadyn, whose music spanned more than the more usual five and a half octaves.

The second time Mary had accompanied her father had been just the year before, when he went to purchase a brace of matching Italian game-pieces. It was certainly not the norm for a young lady to be seen in the gunsmith's, but Mr Cousins, the proprietor, soon realised that Mary was more knowledgeable about firearms than some of the enthusiasts who frequented his premises were. Not that she had ever used a gun – indeed, her father would not entertain the very idea – but she had read much about them and their comparative performances on the battlefield, on the moors and on estates during the grouse-shooting season. When she had started conversing with Mr Cousins about the differences between matchlocks, wheel locks and flintlocks, her father had looked at her with a degree of admiration and apology, lest Mr Cousins should think his daughter a little unladylike. But Mr Cousins had been delighted to talk to her and had even asked her opinion on the raised grape-leaf silver inlay decorating the two Italian flintlock pistols in which Mr Bennet had shown an interest, so that he might clinch a rapid sale.

"Anything is better than that dreadfully florid 'Renaissance' style of engraving you find on some fire-arms," opined Mary, with Mr Cousins nodding in agreement. Mr Bennet was not sure what she meant.

When Mary later commented that she herself rather fancied the Italian percussion blunderbuss, with a pirate's head butt plate, her father drew the line at such silliness and put an end to the visit!

Mrs Bennet, finishing her mouthful of cherry scone and blowing away the remnants of flour on her fingertips as fast as she could to answer the question before her sister could, blurted out, "You are to have some pretty clothes." Swallowing hard, she said, "Your aunt and uncle have decided this, and there is no stopping them once they have made up their minds, though I am sure it will only spoil you."

"Oh, I see," said Mary, looking down at the plain blue morning dress she was wearing. Standing tall and proud, yet stinging with indignation, she smiled and added, "How very kind of you."

On the journey to Summerton the following day, Aunt Philips explained as best she could without hurting her niece's feelings. "My dear, you have so few opportunities to get out and about. You are a very dutiful daughter, but with

22

this trip to Cambridgeshire at the end of the month, you'll need a range of clothes to wear. There will be parties and soirées, balls and visiting. Now, it doesn't matter here in Meryton if you wear the same clothes, because we are all friends, but in other company it does matter."

Mary was beginning to see herself as others saw her now. Always wearing the same clothes! Dull! Dutiful! Indulged and forgiven because they were all "friends"! She also realised that her aunt was genuinely trying to help her to be more acceptable in society, something that her parents failed to do. Was her aunt trying to make her marriageable? Mary had nothing against marriage. Indeed, she would have married Mr Collins, her father's cousin, had he asked her, and she would have made him happy and wiser. But he had not asked her and turned to a dull and unattractive neighbour instead.

So, with the view that there might be two sides to what Mary Wollstonecraft had to say about women's position in society, it was with a good grace and understanding that she embraced the day's shopping.

Summerton was a pleasant, tree-lined town with numerous arcade shops set back from wide pavements. They entered the first establishment, Harvey's Draper's, to buy some pretty fabrics and accessories for evening wear. Her aunt insisted on pink silk, lemon tulle, lilac muslin, cream voile and periwinkle blue taffeta. These were to be delivered immediately to Mrs Snell, the dressmaker, for her to consider appropriate patterns.

Then they went to Simpson's general store, where there was shelf-upon-shelf of day wear materials, stacked so high that to reach the top ones a ladder had to be used. Poor Mrs Simpson, a plump woman, was frequently out of breath and suffering from real palpitations after a bout or two of precarious ascents and descents of the said ladder. She never understood why her customers seemed to ask to see the top bolts of fabric so frequently: her customers never understood why she should keep the most popular ones so high up!

Mrs Philips, undeterred, asked to see the purple velvet roll from the shelf next to the top. "This will do very nicely for your new long-hooded cloak, neatly trimmed with swan's down. This unusually dull weather seems set to continue, so you'll need something warm to travel about in. I am sure Mrs Snell can make you a matching bonnet, with satin ribbons. And you will need a light cloak too, and another shawl for inside. The Russells' house is bound to be draughty. These big houses always are. Let me see what fabrics you have, Mrs Simpson, if you please."

While the good lady was climbing the wooden rungs once more, Aunt Philips took Mary's hand. "How pretty you will be, my dear. My, how I wish I were your age again!"

"The young folks now have such choice," wheezed Mrs Simpson, on her way down the ladder, with rolls of black gauze and pink sarsnet for the cloaks and a roll of the popular Paisley design for an Indian shawl. "In our day we had to make do with a couple of frocks and one shawl, year in year out. Ah, well, times change. But it is good for business, so I am not complaining. Now, is there anything else I can get for you?"

"What would you suggest as something special?" asked Aunt Philips.

"I have got the very thing. I keep it under the counter. It is the new French fabric, made on a Jacquard loom. Here you are," she enthused, producing a length of fine fabric, an intricate cross weave in deep lavender. "Look at the patterns in the weave!"

Mary had read about the modern Jacquard, named after its inventor Joseph Marie Jacquard. It was a kind of apparatus with perforated cards for controlling the warp threads so that intricate designs could be woven.

24

"Just feel the fabric!" Mrs Simpson encouraged both her customers.

Mary took off her glove and gently ran her fingers across the embossed weave, marvelling at the invention which could produce such a delicate fabric on a weaver's loom. When she looked at the material from one angle, the floral patterns in the weave looked light mauve, and when she looked at them from another angle, they appeared to be purple. Like magic!

"It is beautiful," Mary softly said, putting her glove back on.

"I believe the ladies like to have a riding habit made of Jacquard."

"A riding habit!" cried Aunt Philips. "Of course! I had forgotten entirely that you will need attire for riding in your uncle's estate."

Mary had ridden horses from time to time while visiting Pemberley, but she was not a particularly proficient horse-woman.

"Aunt, perhaps this will be an unnecessary expense," she said quietly.

"Please indulge me, Mary! Now, say no more, my dear."

Mrs Simpson continued, "And may I suggest a crisp white cotton chemisette to complement it and complete the ensemble?"

After purchasing cottons for undergarments and petticoat, lace for the hems and a selection of ribbons, netting and feathers to adorn the evening dresses, Aunt Philips instructed Mrs Simpson to send everything over to Mrs Snell before the end of the day. The account was settled and the milliner's establishment was the next port of call, but not before they entered the confectionery shop to buy Mrs Bennet some violet creams, her favourite chocolates, filled with soft violet-scented fondant cream.

At the end of the day, after a delicious dinner at the Crown Hotel, Mary lay in the crisp white starched sheets of her bed, her head fairly swimming with all that had happened during the day: Harvey's array of fine fabrics; Mrs Simpson's breathing problems and the intricate Jacquard design; the milliner who fussed about Mary's hair and said she would have to "do something about it" if any hat was to look its best on her head. Finally, there was Mrs Snell, the tiniest lady, who was not above four feet in height and needed a set of steps to reach up to Mary's shoulders when measuring her and draping materials this way and that, who talked incessantly about fashions of the moment and her favourite book, *The Mirror of Graces: or the English Lady's Costume*, whose anonymous author called herself "a Lady of Distinction".

All the garments were to be ready and sent to Longbourn within a fortnight, and Mary drifted off to sleep with snippets from *The Mirror of Graces* ringing in her ears.

In the morning the arms and bosom must be completely covered to the throat and wrist, the Lady of Distinction was advising.

Mary cheerfully imagined herself visiting fashionable Ely folks and walking along the pavements with her purple cloak swirling around her.

But when she thought about attending balls in one of her new low-cut evening dresses, she was less confident, and not wholly convinced by the Lady's assertion that *the bosom and shoulders of a very young and fair girl may be displayed without exciting much displeasure or disgust.*

In fact, Mary thought fashions of the time had gone too far!

CHAPTER IV

THE UNEXPECTED

"Oh no, sir, you'll not get there tonight." So said Sarah Nonesuch, the serving girl at the Lamb Hotel, the posting house in Ely, which catered for travellers journeying between London and Lynn, Cambridge and Upwell.

"But we have to get there before nightfall," Mrs Bennet insisted.

Not to be deterred, Sarah, who had dealt with many an awkward customer after a tiring journey, tried to mollify this travel-weary lady. "It's a good three mile and only an half hour to nightfall, and no transport to be had at this late hour."

"But what is to be done, Mr Bennet?" enquired his wife peevishly. "Where are we to sleep? Oh! My poor nerves!"

"Be so good as to fetch the landlord," Mr Bennet commanded, almost at the end of his tether.

"It'll have to be the morning. No transport to be had..." Sarah could be heard muttering as she walked down the fifteenth-century oak-panelled hallway, outside and across the mews courtyard to the coach-house where the landlord would be found, there overseeing the new ostler's handling of the hot and steaming post horses which had just brought the Bennets on the second part of their journey.

When Mr Bennet had finally managed to get his business interests completed, it was the first week in August before he, his wife and Mary were able to make their journey to

Ely. Mrs Bennet had been frustrated with the delays, miserable about the wasted days of not being able to see her dear Lydia at the end of July as hoped, altogether out of sorts even at the start of their journey from Longbourn, and worse by the time they had transferred from their own carriage onto the post-chaise in Cambridge.

It had been a long and somewhat uncomfortable journey to Ely, taking most of the day. As the pretty undulating Hertfordshire countryside gave way to the flat and watery lines of Cambridgeshire with its many traditional windmills and a few new power-driven mills and pumps, Mary and her father listened to the fractious grumblings of Mrs Bennet. It was only when they saw "the Ship of the Fens", Ely's towering cathedral, in the distance that Mrs Bennet agreed to look out of the post-chaise window and admitted it was "passable". Let it be said that her comment was an understatement of great proportions, because Ely Cathedral, the ancient seat of Queen Etheldreda, was as fine a testimonial monument to Christianity to be seen anywhere in the land. It looked ethereally beautiful, almost silhouetted against the diffuse, ruddy evening sky.

However, the fact that Mr Russell, Mrs Bennet's brother-in-law, was not at the hotel to meet them was almost the last straw for her, and for her two companions.

"Come and sit in the parlour, Mama," said Mary, taking her mother firmly by the elbow and gently propelling her in the direction of a small front room with leaded windows.

"There is no need to push me so hard, Mary. Just like your father!" she huffed. "Always were, always will be!"

Mary and Mr Bennet looked at each other with eyebrows gently raised in mutual understanding.

Once seated on the crimson, velvet, cushioned armchairs which dotted the room, it would have been possible for Mary to look out on to the main street and see in the distance the spire of St Mary's church set against the mulberry-copper glow of the sunset sky, had Mrs Bennet not continued a ceaseless barrage of complaints, which had to be attended to.

"Father will see to everything, if there really is no carriage," Mary said in as calm a voice as she could muster, and, turning to Mr Bennet she said squarely, "will you not, sir?"

"Ah, yes!" he replied positively, yet he offered no solution to the unexpected problem.

Mary looked directly and steadily at her father. "Surely we can stay the night here and go on to Willow Wood in the morning," she suggested, with a degree of authority and decision.

"Well spoken, my dear," Mr Bennet's spirits were reviving with this sensible suggestion. "Though, rack my brains as I will, I can conceive of no possible reason why my brother-in-law should not be here to meet us, especially after such detailed, precise arrangements.

Mary had to agree. "And not forgetting the daily exchange of notes and instructions between Mama and Aunt Russell, once the visit was agreed. It is all very peculiar, but I am sure everything will be resolved."

Just then, Henry Rance, the whiskered and rotund landlord who had taken over from Robert Genn some eight years earlier, entered the parlour. He and his wife were popular as landlord and landlady, always providing their customers with delicious evening fare of local eels caught in wicker basket traps made by generations of the Gotobed family, or succulent duckling with asparagus, followed by Cottenham cheeses and all washed down with first-class ales. For entertainment, though it might have been frowned upon by some less gregarious souls of Ely, the Rances even had a cock-pit for fighting cocks and gambling, right under the very noses of the cathedral elders.

"Now, in the present circumstances," said Mr Rance, "it seems you'd be better staying here tonight. We have two fine rooms upstairs." Then, looking at Mrs Bennet, whose lips had tightened, he quickly added, "Three, if you'd prefer."

"Three, thank you, landlord," said Mr Bennet, with a slight show of resignation, born of almost twenty years of celibacy. Neither Mrs Bennet, nor he, to be fair, had taken the chance of yet another daughter. Daughters were expensive.

Mr Rance, standing in the doorway, arms akimbo, with an ominous expression developing under his ginger bushy eyebrows: "I'll send over one of the stable lads to Mr Russell's home, to find out how the poor young woman is faring."

"Who do you mean?" asked Mary and Mr Bennet together.

Even Mrs Bennet was gathering herself up to demand, "What poor young woman?"

"Haven't you heard?" Mr Rance paused. The Bennet party were obviously oblivious. "That is why Mr Russell didn't come to fetch you." He stared at the trio, incredulous. "Do not you know? The gossip of the town, it is. Such a sad business!"

"Come on, man!" Mr Bennet said. "Keep us in suspense not a second longer."

But Mr Rance leant back on his heels, folding his arms. He enjoyed a sense of the dramatic.

"Please continue!" Mr Bennet was more than a little concerned. "What young woman?"

"What sad business?" interjected Mary somewhat curtly. She was not disposed to be patient with those who wasted other people's time.

"The governess in his employ is at death's door." Mr Rance paused for effect. Like all who have first or even second hand knowledge of tragedy, and in the style of all good landlords who like to keep their customers entertained long enough to buy more fine ale, nothing pleased him more than a good, juicy story to tell. "A tragedy! I didn't see the accident, you know, but others that did say that she'd brought her governess's chaise to a halt beside a hitching post. She'd no sooner put her foot out on the ground, right beside Oliver Cromwell's house of old, one foot on the right beside the big wheel of the vehicle, the other still inside, than one of our new constables, appointed on account of the rioters…"

"Rioters! Oh dear, Mr Bennet, whatever next?" Mrs Bennet anxiously started to fan herself.

"Oh, yes. You've surely heard of the Littleport rioters." Mr Rance nodded vigorously, enjoying this detail in the retelling of the episode.

"Surely that whole sorry business has been settled," said Mr Bennet, "or we should not have come at all."

"There are still supporters about. They still need to be kept in check, kept off the street, to stop them from rallying. Looters and pillagers, the lot of them!"

"Are we to be killed in our beds?" Mrs Bennet gasped.

"Lord, no!" Mr Rance assured the distraught lady. Remembering his sense of propriety, he said, "Excuse me, ma'am. That is why a new regiment from Bury St Edmunds is here. To keep the peace."

Mr Bennet remembered the account in the weekly periodical. "But surely the five ring-leaders were hanged here a fortnight ago, and the rest of the rioters are in the gaol."

"Not all, you see. Some have been deported for ever to Botany Bay. And their relatives are angry. Who knows what they will do, if not kept in check?"

"Oh dear, Mr Bennet, will we be safe? And poor Lydia, trapped in a very hornet's nest!"

"Peace, Mama," whispered Mary, patting her mother's arm soothingly. Turning to Mr Rance, she said, "Let us hear the rest of the circumstances surrounding the governess. You were telling us about one of your new constables?" Her voice rose in intonation as an invitation for him to continue the original story.

"Stupid fellow with a pea brain tried out his muzzle-loading musket in the street. He was using a stone, on account of none of them being issued with any more lead balls, now that the rioting is supposedly over. He discharged the shot right beside the governess's chaise. Fired in the air, of course, but it was enough to frighten the pony. The poor piebald creature reared up in terror; the door of the carriage closed on the hem of the governess's dress. The animal, wide-eyed and frothing at the mouth, galloped up St Mary's Street." Here Mr Rance interrupted his own narrative to take a hasty breath, but continued right away. "And the carriage, with its huge spoked wheels rattling on the cobble stones and square sets, was careering behind, dragging poor Miss Kenyon along like a rag doll."

"How dreadful!" exclaimed Mrs Bennet, her sensibilities awakened.

"And Miss Kenyon, the governess, is she…?" Mary broke off, sickened by this horrific tale, but needing to know the outcome. She doubted not that there would be none other than a bad one.

Mr Rance, itching to continue this saga of misfortune, continued, "Her gown was caught tight, there was no hope of her getting it free, and her body was fairly broken. It was a red coat outside the garrison up Bugg's Hill that finally brought the horse to a standstill."

Mrs Bennet echoed, "A red coat! Oh, Mary, a red coat!" She looked meaningfully at her daughter.

Mary could feel a faint blush, embarrassed for herself and for her mother's ill-timed remark and insinuation.

Mr Bennet, unaware of his daughter's discomfort, felt the need to say, "That was fortuitous, a soldier of the king standing at the ready, always there in our time of need."

Ignoring this patriotic observation for the time being, though he was as patriotic as they come, Mr Rance went on with his tale of horror. "Doctor Granger was called immediately, and he carried her to Willow Wood in his phaeton. He has been up at the house ever since. They say there is very little hope for her. She was drenched in her own blood, poor lass."

It was fortunate that the landlord's buxom wife, Martha Rance, appeared at the door at that moment, otherwise Mrs Bennet would have swooned.

"I have made you a nice dinner," she informed them, inappropriate in her cheeriness, "and the fire is well and truly blazing in the dining room, so why do not you come through? I am sure you could do with some sustenance after your travels, and now this mishap. Sarah is making up the bed-chambers and lighting the fires as we speak. So cold for this time of year, do not you think?"

The stable lad, baptised Henry after his father and his two grandfathers, later returned with the news that the governess was "very poorly, with every bone in her body broken". After the story which the Bennets had heard recounted by the landlord, they had no doubt that this was no exaggeration.

They also learned with a mixture of relief and apprehension that Mr Russell would send one of his carriages in the morning to fetch them to his home.

CHAPTER V

SAD TIMES

The next morning, Mr and Mrs Rance stood at the door of the Lamb Hotel with expressions which would have admirably befitted a funeral of national importance. The Russells' barouche driver, the veritable Simon Braden, had arrived in full purple, gold-braided livery to take the Bennets to Willow Wood.

He was wearing a black arm band.

Miss Kenyon was dead. She had died during the night.

"She were calling out to the angels who were beckoning her to a better place," confided Mr Braden. "My wife, Elizabeth – she's the lady's maid up at the house – were there when the governess passed away. 'They're beckoning me,' she heard the poor girl cry out, 'to a better place'!"

The luggage was safely stowed in the wooden trunk set on a rack at the back of the barouche, and the coachman ensured that the three passengers were safely aboard.

"Let us proceed to Willow Wood, driver," Mr Bennet sighed taciturnly, with even less enthusiasm than he had shown at the time when the visit had been first suggested a month ago in Lydia's letter and then so readily taken up by Mrs Bennet, to whose entreaties he had finally succumbed.

"It's Simon Braden, sir. The name's Braden," he informed Mr Bennet, with a sense of family pride. "We Bradens have been in service to the Russells for four

34

generations, right back to my great-grandfather, William Braden."

Mr Bennet nodded.

Simon Braden called back to his passengers, having clicked his tongue to the matching pair of bays. "Now hold on tight and hold on to your bonnets, ladies!"

They had travelled no more than three minutes, entering St Mary's Street and approaching St Mary's Green, where weekly horse fairs were held, when Simon Braden brought the vehicle to a standstill outside a timber frame house and made a serious announcement.

"This is where it happened. Right here beside Oliver Cromwell's house. See, there's blood on the roadway even yet."

Mr Bennet cared little for the sensationalism of looking at some poor girl's spilled blood on the cobbles, and even less for ogling, like some common tourist, the house of Oliver Cromwell, the anti-royalist upstart who had almost destroyed the monarchy in *his* great-grandfather's time. "Thank you, Braden."

"Does he say this is where it happened?" Mrs Bennet cried out, inspired to look out over the barouche's open side with more excitation than she had mustered for Ely Cathedral. "How dreadful!" She fumbled about in her reticule, producing her lorgnette, before leaning dangerously far over the side of the vehicle as she tried to discern some speck of blood on the road, her bonnet falling forward and the satin ties almost touching the ground.

"Drive on, Braden, if you please," said Mr Bennet, restraining his wife with a force that she found quite objectionable.

"There is no need for such masculine power, Mr Bennet," she said, adjusting her apparel like a hen adjusting its feathers.

"Would you have me allow you to tumble out on to the roadway, my dear Mrs Bennet, in a strange town with passers-by looking at you with disdain?" he asked, though there was a slight tremor of humour in his voice.

She noticed and responded to him with an acquiescent nod and fleeting smile.

"Not to mention looters and pillagers!" he added, ruining a rare moment of matrimonial near-harmony.

As the light summer carriage rattled over the cobbles along St Mary's Street and up the square sets of the steady incline of Bugg's Hill, towards Willow Wood and in the general direction of London, Mary could not help but flinch with every jolt at the thought of the governess's breaking body, her pain, her cries of agony.

"And this is where the pony were brought to a standstill," said Simon Braden. He had stopped the two horses yet again and was pointing at the very gates of the barracks where the —shire regiment was permanently stationed. "It were a Mr Wickham, they say, what stopped the animal dead in its tracks. Brave fellow, or a daft one, to stand in front of a charging animal!"

"Oh, Mr Bennet! Do you hear? Our dear Mr Wickham! He is a hero!" Mrs Bennet clutched her heart in ecstasy.

"Do you know the gentleman, ma'am?"

"Know him?" cried Mrs Bennet, her face aglow with pride. "He is our son-in-law. Married to my youngest, Lydia, you know."

Mary looked earnestly at her mother, willing her to hold her tongue, lest she divulge too many dark family secrets to a man in service. Not only was Lydia's name besmirched by her unseemly elopement with the said Mr Wickham when only sixteen years of age, but the fact that the youngest of the family was married while Mary remained a spinster, three years on, was a thorn in her side which pained her more and more as each year passed.

Mrs Bennet took a breath, as if to launch into such family histories as Mary feared.

"Father, had we not better hurry on to my uncle's house?" Mary exhorted Mr Bennet with more than her usual directness of address, her brown eyes looking intensely in his direction, willing him to respond positively to her request.

"Why, yes, my dear," he said. Mary rarely called him "Father", so he responded with alacrity to her demand. "Yes, indeed. Driver, drive on, with no further stops and starts, if you please!"

The Willow Wood estate lay three miles distant from Ely, in the direction of Lynn, half-way between the villages of Foxham and Paddleham. There were no distinguishing land features, no hills or hummocks to show the way. The general landscape was naturally flat and watery, but the Dutch engineer Sir Cornelius Vermuyden had etched his mark on a landscape of meres and constant flooding some two hundred years before, creating dykes and drains. These formed a network of canals running between the ebony-coloured, peaty fields, with windmills pumping the water up to the shored-up tributaries of the River Great Ouse, and finally out to sea at Lynn. Now there was some good reclaimed land suitable for pasture, evidenced when the Bennets looked out at a hundred sheep grazing to the right and another hundred to left as the barouche made its way along the lime tree-lined avenue of the Willow Wood estate, which led to the stately home of the family Russell.

"It is most elegant," remarked Mary, once the grand house had come into full view.

"Tush, Mary," scoffed her mother. "What do you know of elegant buildings?"

"From what I read, Mama," Mary patiently answered. She knew it would be difficult to explain about wainscoting, gothic architecture, gargoyles and other such features as were already visible, so she said no more.

"You read too much," was her mother's piqued rejoinder.

"We are nearly here, my dear," Mr Bennet interjected, "so I suggest we put silly quibbles to one side and remember that we are about to enter a house of mourning."

The middle-aged housekeeper, Mrs Brown, a thin stick figure dressed in black, was standing at the bottom of a set of semi-circular marble steps leading up to the front door upon the Bennet party's arrival. On either side of her, two footmen with old-fashioned wigs, powdered and white, stood ready to assist the ladies from the barouche. They were also to take the luggage to three guest apartments designated to the Bennets, all prepared by the upstairs maids in readiness, with dust sheets removed, fresh linen provided, flower petals scattered over the beds, fresh water in the pitchers on the wash stands, and fires already burning in the grates.

"Welcome to Willow Wood, sir," Mrs Brown intoned in a sombre voice, befitting the underlying sadness of an occasion which should have been joyful. "And Mrs Bennet, and Miss Bennet." She dropped a neat curtsy. "I could only wish that circumstances were different."

"Indeed, indeed," agreed Mr Bennet.

"Please come this way," Mrs Brown said, ushering the guests up the sweeping left-hand steps.

Two young downstairs maids were identical twin sisters April and May, so named on account of their entry into this world, one on each side of midnight of April 30 at the turn of the century. They were in service to the family on a temporary basis until their six-month training had been completed to the satisfaction of Mrs Brown. They now came forward nervously, dropping curtsies, and helped to remove the ladies' cloaks and bonnets.

Mr Bennet attended to his own outer garments and handed them, along with his brass-handled cane, to yet another bewigged footman standing in the hallway ready to assist. He was an African. Mr Bennet patted the black fellow on the arm, smiling and nodding, almost as an act of friendship not usually accorded to a servant.

At that moment, Aunt Russell, apparently unable to wait a moment longer for her older brother to enter the drawing room, rushed into the hallway to welcome him.

"Brother, Brother!" she cried, taking both his hands in hers. "I am so glad you are come. What a terrible business!"

She was a pretty and vivacious woman, approaching three-and-thirty, with delicate black curls falling in short ringlets from under her matron's lace cap.

Mr Russell, all affable portliness, followed his wife into the hallway. He was still adjusting his brown wig. He had no inclination to grow his hair and show it to all and sundry simply because it was deemed to be more fashionable. In addition to this, he was balding, so any growth would be patchy.

"My dear sister Bennet, welcome to our home." He took her hand in greeting. "It is too, too long since you were last here at Willow Wood. Let me see, when was it?"

"Oh, sir, I cannot recollect."

"It was in the summer of the year of our Lord 1807, if my memory serves me right."

Mrs Bennet curtsied to her host, smiling, albeit a trifle absently, as she tried to delve into her memory. Not only could she not recollect the date of their last visit, but, had she been asked, she would have had difficulty recognising either Mr Russell or his wife in a crowd.

"We have been so looking forward to your visit, but what will become of our preparations now is unclear."

Mrs Bennet tutted, with a brief comment that it was "a terrible business", echoing her sister-in-law, for what else was there to say?

"Brother," said Mr Bennet, bowing formally to his brother-in-law.

"Brother," said Mr Russell, bowing to his brother-in-law, with whom he had few dealings during the past nine years.

Both men acknowledged one another with a civility tinged with animosity, which Mary assumed had something to do with the fact that an African was in service in this house. The question in her mind was: was he a paid or unpaid servant? A free man or a slave? As things stood, until slavery itself was made illegal, and not just the slave trade of capturing and transporting slaves, it was impossible to tell.

Mr Russell turned to Mary. "And this must be our dear niece. My, how you have changed," he offered.

Of course she had changed in the intervening years!

"Yes, Uncle Russell, I believe I was twelve when last we met," was her patient and polite reply, "when you kindly invited our whole family to Willow Wood."

"What a pleasure, Mary, to have you stay with us again. Had it not been for the unfortunate death of the children's governess, we should have had so many entertainments for you, knowing how you young people love to partake in eight-some dances and other jollities." Uncle Russell smiled on Mary, in the full belief that he knew her character well.

Mary responded with a gentle smile. She looked quite pretty, thought her uncle, but only passably so.

"I am certain that we shall be able to provide some entertainments in a few days, when this unfortunate circumstance has passed," Aunt Russell assured her niece.

Mary knew not how she should respond to now a second reference to entertainment for her benefit. In a house of mourning, it all appeared too unseemly.

"This really is such a tiresome affair, my dear brother," said Aunt Russell, leading Mr Bennet by the arm into the drawing room. "There is a dead girl lying in the cellar…"

"In the cellar, Sister Russell?" commented Mrs Bennet, with raised eyebrows. "How unique!"

"Not at all. It is to keep the body cool, you know, Sister, until we know what is to be done. But before we decide, let us partake of some tea and a glass of Marsala wine."

"In the cellar, Mary, did you hear?" Mrs Bennet repeated this unusual circumstance on her way through to the drawing room. She was quite enjoying the quaintness of this situation, and, had it not been so serious, she might have been tempted to giggle.

Once all the party were seated on the matching cream satin brocade Queen Anne armchairs and settees, Aunt Russell gently commanded the housekeeper, "If you please, Mrs Brown, tea and Marsala."

Mary thought that her aunt was a practical lady, if nothing else, but perhaps too lacking in sensitivity. After all, a young woman had died after a horrific road accident.

Pleasantries were exchanged, but always under the intrusive shadow of the dead girl. Was their journey comfortable? Was the Lamb Hotel to their liking? What was their opinion on the unusually inclement weather for this time of year?

It was only once the tea things and the wine glasses had been removed that Aunt Russell broached the subject of what was to be done with Miss Kenyon's body, now lying in the cool cellar below their very feet.

"She has no living relatives, you know. She had been educated, but was left virtually penniless when her father died this year in January, in America."

"In America!" Mrs Bennet exclaimed.

"Indeed, yes. He was a preacher in the Methodist Episcopal Church, who helped to set up the Free African Society in Philadelphia."

"Humph!" Uncle Russell snorted, but he said no more after a brief cautionary look from his wife was cast in his direction.

Mary was fascinated to learn that in Uncle Russell's household there was an African in service, paid or

41

otherwise, yet he had agreed to employ, as governess, the daughter of a Wesleyan supporter of equal rights for African Americans.

"She was left here in England, to be sent for at a later date." Aunt Russell paused with a sigh. "It was not to be. He died in Philadelphia. Poor girl, she was distraught. And now she has died. But where is she to be laid to rest?"

Mr Russell added, "She cannot be buried in the Russell family vault. That would be unthinkable, as she is not related." With a grin he added, "There is always the burial ground for our favourite cats and dogs at the far end of the estate!"

Mary and her father exchanged looks at this show of flippancy, while Mrs Bennet quizzically mouthed "Cats and dogs?" to herself.

"She was a Methodist," complained Aunt Russell, her attention to practical detail surfacing, "which makes it even more difficult. Otherwise, we might have persuaded our vicar in Foxham to place her in the Holy Trinity churchyard, at the perimeter, you understand, so as not to be in the way. But a Methodist! Pleasant enough young woman, of course. But nevertheless, a Methodist. Reverend Smallwood certainly would not have a Methodist in his church for a service, let alone in his churchyard for eternity!"

"Too true, my dear; our esteemed vicar has his ways."

"Where are they buried, one has to ask," sighed Aunt Russell. "Where does one put a Methodist?"

"There is always the paupers' grave," suggested her husband.

Aunt Russell would not hear of such a suggestion, rounding on her husband. "A young woman in our employ is not a pauper."

"Was not," contradicted Uncle Russell. "Was not a pauper."

The Bennets sat fascinated and silent in the face of this vocal banter, turning to one then the other to hear what would be said next on this unusual topic.

Finally, it was Aunt Russell who terminated the conversation, with the question of Miss Kenyon's interment unresolved, by insisting that their guests should be shown to their quarters and then introduced to Roseanna and Ellen. The young misses Russell were upstairs in their schoolroom being comforted by Elizabeth Braden, the lady's maid, for they had lost their pretty governess whom they had grown to love.

CHAPTER VI

THE CORNISHMAN

Mary woke to a stranger's voice: a man's voice downstairs in the hallway. Had she over-slept? Why had nobody called her? Feeling all the embarrassment of appearing to be a lazy guest, she jumped out of her bed and her slumber. Looking at the time-piece, she was relieved to find that it was only seven o'clock in the morning. Yet who was arriving at this early hour?

"I came as soon as I heard," the voice said sympathetically. "Mrs Brown, pray inform Mr Russell that I have come. I shall wait for him in the music room, my favourite haunt!"

Mary hurriedly dressed in her darkest day dress, the plain Prussian blue one with the detachable white lace collar, leaving aside all the colourful gowns upon which Aunt Philips had insisted, remembering that this was a house of mourning. She pinned her wavy hair neatly back off her forehead and behind her ears in its usual bun, smoothing it down as best as she could with water, then checked her general appearance in the looking glass and descended the sweeping curved staircase before Uncle and Aunt Russell, or her parents, had even begun their morning ablutions.

Mrs Brown greeted her at the bottom of the staircase. "Breakfast is not until eight o'clock, Miss Bennet, though I am sure Cook can make up a glass of freshly squeezed orange juice for you, should you desire it. Perhaps you would care to have coffee with Mr Tremayne in the music room." Mary was about to ask who Mr Tremayne might be, but Mrs Brown gave her no time to form this question. "You know Mr Tremayne, of course," she said. "He loves his cups of coffee." Whereupon she led the way down the hallway and through the Italianate alabaster archway, and opened the double louvred doors into the music room.

"Miss Bennet, sir," she announced before sailing off in the general direction of the kitchens, her skirts luffing and billowing from side to side of her thin mast-like frame.

Mr Tremayne was five-and-thirty, his hair already greying, which gave him the appearance of a much older man. Mary noted his tall bearing and broad shoulders as he rose quickly from where he was seated on the piano stool. His fingers had been gently resting on the ivory and black keys of the latest Broadwood grand pianoforte. He even looked as if he had been about to play.

"Miss Bennet," he greeted Mary, with a formal bow.

Mary felt very self-conscious to be alone in this room with a stranger, a man, with no formal introductions. Was his name familiar? Why did Mrs Brown assume they knew one another? She had no idea who he was. He on the other hand appeared to be relaxed. She wished her uncle Russell would be down soon to greet his guest and help her out of this awkward situation.

"Mr Tremayne?" Mary gave him a neat curtsy.

The interrogative intonation of her address did not go unnoticed. "You are wondering who I am, I think," he said, adding, "yet I know exactly who you are."

Mary felt a pink blush rising in her cheeks. How could this stranger with attractive grey-green eyes know who she was?

"Pray, let us sit," he invited, moving towards a maroon velvet chaise-longue.

Mary moved deliberately to an occasional chair whose cushion was covered in cream brocade. Surely he hadn't intended her to sit in such close proximity to him on the chaise-longue, whether he knew exactly who she was or not!

"Tremayne is a Cornish name, I believe," Mary ventured after a few seconds of silence. She was acutely aware that Mr Tremayne was staring at her. It was very unsettling. So too was another subsequent silence.

"Have you met Roseanna and Ellen?" he suddenly asked.

"Yes!"

"How are they?"

"Unhappy, you know. Understandably."

"Poor souls!"

"Poor Miss Kenyon!" Mary observed. "Did you know her?"

"She was the governess, I the music tutor, so our paths did occasionally cross."

Mary knew now why this stranger had seemed so relaxed in the music room, with his fingers poised over the ivory and black notes of the pianoforte. He was just a music teacher, in her uncle's employ. She knew not what else to say, so she looked out over the lawns which led down to a lake fringed to left with mature weeping willows, and beyond to the far end of the estate, the final resting place of the family pets.

The door opened and in marched Uncle Russell. "My dear Charles!" he said, grasping his guest's hand and shaking it vigorously. "Sorry to keep you waiting. I am sure Mary has been admirably attending to you."

"Yes indeed, John," said Charles, looking at Mary, a friendly smile beginning to soften his angular features.

Turning to Mary, Uncle Russell said, "So how do you like my nephew?"

"Nephew!" Mary heard herself exclaim.

46

"Yes, my dear! I am uncle to you both. Quite extraordinary!" laughed Uncle Russell. "You, Mary, just one-and-twenty; Charles nearly twice your age."

"Really, John! An exaggeration on your part. I am no more than five-and-thirty."

"And here am I only five years older than Charles. Uncle to you both! And my nephew calls me John! And my wife is younger than he is. It fairly shakes up the stability of generations. I hardly know where I stand!" He laughed heartily.

Mary could feel her cheeks burn. Just a music teacher! Surely Charles Tremayne's whole bearing had belied that very idea. And she had abstractedly and disdainfully ignored him by looking out of the window! How rude she must have seemed! She smiled remorsefully, hoping he would not think ill of her.

"Though we are not cousins," Charles said simply. He had seen her blush; he had understood what she was thinking.

"But Roseanna and Ellen are cousins to you both, do not forget!" interjected Uncle Russell, slapping his thigh with mirth, still enjoying the generation labyrinth.

"But we, Mary and I, are not blood relations," added Charles more seriously, continuing his line of thought, looking earnestly at Mary. "If I may take the liberty of calling you Mary?"

Mary inclined her head in tacit agreement. No man had ever taken this liberty before. Her heart was beating so unaccountably fast in her bosom that she thought it must surely have been visible had she not selected her dark day dress to wear. Had she worn one of the more flimsy and revealing muslin or tulle gowns, which Aunt Philips had insisted she wear during her stay at Willow Wood, then these unaccustomed inner feelings would have been less hidden from view.

Charles, for his part unaware of Mary's beating heart, looked with admiration at the sensuous curve of Mary's elegant neck, her shining hair prettily gathered into a neat bun. He had no time for young ladies who adorned themselves with dangling jewellery and allowed their hair to fall over their face in ringlets and unruly curls. He liked Mary's simplicity, her brown eyes, her chestnut hair.

"Anyway, so good of you to come, Charles! At such short notice. All that way, too, from Blixford-in-the-Isle!"

"Just twelve miles, John," Charles modestly corrected him.

"Indeed, indeed!" Turning to Mary, Uncle Russell said, "Charles did tell you he lived in Blixford?"

"We had little time to talk," she replied, somewhat regretfully. She would have liked to have talked at length to him.

"Apprentice to an attorney there," continued Uncle Russell. "Learning the trade, so to speak."

Mary only nodded, remembering Uncle Philips's apprentice, the intractable Mr Bolton.

Recalling who was in the cellar, Uncle Russell continued in more lugubrious tones, "Though what is to be done with poor Miss Kenyon's body is a problem as yet unresolved. As you know, she was a Methodist, with no family." He shook his head sadly, "Your aunt is nearly distracted with worry about the body down below."

Their uncle's words were faintly ambiguous to Mary, with a spectre of a Methodist burning in hell appearing before her eyes. Perhaps the same thought had crossed Charles's mind, for he asked bemusedly, "Down below, John?"

"In the cellar," explained Mary, adding, "to keep it cool."

"Ah! Of course."

"But where is she to be buried?" Uncle Russell's tone was one of near defeat. "I've been tossing and turning in

48

bed all night and can come up with no solution. And Ruby will be down to breakfast in a few minutes, demanding to know what is to be done with Miss Kenyon."

Uncle Russell sat down heavily on the chaise-longue. Mary thought he was about to put his head in his hands. However, it was Charles who put their uncle out of his increasing sense of hopelessness and helplessness.

"My dear fellow, perhaps I can be of assistance. My landlady is a Methodist. She attends the Wesleyan chapel in Blixford. I am sure she could arrange for Miss Kenyon to be buried in the cemetery belonging to her church."

"Capital idea!" Uncle Russell's cheery demeanour had returned.

"I am sure there will be a plot available, as there are so few Methodists in the town, alive or dead," observed Charles. "An odd circumstance when one considers that John Wesley actually preached in the town in the seventies, and the chapel was built only twenty-five years ago."

"Perhaps a contribution to the church funds would be appropriate?" suggested Uncle Russell.

"You arrange for the Ely horse-drawn bier to take the coffin to Blixford on Monday, and leave the funeral arrangements all to me."

"My dear fellow, you are a marvel!" Uncle Russell's face was aglow. "I cannot tell you what a relief this is to me. I quite feared I should suffer from heart failure should the dilemma have lasted much longer."

"I shall go directly."

"Absolutely not! You will have breakfast first," ordered Uncle Russell. "Your aunt will have me thrown to the wolves if I let you depart without sustenance for the journey. Let us go in to the dining room."

CHAPTER VII

CHANGING EMOTIONS

"Another letter from Lydia!" cried Mrs Bennet, seated in the bay window alcove of the drawing room, which overlooked immaculately laid out lawns, flower borders, ornamental fish ponds and a privet hedge maze to the right. "Two in two days!"

"Quite remarkable!" said Mr Bennet. "Obviously, she must be desirous of some benefit which she believes is within our powers to render."

"You always think so ill of your girls. I can safely say that she will wish to send her condolences, now that Mary has sent her the sad news. That will be the sole purpose of her correspondence."

"Shall you open the letter, my dear, or shall we discuss the contents before we know what they are?"

Mrs Bennet adjusted her posture to show her disapproval of her husband's question, and opened the letter. "*Dearest Mama. How exciting!*"

"No condolences, Mrs Bennet?" nettled her husband.

"Shall I continue? Or shall we discuss the contents before we know what they are?" Mrs Bennet smirked at her own sense of victory at repeating verbatim her husband's words.

"Pray do!" Mr Bennet huffed.

"*And what good fortune that the funeral is in Blixford. They say the finest milliner's in the land is there. I shall of course accompany you and my aunt and my uncle Russell tomorrow... a mark of respect.* There, you hear, Mr Bennet. She says 'a mark of respect'."

"She also mentions the milliner's, my dear." Mr Bennet was not going to give in too easily. "Is that the end of this all-important second letter?"

"No, there are two more lines."

"Are you to keep them to yourself?"

"She finishes by saying, *There will be free time for you and me to visit the milliner's and other shops and make some purchases while we are there.*"

"You see!" triumphed Mr Bennet. "I knew she wanted something! And whose money will she be spending?"

"I am sure you can spare a few of your precious pounds," Mrs Bennet said obstinately. "I declare that neither Mary nor I require you to spend much on us, as we are so infrequently in society. But Lydia, as Mrs Wickham, must be fashionable in her attire."

"But will there be room for her in the carriage?" Mr Bennet asked, not wishing to spend a two-hour journey to Blixford the next day and a two-hour journey back, squeezed inside the formal carriage which the Russells had decided would be appropriate for the occasion. With five already travelling in what was meant to be a vehicle for four, the prospect of a sixth, a giddy daughter to boot, inconsequentially and incessantly talking there and back, was intolerable.

Mrs Bennet offered an immediate solution. "Mary, you can stay here and look after your young cousins."

Mary opened her mouth to object to this change of plan. She wanted to support her aunt and uncle, as a show of gratitude to them for agreeing to their stay, and as a mark of family solidarity at the passing of poor Miss Kenyon.

Mrs Bennet continued, "They seem to have taken quite a liking to you. Lydia can take your place in the carriage, for I have so much I long to speak to her about." Folding the letter with deliberation and placing it in her lap, she announced loftily, "There you are, Mr Bennet. The problem is solved. Mary, you shall write directly to Lydia to say that the carriage will call at their lodgings tomorrow morning!"

Mary hoped that her father would come to her defence, but he did not. She herself wanted to dissuade her mother from agreeing to Lydia's demands, overstepping the mark of civility as a guest in someone else's house, but Mrs Bennet insisted that the letter be written immediately and ensured that it was dispatched post haste.

Later that evening, matters became even more compounded when Aunt Russell announced at dinner that Elizabeth Braden requested permission to attend Miss Kenyon's funeral, on account of her "being there when she breathed her last". Simon Braden was to drive the formal carriage with its plush burgundy velvet seats and young Martin Braden was to drive the barouche with its bench seats to accommodate Mrs Brown, the African footman and an upstairs maid.

"I cannot see that there is a problem, Ruby my dear. There is room for another one in the barouche."

"The problem is this: who is to attend to Roseanna and Ellen?"

"Ah! I had forgotten them. Poor souls! Very unhappy… almost inconsolable."

"Mary is to stay with them," Mrs Bennet piped up, in between two mouthfuls of braised turbot. "It is all agreed."

"Agreed?" asked Aunt Russell, with a degree of incredulity. Nothing was ever "agreed" in her household without her express wishes or approbation.

Uncle Russell's fork was poised half-way between his plate and his mouth.

Mrs Bennet licked her lips in a fluster. To divert attention from herself, she muttered, "Is not that correct, Mary?"

"Yes, Mama," was all that Mary could say.

Ruby Russell liked Mary's honesty and her sense of dutiful loyalty to her parents, glad that there was at least someone sensible to take care of her dear brother. Mary had also been particularly sympathetic to her daughters' present needs of comfort, so she smiled in her direction and defused what was an unusual situation in the domestic arrangements of Willow Wood.

"That is most kind and considerate of you, my dear," she graciously said. "They have grown fond of you already."

What Mrs Bennet did not say was that the Russells' carriage was to stop in the main street of Ely to collect Lydia from their lodgings. Mary wondered what her aunt would think about yet another arrangement made without her prior knowledge or approval.

"Yes, damned fond!" Uncle Russell nodded, exhaling loudly, his good humour at least restored.

Early the next morning, when the horse-drawn bier, hired in Ely, came to collect the coffin now containing Miss Kenyon's remains, it was too much for either child to bear. They stood forlornly sobbing in the hallway, wearing identical black taffeta dresses, quickly constructed by Mrs Brown's daughter, who was a seamstress in Ely, to show their respects to their dear departed governess. Mary stood between them, holding a hand of each.

Aunt Russell kissed Roseanne and Ellen's tear-stained cheeks. "You are not to fret, my dears. Your cousin Mary will be here all day with you. We will return before nightfall." To Mary she said, her mind on the practicalities of the daily running of the house, "Just keep a general eye on things, my dear. It is better that the staff know someone is in charge. I have ordered Cook to have dinner ready for us at nine o'clock." She added, "Thank you so much for offering to stay with your cousins. Your uncle and I shall think of ways to show our heart-felt gratitude."

Mary and the children, along with some of the remaining staff, watched the mournful cortege leave the house and proceed down the lime tree-lined avenue on poor Miss Kenyon's final exit from Willow Wood, away towards Blixford and the waiting Methodist churchyard.

The morning passed pleasurably, which was surprising given the circumstances, with Roseanna and Ellen eagerly agreeing to Mary's request to be shown around the gardens close to the house. The highlight of the tour was their expedition into the maze some hundred yards away from the house, when Mary herself got lost and had to be rescued by Roseanna and Ellen, both of whom squealed with delight that the intricacies of the maze, which they had mastered long ago, should be so puzzling to their cousin. How they laughed and danced around Mary in their taffeta dresses, in between hugging her and holding her hand. Poor Miss Kenyon was well on the way to being forgotten, or at least relegated to distant memory.

By late afternoon, the girls had exhausted their repertoire of their favourite pianoforte pieces, playing in the music room as a treat, and it was time for them to go to the nursery upstairs, where they always ate their high tea before retiring to bed for the night.

Mary had time to herself, and, with the family party not expected for at least another hour, she sat down at the grand pianoforte in the music room to practice the first movement, the adagio sostenuto, of Mr Beethoven's *Sonata Number 14, Quasi una Fantasia*. Her sight reading had always been good; indeed she prided herself in her ability to master some of the most difficult pieces known to their circle of acquaintances, and she was always the first to be able to play new pieces of printed sheet music. Even her sister Elizabeth, who played tolerably well, was in awe of Mary's technical skill at the keys.

She played the melody with near-perfect precision, occasionally going back over the fingering of a more complex phrase, but overall she was feeling relatively pleased with her performance.

She suddenly became aware that she was not alone in the music room. Turning her head, she was astonished to see Charles Tremayne standing behind her.

"Why, Miss Mary Bennet, how delightful to hear you play! You have mastered the fingering well."

To cover her embarrassment and surprise she attempted to gather together the sheets of music, and found herself talking rather too quickly, sounding flustered even to herself. "I did not hear you arrive. I was not expecting anyone before seven o'clock, and Cook has had instructions to delay dinner until nine o'clock. Pray, were the funeral arrangements satisfactory? And is poor Miss Kenyon safely interred in the graveyard?"

One of the sheets then fluttered to the floor, only to add to her confusion. Mary was normally so measured in all that she did in life that her clumsiness was out of character. She bent down to pick up the page at the same time as Charles came forward to pick it up for her.

"Everything was as satisfactory as can be expected," Charles assured her, picking up the dropped page.

Mary could feel his breath on her cheek. Oh, how glad she was that she was still wearing her high-necked morning dress! Otherwise, the blush, which had started above her bosom and was travelling towards her face, would have been evidence of her agitation.

"The rest of the party will be here at some time after seven, I fear. They are spending an extra hour in Blixford. Your sister, Mrs Wickham, was desirous of visiting the milliner's establishment with your mother." Here he paused.

Mary was feeling all the humiliation for her sister's behaviour, as well as her mother's. "My sister and mother enjoy each other's company, and visits to the shops."

"They were going to purchase bonnet ribbons to match the crimson dress she was wearing, I understand."

Mary could only give him a look of apology for her sister's indecorous choice of colour for a funeral.

"Our aunt and uncle kindly agreed. They and your father decided to have afternoon tea in the Hunters' Arms while they were waiting."

"My father will not have been pleased." Mary was thinking of the money which he always objected to any of his daughters spending.

"His displeasure was short-lived, once he realised that the hotel was situated beside a river which is famed for its rainbow trout."

"Fishing is one of his favourite pastimes," she offered, but it was a lame explanation.

"I decided to come on ahead to find out how my two young cousins are faring," Charles said.

Mary was on the point of telling him that Roseanna and Ellen had ended their day in much better spirits than they had begun it, from tears to laughter in a few hours, when Charles corrected himself.

"No, Mary. That is not the truth. The real reason is that I came to see you."

Mary was flattered; her breath almost stopped; she knew not what to say.

"I was more than a little surprised to discover that you were not in the carriage, when it arrived at the church."

Mary nodded.

"And I was disappointed, I may add."

Mary was almost spell-bound by this man, a man who had been looking forward to her company. Was he announcing feelings for her? She held her breath, lest she break the spell. She longed to hear what he would say.

"But I cannot understand why or how you were prevailed upon to look after our cousins today."

The spell was broken. Charles's tone of dissatisfaction was unmistakable.

"There was no room in the carriage," Mary said honestly.

"Stuff and nonsense!" Charles expostulated, looking sternly at her.

"Not so!" rejoined Mary hotly. Inhaling slowly in order to calm herself, she told him, "It has four seats. There would have been barely enough room for Lydia, seated between my mother and my aunt. There was no more room. You need not doubt that."

"Your place was surely with our aunt and uncle. And if there was no room in the carriage, as you say, then you should have insisted that you, as their guest at Willow Wood, go with them, and that Mrs Wickham did not."

Mary felt all the justness of this reproof, yet she persisted in her own defence. "It was they who wished that I stay to look after our cousins. You know how distressed they were. And the upstairs maid very much wanted to go to pay her last respects, so there was no one else to stay with them."

Charles simply replied, "Mrs Wickham was a poor replacement."

An awkward silence ensued, Mary's mind filled with annoyance. She was not sure whether it was more because of Charles's censure of her, or because of her own feelings of self-reproach. She, who had always prided herself on her sense of moral rectitude and propriety! Now, in retrospect, she knew that she should have been less acquiescent to an arrangement which had originated from her mother's wish to be with Lydia for the day. She should have insisted on what was politically correct. She remembered with chagrin her aunt's suppressed irritation about plans made without consulting her first, and could only imagine the scene when the carriage had to stop in Main Street to collect the be-crimsoned Lydia.

Mary felt more miserable than she had ever felt in her life, and, as unaccustomed tears pricked the backs of her eyes, she fervently wished that she had never agreed to come to Willow Wood in the first place.

CHAPTER VIII

TEA AND A SOIRÉE

The next afternoon, while Mr Bennet and Uncle Russell went fishing in the lake on the Willow Wood estate, Mary and her mother took advantage of Aunt Russell's offer of the barouche for the duration of their stay. Indeed, Aunt Russell had insisted that they go to Ely to meet up with Lydia. Her man would take a letter to Lydia there and then. No, she would not accompany them; Roseanna and Ellen needed her, she said. Mary was of the opinion that her aunt was endeavouring to free herself from constant contact with her loquacious sister-in-law and her frequent complaints of her nerves.

In reality, Aunt Russell was concerned that, since the Bennets' arrival at Willow Wood, Mary had not set foot outside the confines of the house and the adjacent gardens. She had also noted that Mary had sat in near silence beside Charles at dinner the night before, speaking only when asked a direct question by one of the party. Charles had said not a word to her. Aunt Russell had resolved that Mary needed to get out and about.

It was with a heavy heart that Mary set off in the barouche with her mother. The awkwardness of the prolonged silence between Charles and herself was a memory which pained her at every bend in the road on the journey to Ely for afternoon tea in the Misses Quickly's tea shop.

These two Quickly spinster proprietors were well known for their hot buttered scones and homemade raspberry jam, deliciously cooling cucumber sandwiches, choux pastry éclairs which melted in the mouth, and fine blends of tea. Their teashop was as much of a tourist attraction as Cromwell's house, and, more recently, as famous as the gaol where some of the Littleport rioters were being held for a term of seven years' incarceration.

"You have got a face as long as a fiddle!" exclaimed Mrs Bennet, sitting opposite to Mary at a table in the alcove of the tea shop, as they waited for Lydia. They had been waiting now for twenty minutes past the appointed time. "It quite tires me out just looking at you! And you have hardly spoken a word since we left Longbourn."

Mary smiled weakly at her mother.

Mrs Bennet's maternalism surfaced. "Are you ailing?"

"No, Mama. I am quite well, thank you." Not wishing to divulge the truth of her real feelings, she added, "I worry that Lydia has not yet arrived."

Just then, the door flew open and in came Lydia, parading herself in a flamboyant yellow walking dress, her hat adorned with a mass of floating peacock feathers. She was not alone.

"My dearest Lydia," Mrs Bennet cried, arms outstretched across the table in greeting.

"Dear Mama," Lydia gaily laughed. "What a treat this is!"

"My dear sister." Mary had stood to greet her sister in the more acceptable formal manner of a kiss on either cheek.

"Well, Mary. Just look at you! Not changed at all in three years. And here am I, a married woman of near enough four years. Almost a matron!" Lydia laughed loudly.

Mary was aware of a few faces turned in their direction and wished that Lydia would quieten herself, or at least sit down so as to be less conspicuous.

Then remembering the person who accompanied her, Lydia announced, "This is my dearest friend, Mrs Caroline Moffat." With almost studied civility, she presented her relations: "May I introduce my mother, Mrs Bennet? And my older sister, Miss Bennet?"

To Mary's sensitive ear, the words "older" and "Miss", though absolutely true, were unpleasant reminders that she had been left behind in the matrimonial race. She attempted to put these feelings to one side.

Introductions over, the four ladies indulged themselves, enjoying the finest afternoon tea to be had in Cambridgeshire, but the quality of the conversation was not at all pleasing to Mary. She had hoped to talk with her sister about life in Newcastle, a northern town which she knew was famed for its coal mining and for its cold weather. She had hoped to discover that Lydia's marriage to George Wickham had proved to be more successful than anyone had dared to hope at the time of their quiet, and enforced, wedding three years earlier, when Mr Darcy had intervened.

Lydia appeared to be gay and carefree, but by the time they were eating éclairs, her voice still resounding embarrassingly round the tea shop, Mary became aware of a kind of desperation in her sister's frenetic behaviour, a longing for adventure, a desire to hear gossip, and above all a yearning for social engagements. While she laughed and spoke gaily, there was sadness in her eyes. Mary could sympathise with her sister at this one point in time, the only occasion she had ever felt any affinity with her.

"But when is there to be a soirée at my aunt and uncle's house?" Lydia had been speaking for some time about the dearth of entertainments in Ely. "The regiment has already been in Ely for a fortnight, and there has never been an invitation to visit."

Mary could understand that, if there had not been invitations forthcoming before Aunt Russell had met Lydia, there would certainly be none in the future.

"Caroline, you and I could call on my aunt. To see Mama and Mary, we shall say. An excellent ruse!"

Mary stopped her sister making further ridiculous suggestions. "I believe my aunt and uncle are planning a soirée on Saturday evening. I am sure that an invitation to you and George will be forthcoming."

"And Caroline too, I should hope, as my dearest friend. Her husband is also a captain!" There was no stopping Lydia, for she was in full flight. "And my uncle can send his carriage to collect us. Oh! How exquisite! It will be the talk of the regiment. How everyone will envy us!"

So the conversation, dominated by Lydia, continued until Mary and Mrs Bennet made their farewells and left Lydia and Caroline, the two captains' wives, to enjoy the rest of the day browsing round the shops in Ely, under the ever-present eye of St Etheldreda's cathedral.

The invitation to Mr and Mrs Wickham was dispatched by Aunt Russell with a good grace, as Lydia was her niece, even though she was married to a captain in the militia. However, the invitation to Captain and Mrs Moffat was not extended. Invitations were sent to their colonel, a Colonel Sinclair, and his wife, as was the norm with all the regiments which were stationed for a couple of months or more in Ely. The other guests were Doctor Granger, who had attended poor Miss Kenyon, and his wife; Mr Fellows, who was the local attorney, and his wife; the Morrisons, with their three daughters of marriageable age; Lord and Lady Cuthbert, with their two sons of marriageable age, and Charles Tremayne. With the Russells and the Bennets, there would be three-and-twenty in the party.

Aunt Russell was fastidious in all the arrangements for the soirée. After all, as Ruby Bennet, she was a gentleman's daughter who had learned household management and haute cuisine from the early age of sixteen, when her mother had died. Her brother by then was married with five daughters and living in Longbourn, so the management of her father's house was left to her. At the time of her marriage four years later to John Russell, a man whose estate brought in twenty thousand a year, her father had come to live with them until he died. Ruby Russell, as mistress of Willow Wood, had steadily developed her skills in household management and now had sixteen staff to supervise. On this occasion, her expertise was clearly apparent to their dinner guests, who all but one sent their compliments to Mrs Forbes, the cook, before retiring to the drawing room where various entertainments to cater for all tastes, young and old, had been provided.

"I feel decidedly ill, Mary," whispered Mrs Bennet, fumbling in her reticule for her vinaigrette bottle of sal volatile. "It was the venison, I declare. I thought it had a distinctly peculiar odour. I shall have to retire to my room."

"Come, sit down, Mama!" advised Mary, leading her mother towards the drawing room.

"Do you not hear? I wish to go to my quarters."

Mary made their excuses to Aunt Russell, and accompanied her mother upstairs and into her bedroom.

"Shall I stay with you, Mama?" Mary asked dutifully. Even though she had dressed up for the occasion in the periwinkle blue evening dress which Aunt Philips had bought for her in Summerton, she was not particularly inclined to spend any more time in the presence of Lydia's silly and indecorous behaviour, George Wickham's inappropriately excessive flattery of anyone in feminine attire, including herself, and Charles's solemn and watchful gaze in her direction. She was not at all disinclined to spend the rest of the evening attending to her mother.

An hour later, when her mother was resting in bed, Mary had just begun to read aloud, an activity which always sent her mother to sleep, when there was a tentative tap on the bedroom door.

"Good gracious!" sighed Mrs Bennet, on the point of sleeping. "Whoever can this be?"

Elizabeth Braden entered, dropped a curtsy and carefully enunciated, as if giving a rehearsed speech, "Excuse me, Miss Bennet, but your company is requested below. Mr Tremayne is about to play."

"Mr Tremayne?"

"Oh, yes, miss. He always plays for the guests. Never fails. Such a lovely touch on them ivories!"

"My mother is indisposed. Pray return downstairs and present my apologies."

Three minutes later, there was another tapping on the door, but less tentative than before: in fact it sounded much more authoritative.

It was Aunt Russell. "My dear sister, do forgive the intrusion, but I believe that Mary's presence is required downstairs. Charles is about to treat us to a musical interlude. His repertoire includes works of Mr Mozart and Mr Beethoven." On the mention of this last name, Aunt Russell looked meaningfully at Mary. Whatever could this signify? "I am sure Mary can be spared."

Mrs Bennet opened her mouth to protest, but Aunt Russell stroked her hand.

"I have asked Elizabeth to sit with you. She will read to you if you wish. Come, Mary!" Aunt Russell ordered, coaxing her niece out of the room and escorting her down the long sweeping staircase to the drawing room, where Charles was seated at the pianoforte.

"Ah, Miss Bennet," he said formally, rising from the music stool to greet her. "Perhaps you would be good enough to turn the pages of this composition by Mr Beethoven. I believe you are familiar with this particular piece, Mr Beethoven's *Quasi una Fantasia*."

63

The memory of the sheet of music of this particular piece as it fluttered to the floor and Charles's breath on her cheek, as they both stooped down at the same moment, came rushing back into Mary's mind. Why had he chosen this sonata to play on this evening? Feeling self-conscious, imagining all eyes in the room turned upon her, she quietly acquiesced to his request to turn the pages, and stood beside Charles in readiness.

To her, he quietly advised, "I think it would be more comfortable if you positioned yourself here," patting the long pianoforte stool with his left hand, "beside me, if you please."

Mary's heart lurched and her mind was a whirl. Charles had barely acknowledged her presence during the dinner, even though they were seated opposite one another at the long table. She had deliberately avoided his grey-green eyes, remembering his words of censure. Yet it was he who had insisted that she assist him, and had even enlisted Aunt Russell as a messenger! Outwardly she sat demurely, but inwardly she hardly knew what to think. She took off her white gloves in readiness.

Lydia and one of the Morrison girls were chattering and giggling, while George Wickham had the full attention of the other two. The Cuthbert brothers were sending murderous glances in his direction, as their chances of engaging the two pretty Morrison girls were thwarted. Mr Morrison and Doctor Granger were chortling over some recollection of their boyhood, something about fishing in Waldon Fen for eels which slithered inside their garments. A game of whist was becoming more than a mere pastime, as Mr and Mrs Fellows and Lord and Lady Cuthbert were locked in near-mortal combat over a misplayed card.

Aunt Russell clapped her hands.

"Mr Charles Tremayne, our esteemed nephew, will play for us." She extended a hand in his direction by way of introduction.

Mrs Morrison whispered to Mrs Granger, who was seated beside her on the chaise-longue, "Nephew? He looks old enough to be her father!"

"Mr Tremayne studied music in the Real Collegio di Musica in Milan, and at the Conservatoire in Prague," Aunt Russell added, before taking her seat beside Uncle Russell, her hands clasped neatly on her lap, attentively smiling at Charles in anticipation.

Charles stood to announce that he was to play the first movement, the adagio sostenuto, of Mr Beethoven's *Sonata Number 14*.

"Mr Beethoven wrote this sonata in 1801," he explained, "shortly after he had fallen in love with his pupil, the lovely Countess Giulietta Guicciardi."

Mary looked down, worrying that a comparison was being made between her and the lovely countess. Lydia looked over to her husband romantically, in the hope that he remembered their ecstatic moments of love at the beginning of their affair, but he was all too happy flanked by the Morrison belles.

"To her he dedicated this work," Charles was saying, "naming it *Quasi una Fantasia*, which is Italian for *Almost a Fantasy*."

"Latin was far superior to its descendant," Mr Bennet opined, albeit in muted tones, to his brother-in-law, with whom he had been previously engaged in discussions about the corruption of classical languages.

Charles made a bow, flicked his coat tails like a real impresario over the stool as he sat down, flexed his long fingers above the keyboard, positioned them above the correct keys and began his performance.

Even as he played the first twenty bars of the sonata, every member of the audience in that drawing room fell totally silent, listening to the serenity of the beautifully measured notes. Mary knew the notes and had practised them, but where she struck the notes with precision, he and the pianoforte were as one: he played the notes, caressing them, pushing the keys down, and the keys gently responded, pushing his fingers up again. She was mesmerised. Never had music sounded so melodious, so mysterious, so happy and so melancholy all at the same time. She felt a tingling at the back of her neck. She turned pages and tried to maintain the rigidity of her posture as she sat beside him, but as she felt his body move gently, sometimes touching hers, she felt so warm inside. Her body relaxed, her facial features softened, her breathing became more measured, as if she were in a trance. With each crescendo, a wave of emotion overcame her, so that by the time the last page was reached, and the soirée guests were applauding, her face was glistening with freshly fallen tears.

Mrs Lydia Wickham and Miss Eleanor Morrison came rushing across the room, barely noticing Mary as she slipped away.

"My goodness, Mr Tremayne, who would have believed that you had such talent?" cried Lydia.

"Such talent!" echoed Miss Morrison.

"Do you play dance music, too? I do hope so."

"We do hope so!"

"We could have an eightsome if we push back a few chairs. Oh, no!" Lydia exclaimed, striking Charles playfully on the chest. "That would not do, as we should need you to make up the dance. Mary can play!"

Charles excused himself in order to find Mary, and left Mrs Wickham and Miss Morrison to discuss what he knew to be the impossibilities of turning Ruby Russell's drawing-room soirée into a cheap dance. Far better that they should suggest a proper ball in the Willow Wood ballroom! With that proposition they might meet with some success.

He had seen Mary slip unobtrusively through the open French window, and now found her standing some distance from the house in the light of the full moon, looking out towards the lake shimmering in the distance.

She recognised his tread, but did not turn round, lest he note her tears.

"You will get a chill, I fear," he said gently behind her.

"I am quite warm, thank you," Mary replied.

"Why did you rush away?"

"I needed to be alone," she said, faltering. "I am often alone. There is solace when one is alone."

"Do you play with words to mask your thoughts?"

Mary now turned towards him. "You played beautifully!"

"I think you need this," he said, producing his monogrammed silk handkerchief. "If you will allow me?"

Mary stood still, hardly daring to breathe, as he softly smoothed away the few remaining tears. His touch was as delicate as a butterfly kiss.

"What made you cry?" he now earnestly asked. "Dear God! I hope it was not I, with my harsh words and my even harsher silences."

Taking the handkerchief from his hand, she responded honestly. "It was you."

She heard him sigh in self-reproach.

"It was the way you made the sonata speak."

Charles sounded relieved. "They taught me how to feel the music when I was in Prague. One has to get into the mind of the composer, or to imagine a scene. With this particular piece of music, I imagine this wonderful love affair between Beethoven and his countess." He paused, wishing to convey the depths of his passion for music, of how deeply it affected him.

"But why is this music also so melancholy?"

"It was a love that was not to be."

"Did she die?" asked Mary softly.

"They were forbidden to see one another ever again, and she married someone else."

He was looking out towards the lake.

"I try to imagine what he must have felt. I see him forlornly looking at the moonlight on a lake much like this one, and with each fleeting ripple of shimmering blue-white light he tries to recapture his moments of rapture with his beautiful countess. His memories haunt him like some mystical story which happened long ago. His love affair becomes *quasi una fantasia*. Almost a fantasy."

CHAPTER IX

AN AFTERNOON RIDE

During the following week, while Mrs Bennet took near-ownership of the Russells' barouche in order to visit Lydia at her lodgings, or to indulge in éclairs in the teashop of the Misses Quickly, or to make a few purchases of millinery accessories, Mary preferred to spend time with the two Russell children in the schoolroom in the hours between breakfast and luncheon. They proved themselves to be eager students under Mary's tuition. Equally, Mary proved to be a natural teacher of history, geography, mathematics, art, stories, composition, handwriting and any other educational pursuit that she could think of, except for music tuition, which she knew was Charles's responsibility when he came to stay at the weekends. In the afternoons, either Aunt Russell or Elizabeth Braden played with the children in the nursery or in the gardens.

After breakfast on the Friday morning, as Mrs Bennet was gathering together her coat, gloves and hat in readiness for her day out in Ely with her darling Lydia, Aunt Russell took Mary to one side and said, "Would you not prefer to accompany your mother, my dear? There is no obligation for you to spend time with Roseanna and Ellen during your stay. We have applied to Lowston College for a replacement for poor Miss Kenyon, and a Miss Potter will be here in two weeks. The children can quite easily amuse themselves under the watchful eye of Elizabeth until that time."

69

"I enjoy teaching them. They are eager and pleasing pupils. It is a most pleasurable way of spending the time, and getting to know my young cousins."

"But you are missing opportunities of visiting your sister," Aunt Russell argued. "You will be here only another two weeks."

"I am perfectly sure that my sister will be happier with just my mother as company." By way of gentle explanation she added, "Our tastes differ."

After a pause, Aunt Russell announced, "The two bay mares need to be exercised today. I plan to go out this afternoon. Do you ride?"

"I do, but have little experience, as Father has always been reluctant to allow any of us to go riding. 'If only I had sons,' he often says, 'what fun we should have had together!'" She smiled at the memory.

"I doubt if your father would have ever ventured far from his study, even if he had had sons. He was always a reader, fonder of book learning than anything else, unless there was an opportunity to go fishing!" Ruby Russell looked wistful. "Your father was a very good brother to me. Fifteen years between us, but he always had time for me, always a kind word." Recollecting the present, she suddenly asked, "Do you have a riding habit?"

Mary nodded, thinking of her new Jacquard outfit.

"Excellent! Then we shall exercise those two mares this afternoon."

When the mares, named Shallow Water and Deep Water, were brought from the stables to the mounting block at the side of the house, Mary noted immediately that the saddles were not ladies' saddles for riding side-saddle as she had been taught, but men's. She felt anxious about her skirts and petticoats, and her own sense of decorum.

"Not the social norm, I grant you," admitted Ruby Russell, noting her niece's worried countenance, "but more modern. Much more comfortable and safe, too!" Then she added, "These two stable lads are quite used to seeing my ankles, so it will be of no consequence to them if they catch sight of yours. No one else will see us on the estate. Now come on, my dear girl, and get on to your horse before the afternoon is wasted!"

What exhilaration! What freedom! Mary, as a forward thinker who espoused the modernist views of Mary Wollstonecraft, experienced at first hand the release from at least one rigid restriction: that of riding side-saddle. What would her father say if he could see her now, her skirts flying, her ankles showing as she sat astride a saddle? What would Charles think if he were here?

She and her aunt explored the estate: they trotted through the forest, the horses' hooves disturbing the silence; they walked the mares round the lake, with its hazy reflections of the willows rippling in the light breeze; they cantered across the farthest fields of the estate to inspect the loved pets' burial ground, where the gravestones of Rusty, Toby, Pickles and Moppet were visible.

When they stopped for a rest beside the river which ran lazily through the estate, Aunt Russell, never one for introductory ramblings, got straight to the point with a personal question. "What are your hopes, Mary?"

"To be secure and contented," Mary answered.

"What are your expectations?"

"The security of attending to my mother and father in Longbourn, and this gives me contentment."

"But what kind of security is this?" Ruby Russell demanded. She herself had married at the age of twenty, and here was her niece, aged one-and-twenty, with no husband, nor any beau, nor any real social graces for attracting one. It worried her. Mary needed to do something about herself, to take matters into her own hands and not let the years slip by. She would stir her into some kind of action. "When your father dies, Longbourn will be passed on to my cousin, Mr

Collins. What will happen then? This must surely have crossed your mind."

Her words had completely the opposite of the intended effect. For Mary, the pleasure of the afternoon was dissipating fast. She made no answer to her aunt, but her thoughts were being dragged away from the present afternoon of freedom to the reality of her life. Mary knew that her future was uncertain. Of course it had crossed her mind! But what was to be done? As she projected her mind to a time thirty years hence, with both parents dead, the prospect of being an old maid, dependent on the generosity of relations, was unappealing and dismaying. Marriage was unlikely within the stagnant social sphere at Meryton, and her mother needed her, so she could never get away from that responsibility. What other opportunities were there? Mary Wollstonecraft may have given her ideas, but there were no means of achieving independence or emancipation. She may have defied the norm by riding astride a horse for an afternoon, but she was nevertheless bound by custom, propriety and expected behaviour. There were no opportunities. No, she could never get away.

"Yes, it has crossed my mind, Aunt Russell," she admitted in stoical tones, resigned to her lot.

"We should return to the house," Aunt Russell suddenly decided, to cover up her regret at having broached this topic, which had obviously touched a raw spot. How thoughtless she had been! "The children need to be prepared for their music lesson. Charles should be here within the hour."

How dearly did Mary wish to return to the house and dismount, lest Charles should see her sitting astride the saddle like a man, but her wish was not to be granted.

"And there he is!" exclaimed Aunt Russell, waving at the rider in the distance.

There was no mistaking the meaning of her gesticulation, and Charles was beside them in less than ten seconds, skilfully bringing his fine bay hunter to a halt beside them.

Charles took his hat off in salutation. "Ladies! My dear aunt, and Miss Mary Bennet! What a delightful surprise!"

"Good afternoon, Charles. You see, I am as good as my word. I am showing my niece round the grounds. We have had a delightful afternoon. But now it is time for me to return to the house to see to Roseanna and Ellen. If you would be good enough, Charles, to escort Mary back to the house, I should be so grateful." Without further ado, she pulled on the rein to turn her mare, Shallow Water, and set off at the gallop towards the house in the distance.

Mary had remained quiet, with not even a greeting to Charles. How impolite she must appear! She was trying to understand why he was here beside the river when he had music lessons to give. And what did her aunt mean when she said, "I am as good as my word"? Had Charles desired to meet her, on her own? Had he and her aunt hatched this plan? She was beginning to feel like a pawn in a game of chess, with the superior pieces making all the moves, or like a puppet with the puppet master pulling all the strings. Even now, with Charles at her side, she was still bound and constricted, with no free will or self-determination.

"How do you like the estate?" Charles asked her, unaware of Mary's views.

"Varied," she replied.

"What did you think of the forest?"

"Quiet and secluded."

"And the lake?" Charles dropped his voice. "Was the lake as beautiful as it was last night in the moonlight?"

Memories came flooding back. "Nothing is as beautiful in the daylight," Mary said honestly.

"Ah!" Charles sighed. "I understand." After a pause, brisk and business-like, he said, "I think we should go up to the house. Two little girls expect to learn some new musical pieces. A minuet today: something happy and uplifting."

Mary was aware of the double-edged meaning to her words, and how they had been construed, how they must hurt him. She wanted to explain what she meant. The lake was not as beautiful as it had been in the moonlight. But he had taken her serious comment to encompass him and their fleeting time together as well. Yes, she had been annoyed with her situation in life, but she had not meant to hurt him. There was nothing wrong in his wish to meet her. She should be flattered. There was nothing wrong with her aunt's concern for her future well-being. She should be grateful. She wished with all her heart that she could take her words back. But Charles had turned his horse and awaited her. Together, side by side, they rode up to the house, both lost in their own thoughts.

CHAPTER X

LYDIA'S PARTY

"Mr Bennet, cannot you persuade your sister and Mr Russell to accompany us to Lydia's entertainment?" Mrs Bennet demanded.

"I fear not!" Mr Bennet shook his head. "They are quite determined that they cannot attend, on account of Mr Tremayne's usual weekend attendance at Willow Wood."

"Pooh! He could entertain himself for an evening. He could play the piano to his heart's content!"

"My dear, it is too late. We are already in the carriage."

"It will appear so rude and ungrateful! Do not you think so, Mary? You are usually so fastidious about these matters of manners."

Mary stated the obvious, in agreement with her father: "It is too late. But I do think we should leave now, or *we* shall be too late." She smiled at her own play on words.

"Now, Mary, have you got all that you require for your overnight stay, and clothes for the morrow?" Mrs Bennet had looked askance at Mary's single lady's case, barely commodious enough for a nightgown.

"Yes, Mama. Do not fret!"

"Mr Braden," commanded Mr Bennet, knocking on the front of the carriage with his evening cane, "to Mr and Mrs Wickham's domicile, if you please."

"As fast as the horses' legs can go!" added Mrs Bennet loudly.

Mary was in good spirits. Her aunt's words the previous day had had a startling effect on her. A party, albeit at the Wickhams', was a golden opportunity for her to socialise and to be self-determining. She was therefore wearing the brightest of Aunt Philips's generous provision of gowns, the pink silk, as a statement of her independence, though her own sense of decency forbade her to follow the Lady of Distinction's advice of leaving "her bosom bared", so she wore some delicate white lace tucked into the top of the bodice.

"Good heavens, Mary," exclaimed Lydia, having shown her to the upstairs room where she was to stay the night, "is this all you have brought with you? When I travel I have boxes and boxes!"

"I have all that is necessary, thank you." She took off her purple cloak.

"Upon my word, Mary, you look quite pretty tonight. But remove the lace, dear one. There is one gentleman who is particularly eager to meet you, and he is stylish in his attire. Mr Fitzroy Sinclair is his name. You already know his parents."

"How do I know them?"

"Colonel and Mrs Sinclair! They were at Aunt Russell's soirée. In September, when he reaches his maturity, he will inherit Blanton Estate in Wiltshire. He will be worth thousands. He is an avid reader, like yourself, and if you will play one or two of your favourite Italian opera pieces, he will sing for you. I declare, you have so much in common."

Mr Fitzroy Sinclair stood out from the crowd. Immaculately dressed, with crisp white linen shirt and cravat, a double-breasted maroon waistcoat with a high collar, a navy blue tailored coat, and modern light-brown trousers, he was a dandy following in Beau Brummell's footsteps. Even his short fair hair was waxed neatly in place in the modern style. For a young man of twenty he had established himself, by appearance, as a man of fashion, and his good fortune to inherit a lucrative estate on his maturity cast him in the role of an eligible bachelor.

"Fitz, Fitz!" cried Lydia, taking him by the arm and pulling him across the room to meet Mary. "This is my sister, Miss Mary Bennet, the person whom you so wished to meet."

"I am delighted to make your acquaintance, Miss Bennet." He bowed formally to her when Lydia introduced them.

"Mr Sinclair," Mary acknowledged, with a demure curtsy.

"Call me Fitzroy. Everyone does, except for your sister! It is so much more modern, do you not think?"

"I believe it is, though I do not think my father would approve. He does not believe in a husband and wife using each other's Christian names, even when conversing in their own home."

"Times are changing. Countries have had their bloody revolutions to make change happen. Rioters in Littleport and even here in Ely want change and are prepared to do something to make it happen."

"Perhaps Napoleon's revolutionaries' methods were too drastic, when you consider the thousands of soldiers killed during the war."

"Do not mistake me! I do not sanction violence."

"And what can justify a mob of rioters attacking innocent shopkeepers in the towns, and smashing machinery in the factories up north?"

"I simply admire those who are prepared to move with the times, and dare to challenge the established order of things. As William Blake wrote in his poem *The Tyger*..."

"You know the writings of William Blake?" Mary interrupted, her eyes sparkling. Here was someone who could share her love of literature!

Fitzroy stood elegantly and recited the last lines of the poem:

"Tyger! Tyger! burning bright
"In the forests of the night,
"What immortal hand or eye
"Dare frame thy fearful symmetry?

"Note the word 'dare'! How many of us dare to effect change? In our own sphere, we shall have to embrace the future and what it holds, and not stand back, letting opportunities pass us by."

Had this attractive man read her thoughts of the previous day? "My sentiments entirely, Mr Sinclair," said Mary, already relaxing in his company, looking forward to further conversation with him.

"Call me Fitzroy," he reminded her, "and I shall call you Mary. So much more in keeping with our mutual desire to embrace the future."

The Wickhams' apartments were modest, but afforded sufficient space for ten guests to be seated at the dining table in the room to the rear of the premises. Lydia's serving girl, Nancy Smith, ably served the party with slices of leg of mutton, roast potatoes and some seasonal vegetables. The seating arrangements had been carefully organised. Captain Wilkins, unattached and eligible, sat beside the lovely Diana Moffat, Captain Moffat's sister, who was staying with them for a few days.

Caroline leant towards Mrs Bennet, as they were seated together at the table, and whispered in her ear, "We are expecting a match there. And Wilkie is such a darling! I could not hope for a more delightful brother-in-law."

Mary was delighted to discover that she was to sit beside Fitzroy Sinclair, who continually brought the conversation around to literary figures which interested him. With Mary's love and knowledge of literature, she always had plenty of erudite offerings on whatever topic he chose. It was as delightful a dinner party as she had ever attended, and all the more surprising that this pleasure should have been afforded by her sister, Lydia.

George Wickham filled everyone's hock glasses liberally, so that by the time they had all gathered together again in the front room, there was much jollity. Not even at Aunt Philips's entertainments, which were always happy occasions, were so much fun and gaiety in evidence.

Mr Bennet was enjoying his son-in-law's humorous accounts of various exploits while the regiment was in Newcastle, laughing uproariously and quite out of character at George Wickham's imitation of the peculiar dialect of the inhabitants there.

Mary and Fitzroy were now engaged in easy conversation about the Wiltshire estate he was to inherit.

"But who looks after it at the moment?"

"Since my cousin died, his steward does everything. An absolute marvel, I'm told. He keeps my father informed and will continue to do so until I reach the age of one-and-twenty. Then it will be my responsibility. I shall be a gentleman of means, with a fine house, many servants, a large estate to run. I shall want for nothing..." here he paused, and with a twinkle in his eye he concluded, "...except a wife."

"Where have you hidden your music, Fitz?" Lydia demanded. "My mother wants to hear you sing before she leaves."

"Not hidden, I assure you," he said, moving quickly to the upright pianoforte beside the chimney breast and indicating a number of sheets already placed on the top. Holding out his hand towards Mary, he asked, "Would you be good enough to play for me? I have a couple of pieces I should like to sing."

"Be quiet, everyone!" Lydia called out. "Fitz is going to sing."

Mary sat down and peeled off her white evening gloves in readiness to play the first piece of music. Fitzroy stood dramatically beside her.

"This is an Italian song, *Nel Mio Cuore*," he announced, placing his hand on his chest, "which means *In My Heart*."

As Mary played this and another Italian song, *Si Tu M'ami*, translated as *If You Love Me*, Fitzroy's sonorous tenor voice filled the room. Mr Bennet, who was not fond of music, Italian or English, merely watched this young man with amusement. There was something pretentious in Fitzroy's haughty stance, with his hand pressed against his heart as he sang. Mrs Bennet, her face flushed through imbibing three glasses of wine with her mutton, was nudged by Lydia every time that Fitzroy looked at Mary during his rendition of the first song. During the second piece, it was Mrs Bennet who nudged Lydia, and gave her knowing winks.

Fitzroy's next choice for Mary to play was *Plaisir d'Amour*.

"Sing something in English, my dear fellow!" slurred Captain Moffat. "We have had quite enough of those damn French on the battlefield. Their love songs are not welcome in our fine English houses!"

As Mary began to play *My Love Is Like a Red, Red Rose*, Mr Braden arrived with the carriage to take Mr and Mrs Bennet back to the Russells' house, and to bed.

Mrs Bennet could be heard protesting in the vestibule, "That is not English. It is one of the airs from that Scottish poet. What is his name? I can never remember."

George Wickham, returning to the room after seeing his parents-in-law off his premises, repeated what his mother-in-law had said.

"That is a Scottish air!" he said loudly. "Fitzroy, I insist you desist!" He laughed at his own rhyme. Placing his hands on Mary's shoulders, more to steady himself than as a show of brotherly affection, he wheedled, "Come on, Mary, play us a pretty English ditty." He laughed again at another rhyme. "Pretty ditty!"

So Mary did play an English ditty, *Scarborough Fair*, followed by *Lavender's Blue,* unaware that this was a song often sung in taverns by raucous soldiers and sailors.

"Lavender's blue, diddle diddle, Lavender's green,
When I am king, diddle diddle, you shall be queen.
Lavender's green, diddle diddle, Lavender's blue,
You must love me, diddle diddle, 'cause I love you,"
loudly sang the three inebriated captains.

To the young women present, the lyrics seemed innocent, but Captains Wickham, Moffat and Whitely, in the last of whose lap Caroline Moffat was now nestling, knew their significance. They also knew other lewd verses, which, despite their intoxication and to their credit, they refrained from singing in this mixed company.

So the music and singing continued past midnight and into the early hours of the morning. It was two o'clock when the guests finally left.

Fitzroy was the last to leave, and he held Mary's ungloved hand to his lips so long as he made his farewells that she was trembling at his touch, and captivated by his light blue eyes, which looked into hers with passion, or what she imagined passion to be.

CHAPTER XI

THE WALK

The following morning, it had been arranged that Mary would accompany George and Lydia Wickham to morning service in St Mary's church, after which they were to go to the Lamb Hotel for luncheon. Simon Braden was due to collect Mary from the Wickhams' lodgings at three o'clock.

George Wickham was not in such fine spirits, after the excesses during the previous night's entertainment. He had a pulsating headache and he was suffering from a sore throat, having raucously sung too many popular songs. He would not go to the church service, and, no, he would eat nothing until his stomach settled. Luncheon was out of the question.

"Lord, Mary, if we are to go out and about together, we shall have to do something about your hair," announced Lydia, as Mary was pinning her hair back, as sleekly as was possible with her naturally wavy hair, into her customary neat bun.

Mary remembered the milliner's same words when she and Aunt Philips had been to Summerton: "*You really must make yourself look more modern and stylish*." These were two words which had special significance for Mary in the wake of the happenings of the night before. She therefore did not object when Lydia loosened her hair for her and made a straight parting from her forehead to the nape of her neck. Lydia was deftly able to gather the hair above the ears and secure it on each side with a pair of matching combs, allowing some loose natural curls to cascade as a frame for Mary's face. A pretty blue bonnet, chosen by Aunt Philips, was the crowning glory.

"You look as pretty as a picture. We are now ready to face the world, sister dear. And Ely is all the world at present, until the regiment is relocated in Brighton. Did I tell you we are to go to Brighton next month? Such excitement! You shall visit me there, to rekindle acquaintances."

Lydia continued to chatter incessantly about the attractions that Brighton offered all the way down St Mary's Street towards the centre of Ely, where the Lamb Hotel was located. She suddenly grabbed Mary's arm.

"Look, Mary! Across the street. It is your friend. It's Fitz!"

Mary could not deny that this unexpected meeting was a delight to her, and the additional pleasure of his being regarded as her friend.

"Fitz! Fitz!" called Lydia, picking up her skirts and running indecorously across the road.

Mary stayed where she was, and within moments Fitzroy, the most handsome and stylish man she had ever seen, was raising his hat to her and bowing gracefully, while she dropped him a curtsy.

"This is a delightful surprise," he said with sincerity.

"Oh, Fitz! Tell us what you think of Mary's new hair style!" Lydia eagerly demanded. "Is it not exquisite?"

"It is most elegant," he replied, looking from one side of her head to the other, admiring Mary's erstwhile concealed tresses.

Mary tingled with pleasure at such flattery. No man had ever called her "elegant". Indeed, no one at all had ever described her in that way.

"Is it far you walk, ladies? Perhaps I can accompany you part of the way?"

"Do not be an idiot, Fitz. Of course you can accompany us, and all the way, too. We are going to the Lamb Hotel for luncheon. You must join us."

"Allow me to escort you," he volunteered, offering his left arm to Lydia and his right to Mary, adding, with a significant look at Mary, "and, as nearly a man of means, it will be my pleasure to settle the luncheon account afterwards."

After a huge luncheon, it was Lydia's turn to feel indisposed.

"Lord!" she complained, leaning forwards and holding her midriff. "After last night's enormous helpings of mutton, I thought I should never eat again, and now, with the Rances' delicious fare, I am bloated!"

"Come, Lydia," said Mary, "you need some fresh air." She deemed it best to remove Lydia from the present surroundings, where people could hear her loud and unseemly comments.

"Oh, please, I need to go to bed!" Lydia earnestly implored, as they made their way from the dining room to the front door of the hotel. "I am decidedly ill."

With Mary supporting her on one side and Fitzroy on the other, Lydia was led back to the Wickhams' lodgings, her feet sometimes dragging and her head sometimes lolling, as if she were in a swoon.

In the front room of the lodgings, which had resounded with loud singing the night before, was seated George Wickham. He was now fully and miraculously recovered, it appeared, from the aforementioned afflictions of the head and throat, enjoying the company of Captains Moffat and Wilkins, and two more officers of their regiment. They were playing cards, and there was money on the table.

"Your wife is unwell," Mary said.

"Does she need a physician?" George asked, rising from the card table.

"It is colic, I believe," said Fitzroy.

"I need bed rest," moaned Lydia. Alert to the proceedings in her front room, she tartly added, "Pray, do not disturb yourself, George. Do not break up your little party. Mary can assist to me."

Mary attended to her sister, and only when she was settled and almost sleeping did she venture downstairs. She felt uncomfortable and out of place in the Wickhams' front room. Fitzroy was standing wordlessly by the empty grate, and she was the only lady present. There was no alternative but to sit down, the game suspended by stilted conversation between George and herself, and wait for Simon Braden to take her back to Willow Wood.

"Why do you not meet the carriage half-way?" suggested George Wickham, sensing Mary's discomfort, as well as wishing to continue the poker game. "Fitzroy, be a dear fellow! A fine day for a walk."

Fitzroy willingly took the hint, and to Mary's relief they escaped from the Wickhams' lodgings. As they passed the gates of the garrison on Bugg's Hill, the guard on duty saluted Fitzroy, as a mark of respect to the son of his commanding officer.

"Good afternoon, soldier," Fitzroy said in greeting, and walked on past, tucking Mary's arm neatly into his.

She stiffened and pulled her arm back, for custom's sake.

"It is so much more satisfactory than adhering to age-old customs, do you not think, Mary?" asked Fitzroy, gently but firmly taking her arm and placing it in his. "Much more modern!"

When she did not resist, he patted her arm and smiled charmingly, his blue eyes laughing in the afternoon sunlight. They looked, to any passer-by, as if they were walking out together, like a courting couple with parental approval. Mary's mind was afloat with gay abandonment. She was in high spirits, enjoying the sensation of flouting custom for once, convention thrown to the winds, engaged in easy discourse with this stylish young gentleman. She sincerely hoped that Simon Braden would be late for his three o'clock assignation.

They had walked almost a mile, when round the corner came a familiar figure on a bay hunter. Mary involuntarily gasped, and hastily withdrew her arm from Fitzroy's, but not before Charles had noticed. He dismounted before the couple.

"Miss Mary Bennet." He raised his riding hat to her and bowed. "I had not expected to see you this weekend. I am on my way home."

Mary noted his disapproving look. She now regretted her carefree behaviour of a few minutes before, pleasurable though it had been.

"May I present Mr Fitzroy Sinclair?" she almost stuttered, experiencing all the awkwardness of the situation in which she found herself.

Charles was scrutinising her. She could see he was not impressed with the elegance of her new stylish fashion for her hair. Her hand involuntarily went to her face to push back some curls, which bobbed uncomfortably round her ears.

She continued, "You met his parents, Colonel and Mrs Sinclair, at our aunt and uncle's soirée last week."

"A pleasure, sir."

"Ah, yes!" exclaimed Fitzroy, with no formal salutation. "You are the Cornishman. I have heard about your misfortune. My commiserations, sir!"

Charles's face turned pale, and he answered not a syllable to Fitzroy. He addressed Mary instead. "Your aunt is looking forward to your company. Invitations are to be written."

"Invitations to what, pray?"

"Your sister and mother have worked on the kindness of our aunt and the hospitality of our uncle, and they have been persuaded to host a ball at Willow Wood, at the end of your visit."

"A ball!" said Mary, immediately recovering her spirits at the prospect of an opportunity to be with Fitzroy, on the assumption that he would undoubtedly be invited with his parents. She was looking at him.

"There is much to do," Charles interrupted her thoughts, his expression serious and sad. "The practicalities of such a venture at such short notice are enormous, but our aunt has an indomitable spirit and she is confident that, with your assistance, all the necessary arrangements will be completed in time."

"It will be my pleasure," Mary assured him.

He mounted his bay hunter. "I shall bid you good day, Miss Bennet, and I hope to see you next weekend." There was no mistaking the undercurrent of meaning to his words. He hoped that she would not be spending time with this young man.

To Fitzroy he said, "Thank you for your commiserations, Mr Sinclair. It has indeed been a trying year. Good day, sir." He had no time for this young dandy upstart whose tongue had run away with him, uncivilly broaching a taboo personal topic, which he preferred to keep to himself. It was unthinkable for a stranger to so directly address anyone regarding their fortunes or misfortunes.

Mary had no time to ask Fitzroy what he meant by Charles's misfortune, nor to enthuse about the forthcoming ball. Simon Braden appeared round the corner in the road on his way to the Wickhams' to collect her in the barouche. He was surprised to meet her half-way, and with a young man, but, in accordance with what he knew to be best policy as a servant, his face remained impassive as he bid Mr Sinclair good day and assisted Mary into the barouche.

Mary was whisked back to Willow Wood to help her aunt write the invitations to the ball, with one particular invitation uppermost in her mind. It was only when she had mounted the staircase to her quarters that she remembered that she had left her lady's case behind at Lydia's.

CHAPTER XII

THE MISFORTUNE

Mary found herself alone in the drawing room with Charles the following Friday in the hour before dinner, after Roseanna's and Ellen's music lessons. She had not seen him since they had encountered each other as she was walking with Fitzroy the previous Sunday. The Russells had been visiting friends during the afternoon and had only just returned, and they were now spending some time with their children before changing into evening attire. Mr and Mrs Bennet were in their respective quarters, dressing for dinner, which on Friday and Saturday evenings was always more lavish in preparation of mouth-watering victuals and speciality dishes, on account of Charles's weekend visits.

"Would you care to accompany me for a walk in the gardens, Mary?" requested Charles gravely. "There is something in particular I should like to tell you."

Mary was somewhat wary. She remembered his disapproving looks when they had last met, and knew that he would be advising her against a continued friendship with Fitzroy. She was in no mood to listen to his stern censure, having spent another pleasant afternoon with Fitzroy during the week, when her mother and she had been invited for afternoon tea at the Wickhams' lodgings. Fitzroy had also been invited, and when Lydia had reminded him of his desire to purchase a new cravat pin, Mrs Bennet had had no objection to Fitzroy's request for

Mary to walk with him to Lawsons, the jeweller's in Market Square. In truth, Mrs Bennet believed there was a budding match between Mary and Mr Fitzroy Sinclair, as eligible and fine-looking a young man as she had seen in her life, and one who was to inherit a large estate. She would do everything within her power to encourage their friendship to matrimonial fruition.

"I fear it may rain," Mary ineffectually murmured.

"Come, Mary, if you please," Charles said stolidly, ignoring her comment. Perhaps he had not heard her. "Before your parents and our aunt and uncle appear for dinner."

It was only after they had walked through the shrubbery and entered under the privet archway into the formal gardens that they stopped together and sat down on the sculpted masonry seat beside the ornamental fish pond.

Charles inhaled deeply, and with manifest deliberation, about to address Mary.

She pre-empted, "I know what you wish to say to me, Charles, and I am afraid that your opinion, much as it is of value in most cases, is not welcome at this present time. I am not about to terminate my friendship with Mr Fitzroy Sinclair simply because you have a poor estimation of him, as was evidenced by your curt behaviour to him last Sunday. He is a young man, admittedly, not yet reached his maturity, but he is perfectly amiable. We have already shared some happy times, exchanging our views on modernist thinking, talking of literature, singing popular songs together and even some Italian love songs."

"Peace, Mary," implored Charles warmly at this point. He had heard enough. "You have entirely mistaken the import of what I wish to say to you."

"Is it my changed appearance?" She self-consciously fingered her hair, which now had been dressed into ringlets which dangled at each side of her face.

"No, it most certainly is not. It is something to which your friend Mr Sinclair alluded in your presence. He referred to my 'misfortune'. You must surely recall the circumstance?"

Mary nodded.

"You, with your sense of propriety, cannot condone his impertinence."

"As I recollect, he offered his commiserations," protested Mary, in Fitzroy's defence.

"Mr Sinclair and I had only just been introduced. It was as tactless as it was uncivil to broach a subject of a personal nature." Charles paused, and with softened tones he said, "I am very sorry if I gave offence by what you describe as 'curt behaviour', but I had hoped that the events of the past year would remain within the cognisance of only a handful of friends and acquaintances. It appears I was wrong."

"Misfortune travels quickly, while good news travels not at all," observed Mary, attempting to cover up her chagrin with a wise saying. She sat tensely composed, watching the goldfish near the surface of the pond and the tench foraging for food near the bottom. She remained silent, waiting for him to speak.

"When we first met in the music room, you rightly surmised that my name is Cornish. Let me tell you the Tremayne family history. Tremayne Manor and the lands are situated on the north coast of Cornwall, near Newquay. The estate comprises one hundred acres fenced fields for cattle grazing, with some piggeries, and fifty acres of arable land. On the cliff top are three working tin mines, which have been in existence since Phoenician days.

"My older brother, Matthew, inherited all of the Tremayne estate when our father died four years ago. My mother, who was our uncle Russell's older sister, you already know, died shortly after bringing me into the world. My father, an honourable and good man, endeavoured to ensure that both his older and younger sons, Matthew and myself, would be equal beneficiaries when he died. It was my father's express wish that while my brother would continue to run the estate, I should be responsible for working the three tin mines deep within the land. To that end I have devoted my life to developing wind-pumping machines to assist in the mining process, and to the safety of my loyal team of experienced miners. A sizeable income was to be had, sufficient for a gentleman to live on." Charles paused.

Mary waited for him to continue.

"You will have noted, Mary, with your quickness of recognition of the use of English, that I say a sizeable income *was* to be had. The past tense."

"What has happened to the income?"

"Since my father's death, my brother has become an incorrigible gambler. Perhaps this was a direct result of grief; perhaps temptations were put across his path by unscrupulous rogues. Whatever the reason, with his unaccustomed easy access to money, nothing would stop him, no admonition had a beneficial effect, not one jot of my advice was heeded. He has gambled and lost. Within this past year he has sold off all the land on the Tremayne estate, which has been in the family for generations, to clear his debts. He now resides in lodgings in the Isle of Dogs in London. The Russells responded to his pleas for help and agreed to give him an annual allowance to enable him to live with some degree of comfort and security. I fear he may squander the money on his gaming habit."

"But you are secure, are you not?" Mary's concern showed in the depths of her dark brown eyes. "I mean your tin mines?"

Charles shook his head. "I have no means of financial support from them. Matthew sold all of the estate, tin mines included."

"This surely cannot be!" exclaimed Mary in some agitation. "It was your father's express wish!"

"It was his wish, but, by the laws of inheritance, the estate was passed on to the older son."

Mary knew about the anomalies and injustices of the laws of inheritance, not only for younger brothers, but for women as well, for Longbourn was to be entailed to Mr Bennet's nearest male relative on Mr Bennet's death. "Such laws should be changed! They are a disgrace!"

"The mines belong to the new owners of the estate: the Grimshaws of Cheapside! They made their money from trade and have no interest in running the mines. They have closed them permanently, with no Christian charity or consideration for those whose livelihood depended on them. As a result, my loyal mining families are facing poverty and near-destitution, with no other option but to leave the area in search of work in Bristol or Birmingham. I gave them all three months' wages, to help them make a new start. And so I lodge in Blixford, as you know, with my Methodist landlady."

Mary was shocked that such a terrible change of fortune could happen to Charles. He bore it with such fortitude, with no bitterness, no sense of the injustices of the world heaped on his shoulders, that she could do nothing but admire him. How paltry did her earlier diatribe seem, and how foolish was her consideration that he was critical of her appearance! With such problems as his, how could he find it in his heart to think about her flirtatious behaviour with Fitzroy, or her ringlets?

"I am so sorry!" she said. A simple expression, but it encapsulated all her present sentiments.

"So this is why, at an age when I should be a gentleman of means, all I can do is make a passable living as a humble attorney's apprentice, and as piano tutor to our cousins and to other children of rich parentage. Our aunt and uncle are most generous, and their hospitality here at Willow Wood saves me money on lodgings at the weekends, so that I am able to live comfortably with the appearance of a gentleman, at least."

"Oh, but you are a gentleman," protested Mary, "in every sense of the word. There is nothing 'humble' in your bearing, nor in your prospects. I am sure of that. One day soon, you will graduate from apprentice attorney to a position of attorney in a big town somewhere with many clients, and…"

"My dear Mary," Charles interrupted her hopes for his future. "How kind you are, but I fear that the day you talk about is impossible. Available positions as attorney are usually passed on to family members, as is the case of my apprenticeship in Blixford: father to son, not to me. It is rare indeed to find an attorney who can pass on the position to a stranger."

"But my grandfather, Mr Gardiner, was an attorney and passed on the living to his apprentice, my uncle Philips," Mary earnestly assured him.

"Mr Gardiner was father-in-law to your uncle. The living was passed from father-in-law to son-in-law," he said sadly. "It is virtually the same situation."

Mary could not deny this.

Charles stood up abruptly, sighing with an air of hopelessness, before Mary could suggest any further comforting possibilities. He offered his arm, and she willingly took it. It seemed the most natural thing to do. Together they walked silently back to the house.

Just before they went in, Charles stopped. He took his arm away from hers and quietly said, "I will leave it to your discretion whether or not you apprise your parents of my situation." In a more jovial tone he added, "Let us enter and be merry!"

CHAPTER XIII

DANCE PRACTICE

Throughout dinner, Aunt Russell had been excitedly talking about the forthcoming Willow Wood ball.

"Fifty of the seventy invited guests have replied so far," she announced gaily, "in the affirmative."

"This should be pleasing to you, Ruby," Uncle Russell said. "You have been eager to have a ball for many months, and, with all these replies, a big gathering is already assured."

Musicians from Ely had been hired, and the head musician, Mr Jeremiah Norris, had already been to Willow Wood to discuss with Aunt Russell some of the pieces which she would like him to play.

"Mr Norris is to play a Mozart first minuet. Our first one," Aunt Russell corrected herself, laughing a little, "not his first one, of course!"

Charles and Mary both smiled at this allusion to Wolfgang Amadeus Mozart's amazing ability to compose music from a very early age, his first minuet having been written when he was only four years old.

"And which piece have you selected for the dance we are to lead?" Uncle Russell asked, in the certain knowledge that no practical detail would have been omitted from her agenda of arrangements.

"I have selected a new, lively piece. Perhaps one of you would be good enough to play this for us this weekend,"

Aunt Russell suggested to Charles and Mary, "in order to familiarise ourselves with its intricacies."

"Mary has excellent sight-reading," said Charles. "I suspect she will do the piece more justice than I."

During the rest of the dinner, Aunt Russell regaled them with details of the domestic arrangements: Cook had secured extra staff from Ely to help with the traditional concluding midnight five-course dinner, which would began with soup, include a middle course of venison pie and end with trifle, while Uncle Russell had selected some vintage wines from his cellar which he deemed to be both sufficiently palatable for the guests and enough to satisfy the members of the militia who were to attend.

"These soldiers can drink prodigious amounts, as if each day is to be their last," he complained jovially. "Whether there is a war on or not!"

Mrs Bennet was in particularly high spirits, her mind awash with thoughts that there was to be a ball. She had already decided on her attire and her coiffure for the event. A ball was always an exciting entertainment, and dear Lydia and her Mr Wickham were to be guests, along with a number of the militia. "Nothing pleases me more than to see men in smart militia uniforms," she giggled girlishly.

"My dear, do not expect me to don a scarlet tunic," commented Mr Bennet dryly, "though I give you permission to dance all night, with as many of the soldiers of our king and his regent as your palpitations will permit!"

"Brother!" cried Aunt Russell. "You remind me that we must practise our steps and figures."

Mr Bennet put up his hand and said sternly, "I have no desire to take to the floor on the evening of the ball, so I have no need to practise either steps or figures."

"But you must assist us," said Mrs Bennet, with more firmness than was her wont, "for all of us here do intend to dance. And I do declare," she continued persuasively, "that your minuet was much admired at the Hursts' ball last winter."

"It was you, my dear brother, who taught me the minuet, when I was only twelve." With this hint of nostalgia, it was Aunt Russell's turn to be persuasive. "You simply must indulge us on this occasion."

"Very well, very well!" sighed Mr Bennet, knowing that it was useless to object any further.

Immediately the dessert was finished, and not allowing time for the ladies to retire to the drawing room or for the gentlemen to enjoy a cigar and a glass of port, Aunt Russell insisted that they all go to the ballroom. They trooped after her, across the panelled hall where heads of antlered stags and other hunting trophies looked down on them. Mrs Bennet tripped eagerly behind her sister-in-law, while a disgruntled Mr Bennet took up the rear.

The ballroom was a magnificent feature of Willow Wood, located in the east wing, overlooking the lawns and sweeping carriageway through the lime trees. The stucco work on the ceiling had been exquisitely fashioned by craftsmen in the days of Uncle Russell's grandfather, when the ballroom had been built on to the east wing of the existing manor house. At the same time a matching addition had been built on to the west wing to accommodate an extensive library, a billiards room and a gun room.

"Oh dear!" exclaimed Aunt Russell. "We are only six! How can we practise the quadrille when we are only six?"

"Surely we can imagine the other two," suggested Mrs Bennet, already looking forward to the evening of dancing practice, all palpitations far distant in her mind.

"No, that will not do." Aunt Russell left the room abruptly, returning a few minutes later with Mrs Brown, the thin housekeeper, and the African footman with his white wig and purple livery. Both were looking very uncomfortable in their unaccustomed role.

Aunt Russell was a firm but kind woman, who looked after her staff with understanding. She wished to alleviate their discomfort in some measure. "Mrs Brown, if you would do us the honour of being Mr Russell's partner for the quadrille?" And she herself offered her arm to the African footman.

The quadrille presented many difficulties, as the four ill-assorted couples faced each other in the formation of a square. The head couple was Aunt Russell and the African footman; their opposite couple was Mr Bennet and Mary, the former complaining all the while that he would do himself an injury; the side couples were Mrs Bennet with Charles, facing Uncle Russell and thin Mrs Brown. As the head couple and their opposites moved forwards to meet each other, Mr Bennet could be seen alternately scowling at his sister and smiling encouragingly at the black man. When it was the side couples' turn to advance to the middle of the square, Uncle Russell looked most uncomfortable taking the hand of the diminutive housekeeper. Mrs Bennet made numerous mistakes with the sequence of steps and moves, despite Charles's gentle reminders.

Aunt Russell was adamant that they should complete three repeats of the movements.

"I think we have mastered this one, my dear," Uncle Russell said in a hoarse whisper to his wife, eager to get away from the housekeeper who held stiffly and grimly to his hand throughout.

Mrs Brown and the African footman were excused and thanked for their valuable assistance, and hurriedly escaped from their unusual ordeal.

While Aunt Russell left the ballroom to find a dancing manual in the library, the remaining members of the quadrille sat on the padded ballroom chairs at the side of the dancing area, in order to regain their breath.

Mr Bennet's curiosity, which he had kept subdued since their arrival at Willow Wood, now finally overcame him.

"Look here, John," he said, addressing his brother-in-law unusually by his Christian name, "I have to know under what terms that fellow is here."

"Which fellow?"

"The African," Mr Bennet answered bluntly. "Is he a slave or a servant?"

Mary was also eager to hear her uncle's response.

"A paid servant, of course!" Uncle Russell looked abashed, but slapped his thigh and laughed.

"That is a relief," admitted Mr Bennet. "I was finding it most difficult looking the fellow in the eye." He remembered earlier times. "You and I had our differences, to be sure."

"With some heated arguments on the matter, if I recall correctly," Uncle Russell added, leaning back on his chair. "You were right, in that instance. Slavery was antiquated, even in those days."

Uncle Russell now turned to Mary and Charles and explained, "I used to support slavery all those years ago. Now I am heartily ashamed of such poor judgement. If I had taken heed of the abolitionists thirty years ago, when I was a young man, then I would have changed my mind sooner. But they were evangelical Protestants and Quakers. That was indubitably not my style in those days."

Mr Bennet smiled. "They were called the 'Saints', do you remember?"

"Exactly, and there was nothing too saintly about me then. Far too much young blood in my veins!"

Mary knew that despite Mr Grenville's impassioned speech to the House of Lords finally persuading them that slavery was "contrary to the principles of justice, humanity and sound policy", and despite the passing of the Act for the Abolition of the Slave Trade in 1807, in reality the law did not eradicate the British slave trade. British sea captains still continued to be actively involved in the unlawful trading of captured slaves. If caught by the British Navy, a fine of

£100 was levied for every slave found aboard; this in its turn brought about more actions which were contrary to humanity, because, rather than pay the fines, these heartless sea captains would order the unfortunate slaves to be thrown overboard.

Before Uncle Russell could expand on his unsaintly behaviour in his youth, Aunt Russell returned to the ballroom, brandishing a book from the library. "Here it is. This should ensure that we are as near perfection as possible. We shall move on to the line formation dances next, if everyone is agreeable." She looked especially at the relaxed forms of her brother and her husband, both of whose countenances suggested they were far from agreeable to any further activity.

She opened Thomas Wilson's newly published manual on dancing and read out the title, *The Treasures of Terpsichore*, to the assembled group.

"Never heard of it," protested Uncle Russell. "Terpsichore! Damned silly name, if you ask me!"

"Mary will know what it means," Mrs Bennet declared, and for once she sounded proud of Mary's erudition.

"The muse of song and dance," explained Mary.

"Then why do they not call the book *The Treasures of Song and Dance*," exclaimed Uncle Russell, "so that we can all understand it?"

It was customary for the host and hostess to lead one of the dance formations, and Aunt Russell insisted that two more of the dance formations would be led by the present company. Thereafter, whoever chose to lead or "call" a dance would tell the musicians which music to play and would show the dancers which steps they were all to perform. It was therefore essential that individual sets of figures be mastered by the couples who would be calling the dance, so that the line of waiting couples could observe which steps they were to dance when they had moved up the line and it was their turn.

Aunt Russell read out four relevant passages from Mr Wilson's manual, ending with, "*When the couple calling the Dance has gone down three couples, then the second couple should begin, and so on with all the couples in succession, till after the one that called it has regained the top and proceeded again three couples downwards, where the Dance is finished; and the couple that called it must stand at the bottom for the next Dance.*"

Mrs Bennet was confused. "What does it mean by *three couples downwards*?"

Mr Bennet was even more convinced that he should not partake in this dubious pastime. "My dear sister, much as I wish you success at this ball, leading a dance is absolutely out of the question. It will have to be left to the young ones. Mary, you and Charles will have to do!"

Uncle Russell, about to quit the ballroom, flatly stated, "I need a port and cigar, without further ado."

Aunt Russell, for all her original eagerness, was almost defeated. Mr Wilson's book seemed to take all the enjoyment out of the preparations and anticipation of the ball. "I suggest we return to this practice tomorrow. Come, Sister," she sighed, taking Mrs Bennet by the arm, "let us partake of a soothing glass of Madeira wine in the drawing room."

As the others left the ballroom for the comforts of softly upholstered armchairs, Charles and Mary continued to practise a particular set of steps for the figure which they would use when they led their set at the Willow Wood ball. They engaged in the task with much concentration, making reference to numerous pieces of advice to be found in Thomas Wilson's manual. Together they hummed pieces of music which might best suit their particularly lively arrangement of steps. They eventually decided on the folk melody of the fourth movement of Franz Josef Haydn's *Symphony Number 104 in D major*, the *London Symphony*, whose sonata-allegro form would most certainly be appropriate. They became more and more breathless with each dos-a-dos, interspersed with heel clicks, spirals and turns, with a final gallop between the imaginary lines of participants to the end.

When they decided their dance was perfected, Charles and Mary stood facing one another.

"Miss Mary Bennet," Charles addressed her formally, perspiration glistening on his brow, his hair awry. He bowed graciously, with his palm outstretched towards her, to take her hand for the final rehearsal of their dance. "Would you do me the honour?"

"Why, thank you, Mr Tremayne, it is a pleasure," she responded in all seriousness, standing straight and demure, unaware that her face was prettily flushed and her ringlets were coming loose.

CHAPTER XIV

THE MORNING POST

Whereas the ballroom in the east wing of Willow Wood was light and happy, the library in the west wing was sober and quiet. The ballroom shone bright with glittering chandeliers, white walls, light blue alcoves with chaise-longues and ballroom chairs covered in cream satin brocade to match the window drapes. The library, on the other hand, exuded a dark air of academia and opulence, with floor to ceiling oak bookcases, a range of oak tables and chairs, studded dark green leather armchairs and four Persian carpets of an overall maroon hue. It was so wet and dreary outside, on the morning following the dance practice, that Mrs Brown had instructed the downstairs maids to light the lamps in the library.

When Charles entered the library shortly after breakfast, Mary was already seated at the table beside the front-facing window, poring over a tome which she had extracted from one of the lower bookcases. She had not dared to venture up the ladder to reach up to the higher shelves; it was not that she was afraid of heights, but she did have a fear of falling. She had settled for *The Geographical Features of the West Country*, a book which was within easy reach and with contents which would satisfy her curiosity about one location in particular.

"I thought I would find you in here," observed Charles quietly, befitting the general hushed ambience of the library.

"I cannot resist visiting a fine library, and this is one of the finest, on equal standing with the extensive library at Pemberley, which belongs to Mr Darcy, my brother-in-law."

"Have you an extensive library at Longbourn?" asked Charles.

"Not extensive, and I doubt that it is adequate for anyone of an enquiring mind," Mary answered honestly. "I crave more books, but the more I read, the more my mother complains. I have read and reread all the books in my father's study which he deems to be suitable for a young lady. I borrow what I can."

"What is it you read at the moment?"

Mary closed the book and showed him the title.

"The West Country!" he almost whispered. His heart was a mixture of sadness that he should never see his West Country home in Cornwall again, and elation that Mary should want to know more about the land of his forefathers, the land of his birth.

It was only when he had removed to the far end of the library, and had climbed the ladder to reach one of the uppermost shelves where first editions of Walter Scott's works were placed for security, that Mary reopened her book and avidly read about the high downland of Salisbury Plain, the druid stone circle of Stonehenge and the medieval cathedral in Salisbury, which were the main features of Wiltshire, the West Country county which held a particular interest for her.

Just then, the door burst open and in flounced Mrs Bennet, her mob cap in need of a fixing pin.

"There you are, Mary," she called out loudly. "I've been scouring the whole house looking for you. I am fairly worn out with running hither and thither."

"Whatever is the matter?" asked Mary, closing her book.

Mrs Bennet plumped herself down on an occasional chair beside Mary, and wafted a letter at her. "This is the matter! This letter from your aunt Philips, my very foolish sister Philips, is the matter."

"You do my aunt an injustice, Mama."

"Indeed I do not!

"What possible reason can you have for such a changed opinion of your favourite sister?"

"She expects you to marry Mr Bolton!"

Mary sat speechless at such a notion. Perhaps her aunt was displaying some degree of foolishness in this instance.

"Say something, Mary!"

"Mr Bolton! But surely there is some mistake, Mama. Mr Bolton is engaged to Mrs Maria Tamworth, whose perfections have dominated his thoughts and conversation over these past few months."

"Listen to this, Mary!" Mrs Bennet's voice carried clearly to the far end of the library and to the top of the high ladder there, where Charles remained motionless, and unseen by her. She began to read: *My dear sister, I have such news to tell you. Mrs Maria Tamworth has broken her engagement with our Mr Bolton. Of course, I am not surprised. Such a giddy, silly young woman, all feathers and fine airs, a widow with little intelligence to speak of! The only thing to recommend her is her money. When she came to Meryton last week, there was no indication that she was disinclined to marry him, but then a letter arrived this morning saying that she refused to marry him and how small village life would be the death of her. If you ask me, I should say that he is better off without her. But how fortunate for Mary! This opens a door of opportunity which I had thought to have closed for ever. Mr Bolton is free to marry her now. Mr Philips and I are working hard to that end. Mary is a very dear niece and we wish to secure her happiness as much as you do. In addition, as he is likely to carry on Mr Philips's attorney business in Meryton when he dies, it will keep our father's family business in the family, so to speak. Oh, Sister, I am overjoyed at the prospect.*

Mrs Bennet closed the letter with a crumpling motion.

Mary was displeased. She was very aware that Charles would have heard all this, and she did not wish to say anything in response to this absurd notion of Aunt Philips's.

"What do you say, Mary?" demanded Mrs Bennet.

"We need to discuss this further, Mama," Mary deferred, standing up in readiness to leave the library.

"What is there to discuss? You are not going to marry Mr Bolton." Mrs Bennet's tone was belligerent. "I shall write to my sister directly and inform her that you are to marry Mr Fitzroy Sinclair."

"But, Mama…" Mary's voice trailed off as her mother left the room.

Mary placed her West Country book back in its place on the lower shelf. As she did so, she gave a backwards glance at Charles at the top of his ladder, but he was engrossed in reading and thankfully appeared not to have heard what her mother had so rashly said.

As can be expected, he had in fact heard every word with sad acknowledgement of her family's intentions to marry her off: her Meryton aunt would have her foisted on this Mr Bolton who had been spurned by a rich widow; her mother would expose her to Mr Sinclair, the dandy whose etiquette left much to be desired. Either alternative was inappropriate for a young woman of Mary's sensibilities and education. Charles remained still on his perch for fear of falling off.

Mary followed her mother out of the library to remonstrate with her and remind her that no such engagement had even been suggested, let alone agreed to. Wishing her daughter to be married and married well was to her mother's credit, but her exuberance in presuming a fait accompli was insufferable, no matter how gratifying it would be as a reality.

"Mama, I implore you to write no such letter to Aunt Philips," Mary said hotly, following her mother into the morning room where Mr Bennet was reading *The Times*.

"My dear Mary," responded Mrs Bennet with determination, "I assure you I shall."

"But there is no truth in what you have to say to Aunt Philips. I wish it were true, with all my heart, for Mr Sinclair is a most pleasing young man, but there has been no talk of matrimony between us, except when he said that he will be in want of a wife, when he reaches his maturity."

"There you are, Mary!" Mrs Bennet's tone was one of victory. "That is a clear indication that you are his intended wife. Believe me! Why else would he have made clear those sentiments to you?"

There was no denying there was sense in what her mother said.

"Is Mary to get married?" Mr Bennet, emerging from behind his open newspaper, asked with surprise verging on disbelief.

"No, Papa, I am not. Certainly not to Mr Bolton."

"Mr Bolton! No, I should think not, Mary. A dull young man, and he is to marry a rich widow, I understand."

Mrs Bennet snapped, "You understand nothing! You refused to read my sister's news from Meryton, if you recall. If you had read the letter you would now know that Mr Bolton is no longer engaged, and is now free to marry Mary."

"Preposterous! Mary has far too much sense to marry Mr Bolton. You should write to your sister to say that I do not give my consent."

"She is one-and-twenty, Mr Bennet. Have you forgot that?" Mrs Bennet eyed him smugly.

"Indeed, I have not, but should Mr Bolton ask for Mary's hand in marriage, I repeat, I will not give my consent."

"And I am not engaged to Mr Sinclair!" Mary emphatically reminded her mother.

"Mr Sinclair?" Mr Bennet was attempting to assimilate another potential suitor for Mary.

"Not yet!" Mrs Bennet nodded significantly.

"And I beg you not to write a letter saying that I am. It would be most improper."

"Pooh, Mary! If we were all to take heed of what you consider to be improper, we would allow you to die an old maid!"

Mary could feel tears welling up.

"My dear, I think you have said enough," Mr Bennet advised his wife. "It can only be to Mary's advantage to adhere to the propriety of telling the absolute truth, whatever the consequences. I suggest you write to your sister to tell her about all the excitement of the forthcoming ball, about your trips to Ely with Lydia, and how delightful you find your nieces, Roseanna and Ellen. Do not commit yourself in writing regarding Mary's matrimonial hopes or fears. She is a capable young woman, and of an age now, at one-and-twenty, as you correctly said, to make her own decisions without our help or interference."

Although Mary was being talked about in the third person, as if she were not present in the morning room, she silently thanked her father for his empathy and for allowing her time to compose herself.

Aunt Russell entered the morning room just then, Roseanna and Ellen close behind.

"This has just arrived by special post," she said. "It is news I would rather not have received."

"A negative reply to the ball invitation, Sister?" asked Mrs Bennet, keeping abreast daily of the names of those who would or would not be attending the ball on Saturday evening. She would have so much to tell her sister Philips, and so many things to boast about to Jane and her Mr Bingley during their stay at Longbourn.

"It is from the Head of Lowston College. It concerns Miss Potter."

"She is our new governess," ventured Roseanna.

Ellen tugged at her older sister's pinafore. She knew not to speak unless spoken to by one's elders. How many times had that been drummed into them?

Ignoring Ellen's hint, Roseanna continued, "Read what it says, Mama."

"Very well. *Dear Mrs Russell*," Aunt Russell read, "*I regret to inform you that Miss Potter will have to postpone the commencement of her employment as governess to your two daughters. She has suffered a badly twisted ankle after a fall down the front steps of Lowston, and Doctor Andrews, the physician who attends the college, has advised against travel for a fortnight. I apologise for the inconvenience, and hope that her new arrival date of September 8 will be acceptable to you. Yours sincerely, Miss B M Grafton.*"

Aunt Russell sighed.

Mrs Bennet had never engaged a governess for her daughters, and did not fully comprehend the difficulties of running a big estate with many staff when one had two children in need of care, attention and education for five days of the week. "Do not distress yourself, Sister," was all that she could manage.

"She sounds like a careless sort of young woman, falling down steps just when she is needed," observed Mr Bennet. "You will need to advise her to hold on to stair rails, banisters and balustrades while she is in your employ."

Aunt Russell, who was usually so practical and decisive, now stood before the Bennets, apparently summoning up courage to speak her thoughts.

Roseanna, sensing her mother's reticence, spoke up. "Go on, Mama! Ask them!"

"We, that is Roseanna and Ellen, their father and I, have been discussing this matter," Aunt Russell was summoning up what appeared to be courage, for all her words came out in a rush, "and they and I would like to ask if it would be possible for Mary to stay on here at Willow Wood, until Miss Potter arrives to act as tutor."

"Mary to stay?" exclaimed Mrs Bennet. "Dear me, Sister Russell, I doubt if I can spare her when we return home. She is such a comfort to me with my nerves and helps to run the household."

Little Ellen's face began to show signs of imminent tears.

"My dear, you forget that Jane will be at Longbourn for the fortnight," countered Mr Bennet. "Your nerves will be well looked after by her. You have always said there is no other daughter who is as kind and thoughtful as Jane."

Mary looked down, only too aware of the unfairness of her father's remark. She had spent the last three years being as "kind and thoughtful" to her mother and her father as she knew how. Comparisons were odious, and not the stuff of humour. Constable Dogberry's solecism in Shakespeare's *Much Ado About Nothing*, "comparisons are odorous", may have produced laughter in the theatres, but in reality comparisons were very hurtful. Only a few minutes before, her father had shown her some sensitivity and understanding: now, conversely, he had treated her with a lack of tact. Mary had hoped that she had reached a time in her life when her parents would love and respect her for who she was, and not continue to show her in an unfavourable light in comparison with her sisters.

"And you, Mary?" Aunt Russell addressed her niece on equal terms. "What do you say to the proposal that you stay on? You have shown considerable teaching ability, and the girls adore you, and we could continue just as we are." As an afterthought she added, "I would offer you some remuneration."

"I cannot accept it," Mary emphatically answered.

"Please stay," begged Roseanna.

"Please, please!" echoed Ellen, horrifying even herself with her temerity in challenging the established rules of remaining silent.

Mary looked at little Ellen's imploring face and put her finger to her lips to quieten the child, saying comfortingly, "Yes, I shall stay!"

Ellen was on the verge of jumping for joy when she remembered herself.

Mary addressed Aunt Russell with a purposeful air. "But I will not accept any remuneration. It will be my pleasure to spend more time with my two cousins, and we have just embarked on learning where folk lore stories originated. The children are enjoying the stories and are drawing pictures in a special book, to show you when it is finished. It will be good to have the opportunity to complete this."

"I am most grateful to you, my dear." Aunt Russell actually squeezed Mary's arm in appreciation.

Mary looked over to her father and mother. "And, as my father correctly says, Jane will be an excellent companion for my mother."

If she were totally honest, she would have to admit to herself that there was also an ulterior motive in her agreement to stay on as tutor to Roseanna and Ellen. In the afternoons, she would be able to spend some of her free time at the Wickhams' lodgings, in the hope that a certain Fitzroy Sinclair would also be invited.

CHAPTER XV

SUNDAY WORSHIP

If Mrs Bennet was forbidden to write to her sister in Meryton about her conviction that Mary and the charming Mr Sinclair would soon be betrothed, there was nothing to stop her assisting their natural affection for one another to a higher plane of mutual love and intimacy.

"This will be our last proper Sunday here at Willow Wood, for next Sunday we shall be recovering from a late night after the ball, as well as preparing for our departure the following morning, shall we not?" she pre-ambled during the family breakfast.

"What is this leading towards, my dear?" asked Mr Bennet, finishing off the last delicious mouthfuls of his favourite breakfast dish of smoked haddock baked in milk and butter. How those soft flakes of fish melted in the mouth!

"I should like to attend St Mary's church in Ely, with dear Lydia."

"I shall attend the Reverend Smallwood's church service, as we have done each week." Mr Bennet's tone was one of resignation. Reverend Smallwood's sermons were dull and lifeless, and a waste of time. Mr Bennet would much prefer to stay in the library and internally philosophise on moral issues by reading his two guiding passages from the Bible.

The first of these was from Corinthians 13: *Love is patient, love is kind. It does not envy, it does not boast, it is not proud. It is not rude, it is not self-seeking, it is not easily angered, it keeps no record of wrongs. Love does not delight in evil but rejoices with the truth. It always protects, always trusts, always hopes, always perseveres.*

The second was the fortifying verse from Ecclesiastes 3:
There is a time for everything,
and a season for every activity under heaven:
a time to be born and a time to die,
a time to plant and a time to uproot,
a time to kill and a time to heal,
a time to tear down and a time to build,
a time to weep and a time to laugh,
a time to mourn and a time to dance,
a time to scatter stones and a time to gather them,
a time to embrace and a time to refrain,
a time to search and a time to give up,
a time to keep and a time to throw away,
a time to tear and a time to mend,
a time to be silent and a time to speak,
a time to love and a time to hate,
a time for war and a time for peace.

"Mary shall come with me to Ely." Mrs Bennet's tone was so belligerent that no one was about to argue with her.

Mary knew that Colonel and Mrs Sinclair with Fitzroy would be there too. She was inwardly smiling, grateful to her mother for affording her another chance to meet with this young man, for whom she had more than simple fondness and friendship. She thought she must be in love, but for all her reading, no writer had fully captured the quintessence of love, not even John Donne in his love poems, so she was not sure what love really was.

However, the object of these affections was not present at St Mary's church for morning service. Colonel and Mrs Sinclair were there, but even though Mrs Bennet craned her neck to search every face for the missing Fitzroy, he was noticeable by his absence.

"Wherever can he be?" Mrs Bennet whispered to Mary for the third time. The vicar had begun the proceedings. "This is most aggravating!"

Mary experienced the same aggravation as her mother, with a strange hollow feeling below her heart, but she managed to keep herself composed.

Mrs Bennet turned to Lydia, who flanked her on the left. "Where is he?" she hoarsely asked.

"Oh, Lord, George is indisposed, lying in his bed, after a night of drinking!" Lydia responded, as quietly as she knew how, but a little too loudly for Mary's liking. After all, this was a place of worship; such profanities were unacceptable to her, and would certainly be frowned upon by most of the congregation who might hear.

"Not dear Mr Wickham!" whispered Mrs Bennet impatiently. "Fitzroy! Where is Fitzroy?"

"Gone to Wiltshire, I believe," Lydia airily informed her.

Mrs Bennet turned to Mary. "He's gone to Wiltshire!"

Throughout the service, Mary was only half listening to the vicar's sermon on Christian forgiveness, and, although she usually enjoyed singing hymns, her mind was elsewhere when she stood among the devout people of Ely, who poured forth their harmonious worship of the Lord. Why was Fitzroy in Wiltshire? Why had he not informed her that he should go away? How long would he be away? Would she ever see him again? As she knelt for the final prayer and blessing, the vicar's words did nothing to alleviate her troubled soul. While the rest of the congregation filed out with uplifted spirits through the arched doorway, Mary was downcast and perplexed, Mrs Bennet's state of aggravation had worsened to one of annoyance and an attack of her nerves, while Lydia looked gay and unabashed as she tried to catch the eye of as many unattached young men as she could.

Lydia rushed away across the green in front of the church to converse with one of the men whose attention she had secured, leaving Mrs Bennet and Mary to talk with Colonel and Mrs Sinclair at the bottom of the church steps.

Mrs Sinclair opened up the conversation. "Good morning, Mrs Bennet, Miss Bennet!" The ladies curtsied to one another, and Colonel Sinclair bowed in a more military fashion than was the norm. "This is most fortuitous. I am delighted to meet with you."

"Delighted!" repeated Mrs Bennet perfunctorily.

"Invitations to a little soirée we are having are being sent out tomorrow, but this gives me the opportunity of giving prior notice!"

"How delightful!" Mrs Bennet was recovering quickly from her irritation of a few moments before.

Colonel Sinclair added, "We are inviting Mr and Mrs Russell, too. They have been so kind and generous to us during our stay in Ely."

"We are so looking forward to the Willow Wood ball on Saturday. It will be a much grander event than our soirée, you understand, but we are restricted to only a small gathering in the barracks. Space is at a premium."

Mary had said not a word. She hardly dared broach the subject of Fitzroy's absence, because Colonel and Mrs Sinclair would have been surprised. They would know very little of the attachment between Fitzroy and herself.

Mrs Bennet had no such scruples. "We are given to understand that your son is in Wiltshire."

Colonel Sinclair took it upon himself to explain the circumstances. He was economical and terse in his delivery. "Yes, indeed! He has gone to Blanton Estate, the Wiltshire property which he is to inherit next month, to make some final arrangements with his steward before he takes over. We expect him back on Saturday." He stopped speaking.

Mrs Sinclair's voice was running on, continuing her line of thought from before Mrs Bennet's interruption. "Fitzroy has insisted that we must have the soirée while the regiment is still in Ely, on his twenty-first birthday, and that is on the Saturday following the ball at Willow Wood. We will have just enough room for a few family and friends to celebrate his coming of age! Naturally, there will be a much more formal and splendid celebration when he has moved to Blanton Estate."

"Oh, but my dear Mrs Sinclair," Mrs Bennet cried in sudden realisation, "Mr Bennet and I shall not be here in Ely at that time. We return to Longbourn on the Monday following the ball!"

Mary's mind was in delightful turmoil: Fitzroy wanted a few family and friends to celebrate his birthday, and the Bennets had been invited. She now made a happy and decided response to this all-important invitation. "I stay on in Ely for a fortnight more, so I shall be delighted to accept your invitation."

"My son will be pleased," Mrs Sinclair said, smiling.

This could mean only one thing: that he had spoken to his mother about her! He valued her company, she was a friend, and once he came of age he would be master of his destiny. She believed that she had been singled out to be part of that destiny.

"We shall all meet again on Saturday!" Colonel Sinclair stated, by way of terminating the conversation with these two ladies. He bowed to them and took his good lady by the arm to lead her away to their waiting carriage. "Good day to you!"

For Mary the rest of the day floated deliriously past in rosy hues. She repeated over and over Mrs Sinclair's last words, "My son will be pleased, my son will be pleased". What had Fitzroy told her about their relationship? Why had Colonel Sinclair abruptly stopped Mrs Sinclair saying more? She was to see Fitzroy at the ball and the following Saturday at his coming of age party for family and friends.

At the weekends, it was customary for Charles to play the pianoforte as entertainment for the Russells. On this particular Sunday evening, Charles's mind was troubled by the memories of the overheard conversations of the day before. Mary was to marry Fitzroy Sinclair! How it pained him to the bottom of his soul! How he deprecated himself for his lack of advances towards Mary, to allow her to slip through his fingers and be lost to this dandy upstart forever! He could find no fault with Mary, only with himself. She had responded like any young woman of one-and-twenty to the open admiration of a handsome man who was to inherit an estate and a fortune. They walked out together, unaccompanied! They laughed and had fun together! They sang love songs together!

Yet had he and Mary not hummed dance music together? Had they not laughed together? Had they not been alone together down by the lake and on many occasions at Willow Wood? But he was staid, fourteen years older than she, in addition to the fact that he had never once shown Mary how he felt about her. Although he had commented on her musical talent for sight reading and accurate fingering at the pianoforte keyboard, he had also criticised her lack of feeling and most likely bored her with his advice to put more feeling into her playing. He had made her cry while he played the piano at the soirée, because he had sent for her and demanded that she turn the pages of the sheet music, and had forced her to sit on the piano stool beside him. This was not an inducement for a young woman of Mary's qualities to have any feelings for him. When he had told her about his brother, she had shown compassion. She had told him he was not humble and was to be respected. Respected, not loved. He was simply the nephew of her aunt and uncle, and, while Fitzroy was to be master of his own estate, he had few prospects now that the Tremayne estate was gone.

It was with such intensity of feeling that he sat down to play, selecting Mozart's *Fantasia in C minor*, a storm-tossed piece of music which represented his turbulent troughs of despondency. The dreary pounding of the left-hand chords emulated his self-reproachful heart beatings; the varying moods and the lack of resolution in the whole piece laughed at his irresolute life.

Mrs Bennet, whose spirits had been raised earlier in the day, had heard enough of this dreary piece of music, whether it was by the celebrated Mr Mozart or not.

"Charles, please play something cheerful for your next piece!" she entreated, her hand across her heart. "I declare, that was such a morbid tune that I can feel my palpitations coming on!"

"Mary will be better suited than I tonight, I fear!"

"Are you ailing?" asked Mrs Bennet sympathetically. "It is that music! Mr Mozart's depressing pieces cannot be good for anyone's constitution!"

"Mary, will you do us the honour, please?" asked Aunt Russell, observing Charles's drawn face and unaccustomed desultoriness.

Mary agreed, telling her mother, "Not all of Mr Mozart's music is morbid, you know. In fact, much of it is light and airy." She lifted the book of Mozart's music from the stand, flicking through the pages until she found a lively piece which she thought would please her mother.

"I shall turn the pages for you," Charles offered helpfully, when he saw the difficult sonata she had selected.

"Now listen to this music, mother, so you can revise your opinion of Mr Mozart."

Charles stood beside her while she played the allegretto grazioso of the *Sonata in B flat*, a playful and breezy piece which reflected her happy thoughts exactly. This was one of the most difficult pieces to master because of the intricate finger work as well as changes from major to minor keys every few bars in the third part. When Mary reached the end, she felt exhilarated, her whole body tingling with the music she had created in the drawing room. It was as if a whirlwind had overtaken her body and she had flown through the notes, hardly aware of the intricacies. Charles was astounded by the passion displayed. He was saddened too, for he knew what it portended.

"Excellent, Mary!" Mr Bennet was prompted to say. "Never heard you play better, my dear!"

"Capital!" exclaimed Uncle Russell.

"Play another jolly one, Mary!" commanded Mrs Bennet. "I am beginning to like Mr Mozart, though not as much as a Scottish air!"

"Then I shall play another of our favourites, Mama," acquiesced Mary kindly, leafing through a collection of pieces of sheet music. "*Alla Turca* is here somewhere."

"Damned absurd name for a piece of music, if you ask me!" commented Uncle Russell.

Charles explained, "It is named after the Janissaries, the soldiers of the old Turkish foot guards, originally formed of renegade prisoners."

Mrs Bennet frowned as she tried to recollect this piece of music.

Charles advised her, "It is the popular rondo, the allegretto movement of the *Sonata in A major*."

She was none the wiser for this information.

When Mary found *Alla Turca* and was poised ready to play, Charles was dubious. "Are you sure you want to play this?" he half whispered.

"Do you doubt that I can master the notes?" she asked.

"Indeed, I have no doubts on that score, but can you play them at the required speed? Can you play it all inside three minutes?" He took out his half-hunter fob watch from his waistcoat pocket.

Not only did Mary play the *Alla Turca* inside three minutes, but she played with such delight and passion that everyone unequivocally applauded when she had finished. She sat there laughing, her heart pounding, her whole body quivering with accomplishment and surprise at herself, as she looked up into Charles's smiling face, which was filled with admiration.

"Two minutes and forty-nine seconds," was all he said, though he wanted to tell her how her music had surpassed anything she had ever done, and how lovely she looked with her radiant face and her shining eyes.

Mary now knew what Charles had meant when he said one had to "feel the music" to play well. She had played from the heart, which was filled with love for Fitzroy.

CHAPTER XVI

A FRIGHT

The following Friday, Mary retired to her quarters to write to her older sister Elizabeth, with whom she kept up a regular fortnightly correspondence during the times between her visits to Pemberley. In her letters, she rarely strayed beyond factual accounts of events or giving her opinions on books or articles she had read during the interval since her previous letter. However, Mary's spirit was so lightened and her mind so filled with Fitzroy that she succumbed to writing some of her more private thoughts. Mr Bennet's advice to Mrs Bennet of a few days before, *Do not commit yourself in writing regarding matrimonial hopes*, was ignored now by Mary, and she found herself engaged in an unaccustomed outpouring of those very hopes at the end of her long letter.

You know that I have barely cherished any hope of ever being in love, that I have been resigned to a life of caring for my parents and, when they are gone, accepting the kind offers of generosity of your Mr Darcy and Jane's Mr Bingley. But now, I truly believe I am in love. Fitzroy Sinclair has won my heart, and I am to attend his coming of age party, as one of just a few special guests of family and friends of Colonel and Mrs Sinclair. This can only betoken one thing on which I pin my hopes: that he wishes for us to marry. He told me in a private moment that all he will require when he reaches his maturity is a wife! Our meetings together are filled with happiness, and he is so attentive to my wishes. Would you believe me, dear sister, when I tell you we have even sung love songs together? And he has already claimed the first two dances at my aunt and uncle's ball tomorrow night. My heart is ready to burst. Wish me joy! As ever, your sister, Mary.

The mail coach was due to arrive at the Lamb Hotel at two o'clock for a change of horses and to allow ongoing passengers to partake of some of the Rances' famed victuals to sustain them for their onward journey to Cambridge, the next stop on the route. At Willow Wood, all the stable lads had been commandeered to assist with other necessary tasks in preparation for the ball the following night, so no vehicle could be secured; it therefore seemed to Mary that it would be more expedient to walk to Ely to deliver her letter to the coachman at the Lamb Hotel.

Before setting off on the three-mile walk to Ely, she called to see her mother, who was resting languidly in bed.

"I cannot get anyone to hitch up a vehicle, but I must get to the mail coach before it departs. So I shall walk to Ely."

"What is so urgent that it cannot wait?"

"A letter to Elizabeth."

"Pooh! Elizabeth can wait!"

"Then my news would be old news, and of little value!"

"But is it safe for you to go walking alone? There may be pillagers about!"

"We have been to Ely many times in the past few weeks. Did you see any pillagers on any of those occasions?"

"There may be a highwayman ready to pounce!" Mrs Bennet persevered.

"Dick Turpin resurrected?" suggested Mary with a twinkle in her eye, enjoying the absurdity of her mother's anxieties.

"You mock me, Mary!" sulked Mrs Bennet.

"Do not fret, Mama!" Mary said, patting her mother on the arm. As she paused at the door of her mother's room, she asked, "Is there any message for Lydia? I intend to call on her, of course. No doubt she will want to show me her new ball gown."

"Tell her to tuck her lace tightly into the top of her ball gown. At her own party, she was allowing too much flesh to show. And she has much of it!"

Mary smiled at this, her mother's golden rule for female dress, quite out of accordance with what the Lady of Distinction was advising for the modern woman!

"You may smile, Mary, but it was not long ago, before your aunt Philips started giving you advice, that you would not have bared your neck, let alone your bosom!"

"I shall give her your sound advice, Mama."

Mrs Bennet was not to be quietened so easily. "It might not matter in Lydia's normal social circles of the militia and their wives, but the Willow Wood ball is a very different matter." She sounded like her sister!

"Mama, I must leave, or I shall be too late to send my letter."

"Very well! Go! Go!" Mrs Bennet sighed deeply, waved her hand in dismissal and shut her eyes.

It was a bright, sunny August day, different from the hazy and dull days of most of the past summer. Mary set out wearing her light-weight cream gauze overdress, her Paisley design shawl and her pink bonnet. Her parasol would afford some protection from the sun if it was too glaring. She did not want to have a sun-burnt face the following night at the ball, like some country lass.

Mary did not give Lydia her mother's advice on how to dress for the ball, for it would have fallen on deaf ears. Lydia had never heeded anyone's advice and had learned to live with the consequences of her own actions.

Lydia was surprised to see her sister with no prior notice of her visit, and even more surprised to note that she had walked the three-mile distance.

"But is it safe to go wandering about on your own, Mary? Who knows what sorts of vagabonds there may be roaming the village roads and lanes?"

"You are beginning to sound like our mother!"

"But she is right. There is talk of trouble in the town, Mary."

"You are in the town here, Lydia. Look out of the window! Is there any trouble out there?"

"I think it is something to do with the Littleport rioters," Lydia ineffectually explained. "George knows! Let me fetch him downstairs!"

"I must get this letter to the mail coach! There is little time to waste."

"Then I shall accompany you," said Lydia, putting on her bonnet and adjusting her flimsy white shawl, with no more thought of rioters or vagabonds. "And one never knows whom one might meet!"

If Lydia had hoped to meet anyone of interest, with her husband lying sottishly upstairs on a Friday afternoon, she was to be sorely disappointed. The town was all but deserted, with shopkeepers eyeing any passers-by with suspicion.

Mr Legge stepped out of his boot and shoe premises to give advice to the two young ladies. "You would be best to run along home now as fast as you can. There is trouble afoot."

Mary and Lydia heeded his advice, but found themselves giggling like children at Mr Legge's unintentional wit, once he was out of earshot.

Mary, however, was far from disappointed; when she and Lydia turned the corner of the street, the two horses of his yellow curricle were hitched outside the door of the Wickhams' lodging house.

"That's Fitz's!" cried Lydia gleefully. "I knew we should meet someone of interest today, though, good heavens! I did not think it would be at my very own front door." She ran the last twenty yards.

Mary followed a little more sedately, although she would have run a hundred yards into Fitzroy's very arms, had they been outstretched for her.

"Fitz! Fitz! Where have you been for so long?" Lydia demanded playfully.

"In Wiltshire, dear girl! Organising my estate."

"Life has been so dull without you!"

"How are you, Mary?" Fitzroy bowed and took her hand, lifting it just far enough to brush her fingers lightly with his lips.

Mary did not dare move a muscle, but her heart was pounding.

George Wickham had come downstairs in Mary and Lydia's absence, looking dishevelled and groggy. To Mary, and indeed to Mrs Lydia Wickham, Fitzroy appeared so dandified, dashing and desirable in comparison.

"You see, I am returned in time for the ball tomorrow night," proclaimed Fitzroy with panache, as if he were the chief guest. "Do you remember that I have claimed the first two dances, Mary?"

Not to be outdone, George Wickham slurred, "And I claim the fifth one."

Mary nodded her acquiescence, fervently hoping that he would be in a more sober state by then.

A loud knocking at the door took them all by surprise.

"Stop that row, whoever you are!" George shouted. He aggressively opened the door, which swung back with a wrenching sound on its hinges.

"Captain, sir!" A young militia man stood on the step, saluting. "Orders for you to return immediately to the barracks! And if that is Mr Sinclair's vehicle, I am to

125

request that he too returns immediately to the colonel's quarters in the barracks."

"What is amiss?" demanded George.

"Do not rightly know, sir, but them's my orders. Some say there's trouble a-brewing in the town, but I seed no sign of it."

"Is something wrong?" asked Fitzroy, coming into the hallway.

"Everyone is to go back to the barracks. As I said to Captain Wickham, them's my orders." He saluted and went on his way to other lodgings which housed militia men and their families.

When George came down the stairs and appeared in the front room a few minutes later, he was a changed man: uniform neatly buttoned, hair sleeked back, face shaven and no outward suggestion by his behaviour that he had been drinking. He was ready to leave.

"I would give you a lift, George, but there is only room for one in my yellow bounder," Fitzroy flippantly said, erroneously using the nickname of the fast yellow post chaise for his curricle. He unhitched his vehicle, jumped aboard and, waving cheerily, shouted, "Till tomorrow night, ladies, when we will dance the night away! I bid you good day!" And he was off at the gallop up the street towards the barracks.

On Mary's way back to Willow Wood, with all this talk of trouble, pillagers, vagabonds and rioters, she walked as fast as she could, with frequent backwards glances to check that she was not being followed by some ne'er do well. But no one was following her, the streets were quiet, and, as she walked farther out of the town and into the winding country road, she was already relaxed and thinking about Fitzroy and the two dances she was to have with him. She was even considering what people would think of her if she broke with convention and had a third dance with him. What would the Lady of Distinction have to say about that? And would Mary Wollstonecraft applaud her boldness?

She had reached a sharp bend in the deserted winding country road, about a mile from Willow Wood, when suddenly, out of the hedgerow, sprang two vagabonds. Both were dirty, with ragged clothing, and looked as if they were half starved.

"Give us all you got, lady," the younger of the two barked, "or we'll do you!"

Mary's heart lurched and she was nearly sick with shock, but she was not to be intimidated by two foul-smelling ruffians. She raised her parasol.

"Leave me alone, and be on your way!" she threatened, but too politely.

"What you goin' to do with that?" sneered the older man, making a grab for the seemingly ineffectual weapon in her hand.

She struck him twice across the side of the head and, appalled at her own ferocity as well as astounded by her basic sense of self-preservation, watched wide-eyed in fascination as blood began to pour from the man's ear, down his face and even onto her own clothing.

"You little viper!" he growled, lunging towards the bloodied parasol, more blood spraying over her. Wrenching it away from her, he broke it in half with his bare hands. "That's what these 'ere hands are a-goin' to do to you."

Mary made a dash up the road, her Paisley shawl flying off her shoulders up into the overhanging spiky hawthorn tree.

"Help! Help!" she screamed frantically as she ran, hoping against rationality that there would be people about to save her.

She managed to run fifty yards before she was overtaken by the younger man, who snatched first at her overdress and tore it, partially revealing her underdress. She attempted to run on, but he roughly caught her from behind round her upper body, pinning her arms to her waist. She kicked and tried to free herself, flailing unsuccessfully with her forearms. She was caught as if in a vice, hardly able to breathe, let alone continue her cries for help.

The older man had almost caught up, wheezing with the exertion. "'Old her good and tight!"

He advanced towards her, surveying her squirming body from head to toe. Then he grinned, displaying rotten teeth and toothless gaps. Mary feared what he would do to her, in her helpless, trapped state of near-undress. He roughly grasped and pulled on her ringlets and bonnet, and, firmly holding her head to the side, he tore off her gold necklace, secreting it in some pocket within his dirty, ill-fitting coat. Then he seized her right hand.

"Lookee 'ere, Bert," he sniggered. "We got the bloomin' crown jewels!"

He forced off her two rings, one of which had been her grandmother's christening gift to her, the other a twenty-first birthday gift from her father. Then he pulled at the reticule strap on her left wrist with a twisting and turning motion which cut into her, until it came free. He tore open the tie and extracted all the coins from inside the little bag, then threw it, and the valueless remainder of the contents, into the roadway in disgust.

Mary was so angered, not only by the attack on her person and the theft of her money, but also by the attack on her family and what she valued. She kicked the older man viciously in his private lower regions, making him grunt a dire profanity as he doubled up in pain.

"You little vixen!" he gasped. "Bert, do her!"

Mary kicked backwards with a constant hammering of her heels onto Bert's shins, and Bert, realising that he was suffering more damage than was necessary, let her go.

Mary was as fast as a greyhound released from its starting box, as she sprinted up the road away from her attackers.

"Get after 'er!" she could hear the older man croak.

Then Bert's voice in the distance was arguing, "Nay, we got what we wanted. Let's get away while we can!"

Nevertheless, leaving nothing to chance, she ran for a half mile before stopping. Unable to go any further, she collapsed in the tall grass at the side of the roadway. Clutching her ribs as she tried to catch her breath, she curled up on her side in a state of exhaustion and shock. She could feel her big toe and heels throbbing in time with her heart beat. Her upper arms were bruised. Her wrist was painful. Tears flowed freely now down into her hair and on to the ground, as she thought of her two rings of such irreplaceable sentimental value, which would likely be sold or pawned, never to be seen again.

But she was alive. For that she was thankful. All sense of time deserted her, as she fell into a swoon and drifted into a sleep which overtook her like a soothing balm to her disturbed mind and injured body.

There were distant voices in her dream, calling her name, over and over. She could hear horses' hooves.

"Over here!" someone was calling out. "She's over here, sir."

"Good God!" This was another voice.

Someone was beside her. "She's breathing, sir!"

"Mary! Mary! Can you hear me?" Someone else was close.

Mary came out of her dream, out of her sleep in a timeless zone. When she opened her eyes, she beheld Charles kneeling beside her, distraught.

"Thank God you are alive!" Charles whispered, relief flooding his face. Her bloodied and torn clothing had frightened him beyond belief.

Mary involuntarily groaned as she straightened her body and tried to sit up.

"We are going to get you back to the house," Charles said gently. "You need a physician to attend you."

Mary nodded. "Thank you!" was all she managed to utter.

Mounting his bay hunter, Charles was business-like, yet concerned. "Lift her up to me! Gently, man!"

It was Simon Braden who lifted Mary up. Charles took her in his strong arms, cradling her securely as he rode back to Willow Wood.

He carried her into the house. The family were seated disconsolately in the drawing room, all preparations for the ball suspended, when Charles entered with Mary in his arms. They had been miserably thinking the worst since Mary's empty reticule, parasol and Paisley shawl had been found some three hours earlier by April and May, the two downstairs maids, who had been sent on an errand to get two pails of milk. In their haste to inform the mistress back at Willow Wood, they had run straight past Mary, who lay hidden in the tall grass shaded by the hedgerow at the side of the road.

Mrs Bennet was the first of the family out of her seat, followed by Mr Bennet, Aunt Russell, Uncle Russell and two very tearful children, who all crowded round Mary.

"She is alive!" was all Charles could muster.

"Oh, my poor girl!" exclaimed Mrs Bennet, stroking her daughter's hand with loving kindness.

"I think you could put me down now, Charles," Mary suggested, feeling rather foolish as the centre of attention, and in Charles's arms.

"You will do no such thing, Charles! You will take her up to her room, where she will stay until Doctor Granger arrives!" With the presence of mind of a woman whose latent maternal instinct had strongly manifested itself, Mrs Bennet was the one to take control. "Brother, would you send someone for him, please? Sister, a glass of brandy is required!"

Uncle Russell did as he was ordered, in his own house too!, and went to find Simon Braden again, while Aunt

Russell rushed to the dining room sideboard to fetch a glass of brandy.

Mr Bennet's face was ashen. In all his days he had never experienced anything as traumatic as fearing that a daughter was dead. It made him now realise how much he valued them all, how much he valued and loved Mary!

CHAPTER XVII

THE BALL

"To walk back on your own!" Charles raised his voice. "Had you taken leave of your senses, Mary?" His fright and caring compassion of the day before had been superseded by his anger at circumstances which could have had unthinkable consequences.

"How was anyone to know that those two villains would be there?" Although she was grateful to Charles for his help the previous evening, Mary was filled with a sense of outrage at his tone at breakfast time.

"There was talk of trouble in the town," he hotly rejoined. "You have already admitted that you knew of it."

"There was no alternative." Mary sounded defensive, even to herself. "Mr Wickham was ordered back to barracks. All the captains in lodgings were being ordered back immediately."

Aunt Russell gave her opinion, but with less confrontation than Charles. "I can understand that Mr Wickham must obey orders, but Mr Sinclair should have brought you back in his curricle."

"He was ordered back immediately too!" protested Mary, eager to protect Fitzroy's image in other people's eyes. How she wished her mother had risen early enough to partake of breakfast with them! How she would have supported Mary and defended the charming Fitzroy.

"He is not even in the militia!" snorted Uncle Russell disparagingly.

"It would have been a simple matter to bring you back," Charles persisted, but, noting that Mary's bottom lip was beginning to tremble, muttered his final comment to himself, "like any decent young man of any breeding would do!"

"There was only room for one," Mary lamely murmured.

"Nonsense! A curricle can take two," commented Uncle Russell. "It is a damned disgrace!" But his voice was quietened by the admonitory look which Aunt Russell gave him, for she too observed that Mary was becoming distressed.

"All's well that ends well!" Aunt Russell attempted to lighten the atmosphere, fearing that the evening's ball would be blighted if this conversation were to continue any further.

Mary excused herself from the breakfast table, claiming that she would go and keep the children company and out of the way while staff were busy preparing for the evening's ball. She did go in search of the children, and together they went to see how many goldfish they could count in the ornamental pond, but her mind was in turmoil and she was shaking. She supposed she might be suffering from delayed action shock, which she believed some soldiers experienced after battle, but dispensed with that idea. Yes, she was bruised and her feet hurt, but she was made of sterner stuff than most young women, and was proud of her strength of mind and her independence. Truth to tell was that she was engulfed by others' poor opinions: she was aggrieved at Charles's overt anger at her stupidity, ignoring the courage she had shown the day before; and she was acutely dismayed by her uncle's censure of Fitzroy's behaviour.

When it was time to dress for the ball, Mary was in worse spirits. Although her ringlets had been fashioned to perfection by one of the upstairs maids, when she came to put on her ball gown, the sleeves were too short to cover her bruises, which were a deep and so obvious purple, and her long white gloves were not long enough to reach much above the elbow. When she tried to put on her dance slippers, no matter how hard she tried, her feet were too swollen and painful to squeeze into them. She feared she would be unable to dance, and must forego her two dances with Fitzroy. She sat on the side of the bed for a full thirty minutes while she considered this dismal prospect.

"Whatever are you doing, Mary?" Mrs Bennet demanded, entering Mary's room in her magenta ball gown. She looked almost elegant and ten years younger than her real age. "Everyone is assembled, ready to receive the guests." When Mary failed to respond, she sat down beside her and took her hand kindly. "Are you well? You have been through a dreadful ordeal, my dear, and no one would think it amiss if you were unable to attend the ball. There would be one disappointed young man, I warrant you, but, knowing his sentiments towards you, he will not be deterred."

"Mama, I am well, and I shall attend the ball, but I cannot fit into my dance shoes. My feet have swelled out of all proportion, and my other shoes are muddied and bloodied after yesterday's episode."

"Pooh! Is that all? You can wear mine," Mrs Bennet offered, instantly removing her dance shoes, which were a size larger than Mary's, and handing them to her. "I can wear a pair of day shoes. No one will notice!" she said. "Now do hurry, Mary!"

The ballroom was brightly lit with two hundred candles in the eight pendant ceiling chandeliers and alcove candelabras. The four musicians hired for the night were a sight to admire as well as a topic of conversation for much of the evening. They all sported white wigs and were attired in clothes of a bygone age: luxurious peacock blue brocade tailed coats, white shirts and stocks, white stockings and cream pantaloons.

The musicians were certainly a talking point for the guests who entered the ballroom ready for the first dance, but none could compare with the elegance of Mr Fitzroy Sinclair, who closely resembled Beau Brummell in elegance, stance, attire and charm. Each young lady present smiled prettily in his direction to attract his attention, so that he would claim her for at least one of the seven dances of the evening. Miss Eleanor Morrison secured him for the third dance; he was obliged to dance with his mother for the fourth dance, which was the quadrille; Lydia had already marked him on her card for the fifth dance; for the sixth dance, which was the line dance which Charles and Mary would lead, he was partnered with Mrs Caroline Moffat, and although Mary hoped that he would secure the last dance with her and break convention, he went back to the Morrison girls and engaged the shorter of the two, looking regretfully at the last remaining sister to show that his card was complete!

Charles was disappointed not to be able to engage either the first or the second dances with Mary, and as his aunt and uncle Russell would lead the first dance, the minuet, he was left with little alternative but to ask Mrs Bennet for this dance. She was flattered and as excited as a young girl at the prospect and eagerly accepted, marking her card ostentatiously. Other than the quadrille with a complaining Mr Bennet, her card was to remain unmarked for the rest of the dances.

The musicians struck up the first note, and the master of ceremonies announced that the first dance was the minuet. As was customary, the music was played through as the partners took up their positions for the gentle minuet, a favourite with the older members of the party. The dance lasted a full twenty minutes, allowing for easy conversation, eye contact and smiles. As Fitzroy took Mary's hand at the start of the dance, she was the envy of the whole room as the partner of the most handsome man present.

"I understand you fell victim to some scoundrels yesterday. How good to see you so well recovered."

"There was not much hurt done," she said, making light of her experience, "except for the theft of my favourite jewellery."

"These rogues cannot resist a piece of gold! I always carry a pistol."

"I dare say that a pistol would not fit into a lady's reticule," observed Mary with a smile at the absurdity of the idea, thinking of the size of some of the Italian flintlock pistols in Mr Cousins's gun shop in Summerton.

"Then you need someone to take care of you, Mary!" Fitzroy whispered seriously as they came close together.

For the rest of the dance they spoke hardly a word, Fitzroy enjoying being stared at in open admiration by so many belles, and Mary excited by his closeness and his words "take care of you". All too soon it was over, and Fitzroy escorted Mary back to her seat in the alcove beside her father, at the same time as Charles escorted Mrs Bennet back to the same place. Had Fitzroy been more observant, he would have noticed that Mary was limping. Her painful gait, however, had not gone unnoticed by Charles.

"Good evening, Mr Sinclair," Charles tersely greeted Fitzroy, giving him a perfunctory bow.

"Mr Tremayne," was all that Fitzroy said, bowing with affected gallantry, but a little too smug for Charles's liking.

"I shall return, Mary, for the next dance," Fitzroy added, on the point of joining his parents at the other side of the ballroom.

"I fear not!" Mary stopped him short.

"But, my dear Miss Bennet," he said with affected surprise, "it is promised to me! Look at your card!"

"Card or no card, my feet cannot endure another dance just yet. Please forgive me."

Fitzroy, unaware of the bruising and swollen feet, almost took this rejection as a rebuff, but he bore it with dignity. "Perhaps you will permit me to return after the next dance and we can converse together then. After that, I believe I am engaged for the third dance with Miss Eleanor Morrison." He bowed again and left them. Mary's heart was pained as she watched him deliberately swagger over to the same Miss Morrison and engage her for that all-important and now illusive second dance.

"Permit me to sit with you," Charles addressed Mr Bennet.

"Do you not dance, sir?" asked Mr Bennet. "You should dance while you are still young enough, before gout or any other ailment afflicts you."

"Thank you, sir, but I prefer to sit." Turning to Mary he gently asked, "What is it that gives you pain?"

"She hurt her feet in the scuffle with those ruffians yesterday," piped up Mrs Bennet, answering for Mary.

"Her feet?" Mr Bennet was bemused.

"I told her that the Russells would not be offended if she did not attend the ball, but would she listen? No! And this is the result!"

"Hush, Mama!" whispered Mary. Her mother's voice was getting louder.

"Her feet?" repeated Mr Bennet.

"She is sitting out a dance she had promised to dear Mr Sinclair," continued Mrs Bennet, undeterred.

"After his behaviour yesterday, I should say he does not deserve to dance with Mary today!" Mr Bennet said forcefully.

"Peace, Papa," whispered Mary now to her father, hoping that his voice had not carried, and wishing that his opinion of Fitzroy were more favourable.

Charles sat amiably with the Bennets throughout the third dance, attempting to engage them in easy conversation, but they each had their own thoughts. Fitzroy was in the line headed by Colonel and Mrs Sinclair, who had called the dance and demonstrated steps which they had learnt off by heart and had performed at many balls. Fitzroy was partnered by Miss Eleanor Morrison. He would be dancing twice with her instead of with Mary! This was like an elixir to Charles, who could surmise that Fitzroy's affections might be insubstantial and fleeting. But he felt pangs of pity which stabbed his heart when he perceived how Mary ruefully watched Fitzroy swinging Miss Eleanor Morrison round and galloping to the end of the line with such gay abandon.

At the end of the dance, Lydia rushed over, followed by her husband. "Mary, why do you not dance? You promised that dance to Fitzroy."

"Her feet!" Mr Bennet contributed this unusual information with some incredulity.

Before any more could be explained, Fitzroy and Eleanor Morrison joined them.

"I promised I would be here between dances!" Fitzroy said, with Eleanor hanging on his arm.

"Do not forget the fifth dance is promised to me!" Lydia reminded Fitzroy.

Looking at her cards with a dramatic flourish, Eleanor giggled, "Goodness me! Fitzroy, you are marked on my card for the third dance. Two in a row!" As the musicians struck a chord, she impulsively took possession of Fitzroy by tugging on his arm, "Here it is starting already, and hardly space to get our breath back!"

To Mary, the Willow Wood ball was becoming a nightmare of disappointed hopes. Charles sat with her during the third dance, and when the quadrille was announced Mrs Bennet could sit still no longer.

"Mr Bennet, you did not dance the minuet, but we have practised the quadrille and my card is marked with your name and I insist you dance this, otherwise I shall have a bout of nerves."

"Dear me!" exclaimed Mr Bennet, standing up. "That would never do. Nerves and balls do not mix well."

"And you too, Mary," bossed Mrs Bennet, her erstwhile motherly instinct giving way to parental instruction. "This is your dance with Charles. Your feet will be well rested by now!"

Charles was more considerate when he quietly asked, "Do you think you will be able to manage this, even for a short while? I should not like to be the agent of thwarting your mother's wishes!" He held out his hand to assist her on to the dance floor.

It was unfortunate for Charles that the couple who faced them in the quadrille were none other than Fitzroy and Mrs Sinclair, so there was no escaping the eye contact which Mary and the dandy upstart would have during the following twenty minutes of square dancing. Just when he thought he was gaining ground, he was defeated once again by this soldier's son. The sooner Fitzroy went to Wiltshire, the better.

Mary was elated once more at having danced the quadrille in the same eightsome as Fitzroy, but her feet were now excruciatingly painful. "Charles, you will have to find another partner for the line dance we practised."

And this was why Mary, who had sat at the side of the ballroom watching Fitzroy and a giddy Caroline Moffat dancing and laughing together, could hardly wait till the dancing was over, the midnight feast was consumed and, everyone having gone home, she could go to bed.

She fell into a fitful sleep, with William Shakespeare's words ringing in her ears:

I am giddy, expectation whirls me round,
The imaginary relish is so sweet
That it enchants my sense.

How could she not be disappointed with the miserable realities of life, when her mind had been deceived by the beguiling wishful-thinking of her expectations?

CHAPTER XVIII

DEBT

On the morning of the Monday following, Mr and Mrs Bennet left Willow Wood after their four-week stay.

Mrs Bennet was effusive in her thanks. "Sister Russell, I can hardly express my gratitude to you. Your hospitality, the soirée, the magnificent ball, and giving me the opportunity of spending time with my darling Lydia. It is all too much."

"You are too kind," answered Aunt Russell, kissing her sister-in-law on each cheek. "You are most welcome to stay here again in the future. It will be our pleasure to entertain you, certainly with a soirée or two, if not another ball. However, the regiment remove to Brighton at the end of the week, and Lydia will no longer be in Ely."

Uncle Russell was shaking Mr Bennet by the hand. "Brother, you are welcome any time you want to indulge yourself in some coarse fishing."

"And you must come to Longbourn for some fine grouse shooting," replied Mr Bennet.

Mrs Bennet took Mary by both hands and said, "Dearest Mary, do look after yourself and return to Longbourn safe and sound, though how I shall do without you for two weeks, I do not know."

"Remember, Mama, Jane will do very nicely in the interim." Mary smiled as she said this, no longer feeling piqued at comparisons. They were meaningless in the face of the genuine love which she now realised her dear mother felt for her.

"I forbid you to go anywhere unaccompanied!" commanded Mr Bennet, as he got into the carriage. He was unusually dictatorial this day, born of his epiphanic experience of the weekend scare.

While her aunt and uncle retired to the conservatory at the rear of the house, and once Roseanna and Ellen had finally finished waving to the departing carriage as it wound its way down the carriage sweep, under the lime trees and into the far distance, Mary took her cousins by the hand. Together they ascended the stairs to the schoolroom which adjoined the nursery for their lessons. They continued the previous week's history lesson about how the Romans had built viaducts. This was followed by both children drawing a picture of a viaduct and a Roman soldier.

"Why did they wear short skirts?" asked Ellen.

"It was the custom in Roman times," Mary answered. In fact she did not have a proper answer.

"It is very strange!"

"Like the men in Scotland today," observed Roseanna, by way of explaining this peculiar mode of dress.

Later in the morning, when it was time to practise their music pieces on the harpsichord in the nursery, Roseanna put on her appealing facial expression, which was reserved for a special request. "Please may we practise on the pianoforte in the music room? It sounds so much better, and Cousin Charles is always telling us that we must allow the keys to push our fingers up, and we cannot do that with the harpsichord. It sounds different, too," she added as an extra inducement.

"Please! Please!" begged Ellen, though it was doubtful if she fully understood the concept which Charles was trying to instil in them.

Mary succumbed to the children's entreaties. They were very hard to refuse. Also, as their parents were out of earshot in the conservatory, she could see no harm in this. "Very well, as a special treat, seeing that you were as good as gold all weekend. Take your music and go down now. I shall follow you directly."

The children ran down the sweeping staircase two steps at a time, a method of descent frowned upon by both their parents as highly dangerous, and disappeared into the music room.

No sooner had Mary reached the top of the staircase than Roseanna and Ellen came running out of the music room, down the hall and up to where she stood. Both children were distressed.

"Oh, Cousin Mary!" cried Roseanna in much agitation. "Cousin Charles is in there."

"Charles is here?" asked Mary doubtfully. "On a Monday?"

"You must go to him immediately!" Roseanna begged.

"He is crying!" piped up Ellen, clearly upset at an adult in tears.

"He has got his head in his hands," corroborated Roseanna.

"Go to your nursery now and practise some of your tunes on the harpsichord!" ordered Mary. "And stay there until I come to you! Do not worry about Cousin Charles! Everything will be all right," she added, shooing them back towards the nursery.

It was with some trepidation that she politely knocked on the music room door before she entered. She was incredulous. Was Charles really crying? Whatever could have occasioned this? Perhaps the children were mistaken or exaggerating?

But when she entered she could see that Roseanna and Ellen were far from mistaken. Charles was seated on the chaise-longue with his head buried in his hands.

"My dear Charles, what has happened?" she cried.

He lifted his head from his hands, and his face was dampened with tears. Mary had never seen a man cry; men were always there to support women who wept, and her sympathetic heart was moved to near distraction as she fought to keep back her own tears.

She ran towards him, uncertain whether she should or should not extend her hand to him. What would be deemed appropriate in the circumstances? What were the circumstances? What calamity had broken this strong man who sat looking up at her so forlornly?

"What is the matter?" she whispered compassionately. "Please tell me!" Allowing her humanity to take over from her questions of propriety, she instinctively put her hand on his tear-stained cheek in a soothing caress.

He cupped his hand over hers and pressed it to his cheek for a moment and sighed. Recovering himself, he stood up abruptly, shook his head and took two pieces of paper out of his pocket. "These letters came this morning." He handed her the first one. "Read this! It was written a week ago."

It was a scribbled note from Charles's older brother, Matthew.

Bow Street Runners came for me. Magistrates court found me guilty. In Marshalsea Prison for debtors. I owe £5 to my landlady. £30 gambling debts I cannot pay. My money is gone. No hope of release. I am desperate. There is no help. I will have to end it all. Goodbye my dear brother. I am sorry. Goodbye. M.

Mary took a deep breath. "Oh, Charles! This is dreadful news indeed. Surely he cannot mean to end his own life? I hardly know what to say. What can be done?"

"There is worse." He handed her the second letter. "It was written just two days ago."

It was from the chairman of the Trustees of Marshalsea Prison in London.

Sir, I regret to inform you that your brother died last night, after taking too much laudanum. He rests in the morgue here and will be buried in the paupers' graveyard of St Saviour's church in Southwark on Wednesday, unless you wish it otherwise. Yours etc.

When Mary had finished reading the letter, neither of them spoke for a full half-minute.

Charles was miserable and alone in his thoughts: he was tortured by the images of the ignominious demise of his only brother; he was appalled that Matthew should have died by taking an overdose of laudanum, that reddish-brown "tincture of opium" which tasted as bitter as gall; he was stupefied by the rapid fall of such a man of wealth and status; he was crushed by his own sense of helplessness; he was saddened by the thought of the mental suffering and anguish which had led to his brother's wish to end his life.

Mary was considering the implications of both letters. It was clear that Matthew would have to be buried as befitted a gentleman and not in the paupers' graveyard. He was still a Tremayne, the son and heir of Tremayne Manor, which had been the family seat for generations. Whatever had befallen him in life, nothing could take this away from him.

The problematic question of suicide whirled round Mary's mind. Could Matthew be buried in consecrated ground? Times were changing, she knew, but how far? There were still those who clung to William Blackstone's ideas that suicide was a crime against God and King and to John Wesley's belief that suicide was murder of the self, and who even went as far as to assert that failed suicides should be hanged. However, there were others who aspired to the new Romantic ideals of suicide as the last act of heroism of free men and women. Even Mary Wollstonecraft, a woman of great strength and determination, had plumbed the depths of despair and had attempted suicide with a laudanum overdose. Mary was more inclined to view those who committed suicide as victims of psychological and sociological problems, who should not be condemned on religious or philosophical grounds.

It was clear that it was of paramount importance to keep the contents of Matthew's letter to the immediate family. If anything were to be done, it would have to be done immediately.

Mary broke the silence. "This is very sad news. Let me get you a glass of brandy. Her business like tone belied her sympathy for Charles, who still stood with his strong shoulders now drooping and his rugged face now haggard.

"Please stay," Charles begged her, his voice breaking. When he had sat down, he put his head once again in his hands. In a muffled, hopeless voice he admonished himself, "I could have helped him, had I known."

"You could have done no more," Mary wisely but gently argued. "You nearly pauperised yourself, too! You had no more to give."

"I could have sold my horse!"

"And then what? The clothes off your back?" Mary sounded stern. "I tell you there was nothing more you or anyone could have done. Remember, he sold the family estate; he ruined your means of livelihood. You said yourself that he was an incorrigible gambler!"

"Yes, I did," said Charles, "but he was still my brother."

Mary straightened herself up. "Our aunt and uncle must be informed. Would you like me to break the news to them?" she offered.

"If you would be so kind," Charles sombrely agreed to her suggestion. He did not trust himself to remain composed. "Take the letters with you."

As Mary walked to the doorway, she said, "And I shall ask Mrs Brown to bring us all a glass of brandy."

145

She left the room, taking the letters with her, and ran all the way to the conservatory. She found her aunt and uncle seated on wickerwork chairs at a wrought iron table, sipping coffee made from freshly ground coffee beans that morning. The distinctive fragrance of giant chrysanthemums filled the air, and at the far end of the conservatory grew an orange tree laden with fruit, hanging over the geraniums of many hues which were the pride and joy of the head gardener. When Charles had arrived they had not heard the front door bell-pull, which only sounded in the kitchen quarters, and consequently they were unaware that they had a visitor.

"Charles is here!" Mary panted.

"Here?"

"He has some very bad news. He asked me to tell you." Mary took a deep breath. "Matthew is dead."

"What!"

"Oh, no!" Aunt Russell paled with shock.

"Dead? How is he dead?" Uncle Russell raised his voice, sounding simultaneously astounded and fearful.

"I do not understand." Aunt Russell was choking back her tears.

"Read these!" Mary said, handing her uncle the two letters. "This is all the information there is."

Together, in a silence which grew more laden with disbelief and sorrow, her aunt and uncle digested the contents, and then they held each other's hand.

As Mary watched them, she grew tearful at everyone's distress. "I am so sorry," she whispered.

"We must speak to Charles without delay." Uncle Russell stood up briskly. "Where is he?"

"In the music room," Mary managed to reply as composedly as possible.

On their way down the hall, Mary excused herself, impatiently brushing away her unwanted tears, to ask Mrs Brown to bring four glasses of brandy and the decanter to the music room and to make haste. Mrs Brown was surprised, as it was not even midday, but she did as she was requested.

In the music room, Charles had stood to receive his aunt, whose outstretched arms promised comfort of a kind, though he longed to be in the comforting arms of Mary. He would remember her soft hand on his cheek forever!

As Mary returned to the music room, Aunt Russell sat down beside Charles, placing her hand over his. "This news is unbearable," she murmured, and, out of grief for her dead nephew, she began to weep. "I can hardly believe it. Oh, poor dear Matthew!"

"Charles, this news beggars belief!" exclaimed Uncle Russell, the unfortunate choice of cliché in the present circumstances completely escaping his notice. "In a debtors' prison! To commit suicide!"

"Uncle Russell, I believe that we should keep this information to ourselves," warned Mary. "I urge you to keep your voice at bay, for fear the servants should hear."

"Too true, my dear." Uncle Russell looked grave. He was more troubled than upset that his nephew had died in this shocking manner.

He seemed to be on the point of divulging his thoughts when Mrs Brown entered with the tray of brandy, placing it on the occasional table beside the chaise-longue where Charles and Aunt Russell sat.

When she had left, and he deemed her to be out of hearing, he blurted out, "It is I who am to blame!"

"No one is to blame!" Aunt Russell sniffed. "And least of all you, my dear John."

"I repeat, I am to blame!"

"I must contradict you, John," Charles said with a tone of finality. "You did more than anyone could have reasonably expected."

Uncle Russell harrowingly groaned a negative as he shook his head from side to side, his complexion becoming redder and redder.

Mary handed him a glass of brandy, as a priority. "Sit down, I pray. You are unwell!"

"I am not unwell," shouted Uncle Russell. "Would that I were struck down at this very moment for what I have done!"

Aunt Russell stopped her crying and stared at her husband. Mary was aware that Matthew's death had opened up some unknown and terrible wound of guilt. Charles picked up a glass of brandy from the tray and downed it in one fiery gulp.

"You have done nothing to be ashamed of, my dear." Aunt Russell, recovering some of her usual pragmatism, stated her conviction. "All of your life, you have been the pillar of goodness and moral rectitude!"

Uncle Russell put up his hand, inhaled deeply. "There is something I must now divulge to you. Sit down, Mary, I pray you." He poured himself another brandy.

Once Mary was seated in the occasional chair on the other side of the chaise-longue, Uncle Russell paced to and fro before them and began his story. "In the last week in May, I received a letter from Matthew. It was another begging letter."

"Surely you paid him a year's rent and living expenses in April."

"You are correct, my dear Ruby. However, he had spent it all by the end of May. He applied to me for more, a 'loan' as he called it, to pay off his debts."

"Gambling debts, I surmise," interrupted Charles sadly.

"You cannot doubt it," agreed Uncle Russell. "However, I took him at his word, assurances that he would find gainful employment and endeavour to pay me back as soon as he could, and that he would incur no more gambling debts. I sent him thirty pounds, to cover his debts and living costs for a further six months."

"Thirty pounds! John, this was more than generous!" Charles was amazed. After all, his own meagre salary amounted to no more than twenty pounds per year! "Not something to blame yourself for."

Uncle Russell cupped his warm hands round his brandy glass and took a deep breath, endeavouring to enjoy the fumes rising from this eau de vie and to savour a mouthful before continuing with his story, but his senses were dulled. These normally pleasant sensations gave him no solace.

"Another letter from Matthew arrived four weeks ago. The same request for money, the same assurances! I sent an immediate reply stating that there would be no further money coming from this quarter, and not to apply to me again. He had squandered his own family estate through gambling; he was not going to do the same to mine." He stopped here and looked helplessly round the three faces. "So, you see, it was my fault that Matthew felt so 'desperate' with no hope. It was I who drove him to suicide, do you understand? It was I!" He slumped in the armchair beside his wife and stared desolately at the pianoforte straight ahead.

In the ensuing silence, Mary stoutly made a suggestion. "He showed that he could not be helped, but if you could not help him in life, you can help him have a decent Christian burial, with a fine headstone to preserve the dignity of the Tremayne family name. He was a Tremayne who simply lost his way in life, like the parable of the prodigal son, you know."

Uncle Russell knew his Bible "Luke, chapter fifteen," he remembered. The words were like a light at the end of this dark nightmarish tunnel.

Charles said, "I suppose we must act quickly to get him decently interred and not in a paupers' graveyard."

Mary uttered some of her earlier thoughts. "If he is to be assured of a Christian burial, none of us should breathe a word of suicide to anyone else."

"Come, Charles, not a moment's delay!" Uncle Russell exhorted his nephew. He was transformed and galvanised into action, jumping up out of his armchair with alacrity. "If we are to stop this burial in the paupers' graveyard, we must be on our way immediately. Where is this God-forsaken prison?"

"It is in High Street on the south side of the river," answered Mary, with her usual penchant for delivering facts gleaned from her reading. "The Tower of London is on the other side of the river, directly opposite."

Uncle Russell took his wife's hand. "Charles and I shall go alone, my dear. It will not be safe for you on the murky streets of London with all manner of vagabonds and body snatchers roaming about."

Aunt Russell, in her turn, was truly concerned for their safety. She insisted, "Take your pistols!"

Mary focused on the practicalities of their travel arrangements. "You must break your journey to London at Longbourn tonight. My parents are just a few hours ahead of you, and Mrs Hill will make you up rooms. Uncle, do not shake your head! I insist that you stay. You will both have a good dinner when you arrive, and a hearty breakfast to sustain you tomorrow."

"That is sensible and kind, Mary," said Charles stiffly, recovering some equanimity after the distressing news of his brother's impecunious circumstances, incarceration and suicide. Mary's reactions in his time of need had been instrumental in saving him from near despair. He would be eternally grateful to her for that, just as he knew he would always love her, despite the fact that her affections lay elsewhere. But he wished that his words had sounded more heartfelt.

CHAPTER XIX

THE LONG WAIT

When Uncle Russell and Charles were gone, Mary could barely contain her joyful anticipation of the Sinclairs' party, but kept herself busy each morning devising new schoolroom activities for the children.

On Tuesday a letter arrived from Uncle Russell.

"Let me read you this letter, Mary," Aunt Russell suggested at breakfast. "It is from your uncle. He and Charles have arrived safely in Longbourn." She read, "*Ruby dear, a quick missive before we leave for London. Your brother and Mrs Bennet were astonished when we descended from the hired carriage outside their very door, not more than three hours after they had arrived home. We feared Mrs Bennet would have to retire to her chambers with no one to look after her nerves, but she rallied and ordered the jolly housekeeper, the redoubtable Mrs Hill, to make up beds. Tell Mary that Mrs Hill provided the promised excellent dinner and a hearty breakfast too! Mrs Bennet has even insisted that we return to Longbourn to stay for a few days, as Jane and her husband, Mr Bingley, will be here by then. This should cheer us after our harrowing visit to London, and some grouse shooting in the grounds of Longbourn is an added inducement to return here! Charles managed to secure some days away from Blixford – his employer is a damned good sort in my opinion – so we have accepted her kind invitation. I cannot* write more, my dear, as the carriage to London awaits us. The business in store for us there is unbearably grim to think about, and the sooner it is concluded the better. I shall write again when it is. Your husband, John."

"Let us hope they are not too late," commented Mary. "The body may have already been committed to the paupers' burial ground."

"Then they will have to get it exhumed and buried properly, as befits his true status," Aunt Russell said decidedly. She agreed heartily with Mary's views that Matthew should be interred decently, with dignity, with a proper headstone in consecrated ground. "We shall have to be patient and wait for further news from your uncle."

Mary spent the morning, as she spent each weekday morning, teaching Roseanna and Ellen upstairs in the schoolroom. She had been working on a series of educational projects which linked together different disciplines. History linked with art was evidenced by her examination of the Romans' engineering feats and the uniform of the soldiers of Julius Caesar's empire. Today she would talk about Laki and Tambora and explain what happens when a volcano erupts. She had also arranged with Cook to show how lava flowed, by allowing the children to drop icing onto newly baked buns to watch its slow motion downwards and eventual hardening. They would then eat a bun apiece. Later in the week she planned to teach them what she knew about birdsong and link this information to the names of garden birds. They would go into the gardens to identify birds which came close. In Charles's absence, she would give her charges a music lesson, and they would invent two pieces of music, Roseanna on the pianoforte and Ellen on percussion instruments. One piece would represent an erupting volcano, and the other birdsong, though which was to be which was still undecided!

However, no matter how hard she worked with her tutoring, her mind would involuntarily wander to Fitzroy and the joyful anticipation of his birthday party in the barracks at the weekend. Her heart would miss a beat when she imagined differing scenarios: talking to Fitzroy, whist with Fitzroy, dancing with Fitzroy, laughing with Fitzroy, discussing interesting topics with Fitzroy, simply being with Fitzroy for all of one glorious evening.

By Thursday, she was tempted to go into Ely, ostensibly to visit Lydia and purchase some pink and white accessories to adorn her ringlets at the birthday party. In reality she hoped to glean some information from Lydia about Fitzroy, or better still to meet with him in the town.

"Oh, Lord, no!" chirped Lydia. "He's not here. He's gone!"

"Gone?" asked Mary, her heart missing a beat for a very different reason from before. She feared she would see him no more, that he had left without a word.

"They have all gone, the whole family, gone to Wiltshire to visit relations as a pre-birthday celebration. It was Colonel Sinclair's cousin, you see, who died and left the Wiltshire estate to Fitzroy. Lucky old Fitz! No other male relations to leave it to."

"Like Longbourn being entailed to Mr Collins," observed Mary, though the analogy could not have been more different. Mr Collins was gauche and dull, whereas Fitzroy was dashing and charismatic.

"Let us go and purchase your hair decorations. Oh, how I wish we had been invited to this party!"

"Are you not?" asked Mary with surprise.

"Just Lieutenant Colonel Timmins and his wife, and Major Bisley and his wife. The captains are a rank too low for the colonel's parties!" Lydia laughed gaily, but Mary could discern her bitterness at this seeming slight; an invitation to members of her own family had been extended, but none to her. "It is a silly notion!"

The next day, Friday, another letter from Uncle Russell arrived. During the afternoon, when Aunt Russell normally spent time with the children, she entered the conservatory where Mary was reading.

"Another letter from your uncle," she said, as she handed Mary the two pages of bold handwriting. "You must read it."

Mary noted her aunt's unusually pale face and drawn features and imagined the worst. "Is it as I feared? They were too late?"

"Read what he says!"

My dearest Ruby,

We are both in a state of shock. Our wish is to spare you details of the squalid conditions of Marshalsea Prison, where my dear nephew spent his last days, but it is fitting that you should know and understand something of what must have driven him to the end which he chose for himself.

Charles and I have no doubt now that he must have committed suicide. No man of breeding could tolerate for long the noise of miserable mortals crying out for help or forgiveness while others hurl obscenities and curses at their gaolers and all humanity. One of the trustees, a Mr Jenkins, took us through the prison to reach the morgue where Matthew's body lay. The stench of urine running along the open gutters is so putrid that Charles and I had to untie our stocks and use them as masks over our faces. Mr Jenkins informed us, with misplaced pride, that the prison is hosed down once a year to keep it clean! Some prisoners reached out to us for alms, their imploring hands caked in dirt, while others lay huddled and inert on dirty, infested palliasses in cramped cells, three prisoners occupying no more than ten feet square. Mr Jenkins revealed that when the prison gets overcrowded – dear God, how much more cramped do conditions have to get for the prison to be deemed overcrowded? – they send prisoners to the hulks which are anchored in the Thames Estuary, ready to be transported to the colonies. On the north side of this three-storey building,

154

little light penetrates through the small barred window of each cell. I dread to think how cold these cells must be in the depths of winter. To be imprisoned here is a fate worse than death. Indeed, Mr Jenkins told us dispassionately that many prisoners choose death and that suicides are quite common.

How we as a country can stand back and let men and women be treated as worse than animals is a terrible reflection on our moral responsibilities. When I return home, I shall press for prison reform.

Our business is concluded satisfactorily. Matthew's body had been placed in a roughly constructed wooden box, awaiting a cart to transport it to St Saviour's church, renowned for its interments of "fallen women" and paupers. However, after discussing terms with the vicar of St George's church, across the road from Marshalsea, we committed him to the graveyard there without delay in a very dignified funeral ceremony. The vicar, Charles and I said the Lord's Prayer together as two gravediggers lowered the coffin into the ground.

We have found a monumental mason who has been paid to fashion a fine granite headstone with the simple inscription, "In loving memory of Matthew Tremayne, of Tremayne Manor, Cornwall, who died aged thirty-seven, 1816". This will be placed next week in St George's graveyard. It was Matthew's last wish to be transferred to the brighter south side of the prison so that he could look out on to the sunny St George's church and graveyard, so it was fitting that he should be buried there.

We return to Longbourn tomorrow, to recuperate.

With love, as ever, John.

Aunt Russell remained forlornly by while Mary read this letter. The prison conditions were much worse than Mary had expected from her reading, and hearing of them from a first-hand observer brought it all the more into reality. She rose from her seat and put her arms round her aunt's shoulders in order to offer some kind of comfort. Aunt Russell relaxed into her niece's tender embrace and let her tears fall.

Mary uttered not a word. There was nothing that could be said to soften the fact of a dead nephew, killed by his own hand, in such a place. Mary shared her aunt's sympathy for Charles, who had lost his only brother, but words would have seemed mere platitudes, and nothing should be said to lessen her aunt's misery born of deep love for her husband, who had been irrevocably scarred by what he had witnessed in that dreadful house of correction.

"Thank you, Mary," was all Aunt Russell said, as she left the conservatory.

That evening Mary found herself playing the melancholy Mozart piece which Charles had played: the one which her mother had so criticised as being "morbid". The storm-tossed, turbulent music of Mozart's *Fantasia in C minor*, with its dead march left hand and varying moods, seemed to reflect the thoughts and feelings which all the family must be experiencing. Yes, they were mourning for a lost close relative, but what torment and self-reproach he had put them through! He had become a lost soul in abject misery, yet he was the one who had thrown away everything and damaged others in the process.

Saturday finally came. Mary woke with a smile and jumped out of bed. She pulled back the curtain drapes, fully expecting nature to correspond with her thoughts of optimistic anticipation, but the sullen, overcast day presaged no such assurances of success or safe hopes. Through the drops of water which rolled down the windowpane, she watched flurries of rain sweep across the gardens, and her spirits dampened as the lake at the far end of the estate was obliterated by a watery mist.

At breakfast, Aunt Russell remarked, "We shall have to lift our skirts above our ankles again, my dear, if we are to keep them free of mud this evening!"

Mary smiled. Her aunt was back to her practical self.

With a twinkle, Aunt Russell added, "One hesitates to imagine what the barracks' courtyards and parade grounds will be like. Horses can be such a problem, do you not think?"

The rain did not abate all day, and, as the Russells' carriage made its way to Ely barracks, there were occasions when Simon Braden was sure that the flooded roads would necessitate turning back or, worse still, they would be stuck in the mud.

"Drive on, Mr Braden!" commanded the intrepid Aunt Russell.

Their carriage and passengers were identified at the gates of the barracks and, when Mary and her aunt descended on to the wet square sets, the rain had stopped and the last rays of the sun were filtering through the remaining mist.

"Such dreadful weather!" exclaimed Mrs Sinclair, as an impromptu and unusual greeting to Aunt Russell and to Mary as they entered the drawing room. Remembering protocol, she said, "Welcome, my dear Mrs Russell, and dear Miss Bennet!"

The three ladies curtsied.

Mrs Sinclair resumed her discourse on the weather. "There is flooding everywhere! Ely will become an island very soon!"

"It is called the Isle of Ely," commented Mary, used to her role as instructress, "and now we can begin to understand why."

"Thank goodness we returned from Wiltshire yesterday, or we may not have managed to get through."

"Wiltshire?" asked Aunt Russell.

"Yes, to visit our cousins. Our son inherits Blandon Estate in Wiltshire today, from Colonel Sinclair's cousin who died some time ago. Fitzroy stayed on for an extra day, but has not yet returned. He travels with his second cousin, but I fear the rising waters may delay them some time."

"Uncle Russell is unable to be here," apologised Aunt Russell. "There has been a death in the family and funeral arrangements to see to in London."

"My commiserations, ma'am. Sadness and Joy always ride together," Mrs Sinclair philosophised, sighing sympathetically. Changing the subject abruptly, she became the hospitable hostess. "Now do let me introduce you to Major Timmins' wife."

Introductions and conversations continued for another hour, and still there was no sign of Fitzroy and his second cousin, whatever his name was. As the evening wore on, the colonel and Aunt Russell became more and more perturbed. Mary was agitated in extremis and could barely keep up the social graces required of such an occasion. Wines and canapés were handed round and, as the guests became more and more jovial, Mary became more and more anxious.

Just before ten o'clock, a carriage was heard outside, and Mrs Sinclair flew to the door to admit her adored son, who was now one-and-twenty.

"Mother, what a terrible journey!" Fitzroy exclaimed as he entered. "We thought we should never be here in time for all the festivities. But here we are, safe and sound," he said expansively, posing at the doorway. Some of the guests made an attempt to applaud.

"Such a handsome man!" Mrs Timmins whispered to the lieutenant colonel's wife who sat beside her. "A matchmaker's paradise!"

Everyone smiled in his direction, as he still stood poised at the doorway, holding the door open.

Then Fitzroy formally and proudly announced, "My honoured guests, please may I introduce you to my second cousin, Miss Matilda Sinclair?"

In walked a pretty, blonde-haired young woman of no more than eighteen, innocent and nervously smiling.

Extending his hand to her, Fitzroy said, "Matilda has done me the great honour of agreeing to be my wife."

CHAPTER XX

DARKNESS

Mary should have felt considerable pride in the stoical and composed manner in which she conducted herself in the longest two hours of her life before Simon Braden returned to take her and Aunt Russell back to Willow Wood. But she experienced nothing but self-criticism and darkness. She should have been pleased that her natural good sense and propriety had prevailed and she had conversed politely with all the guests. But her mind was awash with deluging waves of misery. She should have been outraged by the open betrayal which had been hurled at her so cruelly and so publicly by Fitzroy Sinclair. But she reprimanded herself on her own foolishness and vanity in imagining that the handsome and desirable heir to a large estate in Wiltshire should be attracted to her. She should have prided herself in her aplomb when she smiled and wished Fitzroy and Matilda joy. But she compared herself with the beautiful young bride-to-be and felt humiliated by her own inadequacies and ineffectual attempts to make herself truly attractive to Fitzroy.

Lord Byron's poem *Darkness* was swimming round and round in her head:

I had a dream, which was not all dream.
The bright sun was extinguish'd, and the stars
Did wander darkling in the eternal space,
Rayless and pathless, and the icy earth

Swung blind and blackening in the moonless air;
Morn came and went – and came, and brought no day,
And men forgot their passions in the dread
Of this their desolation; and all hearts
Were chill'd into a selfish prayer for light.

Mary had fallen into a fitful and tearful sleep, but her weary, saddened soul finally succumbed to a deep and remedial slumber. She would have slept all the next day, but John Donne's *busy old fool*, the *unruly Sun*, streamed in through the curtain. How welcome this change in the oppressive weather would be to the farmers, but how unwelcome to her, to unmercifully illuminate her misery and force her to rise and be merry!

However, like the ancient mariner's spell-bound wedding guest who could not choose but hear his tale, she too was wiser the following morning, after the events of the previous evening had been forced on her.

Mary rang for the upstairs maid to fetch her some warm water.

"Now, Susan, I shall require you to wash away all trace of these ringlets," she ordered the young girl who was pouring the warm water into the bowl on the wash stand.

"No! Not all them pretty ringlets, miss!" Susan blurted out, scandalised out of decorum at such a suggestion. Ringlets were evidence of status!

"All trace!" Mary repeated soberly. "And when my hair is as straightened as it can be, you will assist me to pull it back into a neat bun at the nape of my neck. Like the one I had when I first arrived here."

"Yes, miss," agreed Susan, but with a distinct lack of enthusiasm for such sacrilege!

Next, Mary went to the wardrobe to pull out all the pretty evening gowns which Aunt Philips had bought for her and placed them one by one on the bed. She surveyed and stroked each of them in turn, finally patting each one as if she were saying farewell. Susan stood motionless, scared and perplexed by Miss Bennet's deliberately measured actions, daring not to interrupt what appeared to be a kind of ritual.

"These are of no further value at present. Put them in my packing case, please."

Mary instructed Susan with calm determination, her crying finished. She was not going to let fall any more tears over Fitzroy, her own silly aspirations or her failed hopes. She doubted if these dresses, as poignant reminders of her time in Ely, could ever be worn again.

"Yes, miss."

"And I should like you to have these ribbons for your bonnet."

"Ooh!" Susan's excited gratitude came out as a shriek. "Thank you, miss!"

At breakfast, Aunt Russell immediately noticed Mary's changed appearance, her hair, her high-necked day dress, and that, although her facial features were controlled and demure, her eyes were red-rimmed, telling of uncontrolled abandonment to tears.

"Are you quite well enough to attend morning service, my dear?" she asked kindly.

"Yes, indeed, Aunt."

Not wishing to waste time on niceties, Aunt Russell said directly, "It was a shock to discover that Fitzroy was to marry. He never mentioned, certainly not in my hearing, that he was betrothed. You were very fond of him, were you not?"

"Yes, I was, but, as has been made abundantly clear, it was all foolishness on my part."

"You are not foolish, my dear. I dare say he led you on."

"I thought that he enjoyed my company, that he even had some affection for me," Mary admitted. "I was deceived."

"Indeed you were!" Aunt Russell, hardly able to restrain herself, utilised this ambiguity to full advantage. "You were intentionally duped!"

"Not intentionally, Aunt," Mary contradicted, unwilling to admit to her aunt what she herself knew must have been the truth. She had indeed been duped, and now it was crystal clear that it was deliberate. However, she kept these thoughts to herself, and stated truthfully. "I misread his apparent friendliness for real affection."

"It is quite insupportable!" Aunt Russell was getting angry at such treatment of her dear niece. "To knowingly show such friendliness, when all the time he knew he was betrothed to his second cousin."

How could Mary deny that this was so? He had deliberately engaged her in conversations which were more than of just a casual nature. What she had written to Elizabeth of her love for Fitzroy and her matrimonial hopes, these had not emanated from some childish dream. Time and again he had led her to believe that she was favoured, that he wished to be with her above all others. She was ashamed now to think that she had flouted the rules of convention in walking out alone with him, and that she would have danced that third dance with him, had he asked her.

"He has treated you abominably," continued Aunt Russell, "but I admire your spirit, my dear. Your uncle will take a very dim view of this treatment, not only by Fitzroy himself, but by the colonel and his wife, who must have had some inkling of their son's relationship with you. I am relieved that they leave Ely at the end of the week. They will be no loss, I can assure you!"

Although Mary would have persisted in preserving Fitzroy's good name in the face of censure, she was nevertheless grateful for her aunt's staunch support. It fortified her resolve to return to her own values, to be true to her own self, and to nurse her broken heart in private.

The Reverend Smallwood's choice of the twenty-third psalm gently aided this resolution, and when Mary left Foxham parish church she believed with earnest conviction

163

that the Lord was her shepherd, who led her by quiet waters, who was with her, his rod and staff comforting her. But later in the day she was unconvinced that her cup overflowed. To her it seemed empty. And she could only hope that her soul would be restored again, in time.

After dinner Mary sat down, as was customary, to play the pianoforte for her aunt. Only a few days before she had played Mr Mozart's allegretto grazioso of the *Sonata in B flat* with such exhilarating passion, fuelled by her love for Fitzroy. Now she turned to the second movement of the same sonata, the slower, more emotional andante cantabile. It suited her inner dejection, played with such intensity, seeming to come from Mary's very soul. The gentle and melancholic cadences spoke of Mary's love, and the dissonances were interpretations of her lost hopes.

As Aunt Russell listened to the music, she knew not which of her own emotions ruled her the most: pity for Mary who had been led down a primrose path by Fitzroy to a hell of sadness; admiration for a young woman who was able to courageously withstand an attack of deliberate deceit; or anger that the young, dastardly Fitzroy would leave and live a honeyed existence in Wiltshire, while Mary faced an uncertain future. She would do all in her power to help Mary, the loved niece for whom she had the utmost respect. Things would get better; of this she was certain.

However, things got decidedly worse.

CHAPTER XXI

THE GRAND PLAN

At breakfast the following morning, a letter from Mr Bennet addressed to Mary arrived. Mary's instinct told her that there must be something amiss, because her father disliked correspondence, both receiving letters and writing them.

"This cannot be good news, Aunt. My father rarely puts pen to paper."

"The best policy is to open it immediately and not trouble yourself thinking the worst," advised Aunt Russell.

Mary broke the seal without further ado.

Mr Bennet wrote in a sloping Italian copperplate hand, having been taught penmanship from John Sealy's manual *The Running Hand*. He had insisted that all his daughters had access to this same manual when it came to learning penmanship. All but Lydia had exercised the patience to learn to write in this neat and attractive hand, with Mary excelling. Mr Bennet's letter was brief.

My dear Mary,

It pains me to have to be the bearer of unpleasant news, but when a certain matter came to my attention, there was no other alternative but to inform you immediately of circumstances concerning Mr Fitzroy Sinclair. Your sister Kitty, who is staying at Pemberley with the Darcys, received the accompanying letter from Lydia, and thought it best that I should consider the contents first in order to advise you accordingly. Kitty is most distressed by this news from Lydia, and wishes to say that she had no prior knowledge of the grand plan.

My advice is that you immediately cut off all discourse with Mr Sinclair, return any trinkets which he may have given you, and apply to your aunt for guidance and comfort at what will be a distressing time for you. Your mother is amazed at such a turn of events, as she fervently hoped, indeed she believed, that you would be the next Mrs Sinclair by the end of the year, and, were Jane not here, she would have taken to her bed for days with her nerves.

My thoughts are with you. Your father.

Mary handed this letter to her aunt to read, while she unfolded Lydia's untidily written page. Jangling like a discordant bell, the words "grand plan" had an ominous ring to them. She steadied her shaking hands and took a deep breath, preparing herself to discover what was thought to be so unpleasant about the news which Lydia had imparted so conspiratorially to their sister Kitty. News which Kitty had deemed so bad that she had to pass it on to their father, and not just to her! Mary began reading Lydia's letter with apprehension, caught between a burning curiosity to discover the significance of the "grand plan" and a reluctance to discover what could be so distressing.

Dearest Kitty

You will be having a thrilling time with the Darcys at Pemberley, soirées and balls and all manner of delicious social engagements. How I wish my dear George and Mr Darcy were good friends, so we too could enjoy all this fun! But Mr Darcy refuses to have anything more to do with him. Such a horrid man, in my opinion!

But we have our own fun. Anything to liven up the last few weeks here in Ely! When we – that is George and I, Captain Moffat and his dear wife Caroline, and Captain

Wilkins – knew that Mary was to visit, we devised a grand plan.

What a lark!

You know how dull Mary is, rejecting the very idea of love? Miracle of miracles! I have persuaded her to style her hair in ringlets, and to dress more alluringly, showing more bosom! I pride myself that she looks passably pretty now. We engaged Fitzroy Sinclair, the colonel's son, a handsome dandy, to pretend that he found her irresistible. A good sport! He's a real Don Juan!

George has a wager of ten shillings with his two captain friends that Mary will fall in love with Fitzroy by the end of the regiment's tour here. And hurrah! George is on the point of claiming his money. Mary shows all the signs of deep affection. Even our mother is convinced that Mary and Fitzroy will be wed before the year is out.

I can hardly write for laughing!

Your loving sister, Lydia.

When Aunt Russell had read this second letter, there followed a stunned silence. Mary looked down into the dregs of her teacup as if she would divine some vestige of order in a world of deceit and betrayal. Aunt Russell folded Lydia's letter most precisely with her fingertips and placed it before her as if it were some distasteful specimen.

"Sad, sad Lydia!" she sighed, shaking her head. "Her life must be so very empty and deficient, to search for fun at her sister's expense. I cannot doubt that she knew this would cause you distress. And then to boast and laugh about the success of the 'grand plan' is reprehensible. I am so sorry, my dear!"

Mary sat quite immobile, her mind in turmoil. To be tricked into believing Fitzroy cared for her was but a drop in the ocean compared with the duplicity of her sister, her own flesh and blood. Despite all her reading of unkind familial acts in stories of ancient Greece, and even in the Bible,

167

Mary's sheltered life in Meryton and her naïvety could not have prepared her for Lydia's total disregard for the Christian values to which the Bennet family aspired. To think that Lydia and her friends had watched Fitzroy and herself, as if they were actors in a scene from a cheap comedy in the theatre! Or, worse, as if she were a stringed puppet, at the mercy of their whims, dancing to their unkind tune! How they would have roared with laughter together when she was elsewhere! She choked back her tears of anger and humiliation and would not let them fall. She could hardly trust herself to speak.

Aunt Russell tentatively asked, "Would you like to go back home? I can arrange for you to leave today, should you so desire it."

Mary inhaled slowly and deeply before replying, decisively and in measured tones, "That would be running away."

"What will you do?"

"I shall speak with Lydia. This needs to be brought out into the open and aired in a level and civilised manner."

"Shall I accompany you for moral support?"

Mary thought about this proposition for a few seconds before answering, "I appreciate the offer, Aunt, but I would rather confront Lydia on my own, face to face, one to one."

"Quite the best policy," agreed Aunt Russell.

"Can you spare me this morning?"

"Certainly, my dear. Anything you wish in order to get this unpleasant business over and done with!"

After setting Roseanna and Ellen some schoolroom drawing and writing tasks for the morning, Mary dressed with care in a blue walking dress, ensuring that her hair was neatly tied back in a bun and donning a simple matching blue bonnet. Her Paisley shawl which had before caught on the hawthorn tree branch, now laundered and ironed, completed the ensemble. Before descending to Simon Braden and the waiting barouche, she carefully scrutinised her appearance in the looking glass in her chamber, to satisfy herself that this reflection was again her real self, and to give her confidence to speak her mind to Lydia.

Lydia was not at her lodging house when Mary arrived.

"No, miss, she's not here," the Wickhams' housemaid informed her. "She and that other captain's wife have gone to the Lamb Hotel. Shall I give her a message when she gets back?"

"I think not," said Mary. Despite herself, she smiled inwardly at the thought of this simple housemaid's retelling of all that Mary had to say, if she had recounted it to her.

Simon Braden had waited to see Mary admitted into the house, no one wishing for her to be alone in Ely with the possibility of a repeat of a robber's attack on her person, and he now was instructed to take her to the Lamb Hotel. Mary had given herself half an hour, which she had deemed to be adequate to carry out her task, before Simon Braden was to collect her again.

Lydia and Caroline Moffat were seated in the dining room of the hotel, awaiting the extravagant luncheon for which the Rances were famed. Mary grimly wondered whether Lydia was spending some of the ill-gotten gains from the wager, which had been won at her expense.

Henry Rance recognised Mary immediately. "Why, it is Miss Bennet, if I am not mistaken. Are you and your family here for luncheon?"

"Unfortunately not today," Mary politely responded. "Would you be good enough to ask Mrs Wickham if she would join me? I have words to speak with her which are of a private nature."

"Private, eh? Would you care to avail yourself of the back parlour? A nice fire is burning in the grate," Henry Rance offered. "There's nobody in there, and do not you worry, I'll keep anyone out till you are done."

Mary sat down and composed herself before Lydia came bursting into the snug little room.

"Mary!" cried Lydia. "This is a surprise! What's all the secrecy? Mr Rance said you wanted to see me in private! Very clandestine! And good heavens, look at you! Whatever has happened to your hair? It is all scraped back again like some Quaker's!"

"Please sit down, Lydia," Mary said coldly. "I have come about this." She took her time to undo the ties on her reticule, and to produce and unfold Lydia's letter to Kitty. "Do you recognise it?"

"How can I recognise a bit of paper?" Lydia stalled, suspecting immediately what it was.

"Why not read it, to refresh your memory?" Mary coolly commanded, handing the page of untidy scrawl to her.

Lydia's face paled. She had been caught out, but was on the defensive, like a cornered cat. "How did you get this?" she demanded, the colour in her cheeks coming back with a rush. "Did Kitty send it to you? It wouldn't surprise me – she's such an empty-brained snake-in-the-grass."

"She sent it to our father," Mary replied dispassionately. She amazed herself with how calmly she was dealing with Lydia's exclamations and questions. She presumed Lydia must now be feeling some embarrassment, if not guilt. She doubted if Lydia felt any remorse!

"What right has he to read other people's letters, and what right had he to send it to you? What right had Kitty to share my private correspondence to her with anyone else? It is shameful!" Lydia's voice had risen to a shout during her outburst.

"Shameful! We are agreed on that," agreed Mary, smiling politely. "It is indeed shameful to abuse a sister in any way."

Lydia sat very still, her face ablaze. There was something unsettling in the way Mary spoke so serenely, and so pleasantly.

"A sister should always stand by her sibling, in the face of disrespect by others. Would you agree, dear Lydia?"

Lydia stared unblinking at her sister.

"A sister should defend her family in the face of laughter or scorn by others. You cannot disagree, Lydia dear." Mary paused to return Lydia's stare. "Your sisters and whole family circle supported you when you brought shame on their name. Do you recall?"

Lydia frowned pettishly.

"It is shameful when a sister devises a grand plan – yes, those are the very words – a grand plan to trick and humiliate her sister."

Lydia looked down, with what may have been the first signs of contrition.

"A sister should not entertain the idea of a common wager, let alone enjoy the spoils at a grand luncheon in the Lamb Hotel. What say you, my dear Lydia? Is not this all shameful?"

Mary stopped speaking and waited for Lydia to look up. Lydia's face was screwed up in an odd melange of defiance, guilt and sulkiness.

"Is not this all shameful?" Mary simply repeated her question and waited for Lydia to reply.

"It was just a game," Lydia answered with a shrug.

"Not to me!"

"Anyway, George thought he would lose the bet, that you were so dull and book-learned that you would never succumb to Fitzroy's charms. There was no harm in it."

"Harm was done, Lydia."

"Pooh!"

"You could have stopped it," persisted Mary. "You saw what was happening, but you even arranged meetings between Fitzroy and me."

"What if I did?" Lydia was rallying to her own defence. "Fitzroy was enjoying himself too much. So were you, Mary. Why should I stop it, if you were having such fun together? It was just a lark."

"But you deliberately encouraged me in the hopes that Fitzroy and I would one day marry. And you knew all along that he was betrothed to his second cousin."

"What! Betrothed?" cried Lydia, in genuine surprise. "He kept that secret. The rascal!"

"Which makes him all the more culpable, but you are still very much to blame," insisted Mary.

Lydia failed to comprehend the notion of culpability. Mary could see that Lydia was unchangeable, that continuing to berate her would be ineffectual.

"Betrothed!" Lydia shrieked with delight. "What a dark horse! George should have had a wager on that!"

Mary stood up, eager now to terminate this discussion. "I leave Ely on Saturday. This will be our last meeting."

"Come and join Caroline and me for luncheon!" Lydia suggested, quite unconcerned, and ignoring the import of the preceding conversation, as she made ready to quit the back parlour. She added, laughing, "You may as well enjoy the spoils too!"

"I have to return to Willow Wood."

"Just as you like." Lydia was dismissive "Heavens! I am dying of hunger!"

"Goodbye, Lydia."

"Goodbye, sister dear!" Lydia airily waved her hand.

Before Lydia stepped jauntily out of the room, Mary had time to say, "A word before you go! When you are in Brighton, please do not invite me to stay, for I shall have to refuse. I have no matrimonial hopes, wager or no wager."

"Oh, Lord! Just wait till Caroline hears about Fitzroy!" Lydia rejoiced as she left.

Mary thought back to Aunt Russell's description of Lydia as a "sad, sad girl", and all her own sense and sensibilities forced her to accept with dismay that this was apt. Poor Lydia!

CHAPTER XXII

THE RETURN

Uncle Russell and Charles were to return on the Thursday, two days before Mary was due to leave Willow Wood, but in the event it was only Uncle Russell who travelled back from Meryton. He was fatigued after his long journey on the mail coach, which had travelled almost non-stop from Hertford to Ely, only stopping at the toll gates, or at the post houses to change horses and for travellers to hurriedly avail themselves of any facilities. It was late afternoon when he finally arrived.

"A dashed peculiar decision, if you ask me!" opined Uncle Russell, as he relaxed in his comfortable armchair in the drawing room. "But nothing would induce Charles to leave Meryton, until he had helped Mr Philips."

"In what way could he help?" Aunt Russell queried.

"They are both attorneys at law," Mary suggested.

"The Philips insisted we should attend one of their soirées, and a very jolly evening it turned out to be, and most welcome after Matthew's death and the ensuing trauma of our experiences in London. Charles and Mr Philips engaged in numerous discourses on legalities and acts of parliament and appeared to value each other's opinions."

"They have a lot in common," commented Mary.

"Mr Philips asked him to help finalise a complex legal case involving patents."

"Patents for what?" asked Aunt Russell.

"It turns out that Charles is quite an expert in mining patents, relating back to when he ran the tin mines on the Tremayne estate."

Remembering a conversation she had had with Charles shortly after her arrival in Ely, Mary now explained, "He had developed sufficient wind-powered pumping machines to pump out the sea water seeping in at the base of his mines. Next he wanted to install a high-pressure engine to raise the ore from the mines, like the one developed by Richard Trevithick for the Ding Dong mine in Penzance."

"Ding Dong, eh!" chuckled Uncle Russell.

Aunt Russell and Mary both smiled with him at the odd name for a mine.

"He had been investigating patents at that time," Mary concluded.

"Be that as it may, Charles will return on Sunday. No doubt he will wish to regale us with all the details when we next see him. So, Ruby dear, you will have to take him into the library, where you can exercise your patience and listen attentively to what he has to say. I shall be elsewhere. I cannot abide all that legal jargon! And you, my dear niece, shall be spared, as you will be safely restored to the comforts of Longbourn."

"In actuality, Uncle, I shall be very sorry to leave," Mary assured him.

"From what I hear, I thought you would be glad to get away from any reminder of that arrogant trickster."

Mary was embarrassed. She had forgotten that others would know of the scandalous behaviour of Fitzroy and how she had been the butt of her sister's game. It was a painful reminder.

Uncle Russell continued, "I should certainly like to give him a good dressing down, pistols at dawn sort of thing! We all thought so at Longbourn, once Lydia's letter became known. I shall tell him to his face that he is a damned disgrace, and that he is no gentleman."

"I should prefer that you did *not*, Uncle Russell," Mary said, so emphatically that both her aunt and uncle looked at her in some amazement. By way of explication, with more composure, she added, "It would serve no purpose and would only give him additional fuel for his idle amusement."

"True! True! Well spoken, my dear. Let sleeping dogs lie!" Uncle Russell brought his cupped hands together to produce a clap. "Now, where are my two little angels? I have their promised gifts."

When her aunt and uncle had left the drawing room, Mary agonised over how she would appear in Charles's eyes. How foolish and naïve she would appear. Would he now pity her? Would he censure her, again? Would she actually ever see him again? And what did Jane think, and her Mr Bingley, both such sweet and innocent creatures? Even they, who never criticised anyone, would surely be surprised at her stupidity.

As these negative thoughts swirled round her mind, she considered her future. After her whirlwind "romance", normal life paled into humdrum insignificance. However, she was comfortably resigned to going back to the usual Meryton social rounds, interspersed with attention to her mother's nerves and vapours, with Mr Bolton hovering in the immediate background. She continued to sit for an hour, ruminating over the lack-lustre years which stretched out interminably before her.

That evening, Roseanna and Ellen were permitted to stay up late and have a grown-up dinner with their parents and Cousin Mary in the dining room. This was a very rare occurrence, but Aunt Russell believed that both daughters had been pining for their father while he was away, and she knew that he would have missed them. This would be a good restorative. They each were allowed to sit down with the gifts which Uncle Russell had brought back for them: a lovely moulded composition lady doll apiece, made out of papier mâché.

"It is marvellous what they can do nowadays!" Uncle Russell announced. "These dolls look so lifelike with the thin covering of wax. You would swear it was real skin! Feel it, Mary! It even feels like real skin!"

Mary was invited to admire every feature of these dolls from their rosebud lips and golden mohair ringlets to their fashionable pastel silk gowns. They even wore little white slippers!

Mary was fascinated by the realistic "paperweight" eyes, which had been made from blown glass, and she watched with delight as Ellen demonstrated how the weighted eyelids closed when the dolls were lying down and opened when they were sitting up.

In the drawing room afterwards, the children entertained their parents with performances of their pianoforte pieces, which Mary had helped them to perfect in readiness for Charles's next lesson with them. Nothing would suffice other than the dolls being placed on the sofa to constitute their captured audience.

Roseanna sat down to play her first piece, accompanying Ellen singing *London Bridge is Falling Down*.

"Bravo!" Uncle Russell enthused, after the performance.

Ellen played a tuneful ditty to which Roseanna recited the nursery rhyme *Little Miss Muffet*. Roseanna's relevant actions, to show Miss Muffet sitting down, eating her curds and whey, and being frightened by the dangling spider beside her, were humorously theatrical.

"Bravo!" cried Uncle Russell again.

Aunt Russell and he were genuinely surprised that Ellen could play so well, remarking to one another that she had a natural talent. They had found Roseanna's dramatic representation of the rhyme very amusing, but hoped she, as the daughter of a gentleman, would have no aspirations to go onto the stage!

The two girls sat down together at the pianoforte, Roseanna at the lower notes and Ellen at the higher notes, to play a charming duet which Charles had composed especially for them, entitled *Bluebells in Spring*.

"Very pretty, my dears," commented Aunt Russell at the end, smiling proudly at her children. "Cousin Charles will be very impressed."

"Will he come tomorrow?" asked Roseanna. "It will be Friday."

"I fear not. He has business to attend to in Hertfordshire. He will be here on Sunday."

Mary realised with a pang of regret that she would have departed from Willow Wood by the time Charles arrived. Would their coaches pass on the journey? Would she ever see him again?

Her thoughts were interrupted by Uncle Russell. "Would you play solo for us now, Mary!" he urged.

Mary deferred, "The girls have two sets of dances they would like to show you. I shall accompany them on the pianoforte. Perhaps that will suffice."

Mary played the second, adagio movement of Johann Sebastian Bach's *Brandenburg Concerto Number 5* to accompany the children in demonstrating the five positions of dancing. These were described and illustrated by none other than the same dancing master as before, Mr Thomas Wilson, this time in a less obscurely entitled manual, *The Complete System of English Country Dancing*.

"Well done, my dears!" cried Uncle Russell, applauding, obviously impressed by his daughters' elegance and abilities. "You will be able to teach me some of your steps!"

"Papa, they are called positions," little Ellen informed him pertly.

"Positions, eh?"

"There are five of them: one, two, three, four and five," she added, doing each one again in turn. "Ballet dancers do them. A French man made them up, but I forget his name." She bit her lip and looked towards Mary for a reminder.

"His name was Monsieur Beauchamps," Mary advised her.

"His name is very hard to say!"

Mary now nodded to Roseanna, who was waiting patiently to introduce their next dance. "If you please, Roseanna!" she said, placing the next sheet of music on the pianoforte rest.

Roseanna now stepped forward to introduce their next dance. With considerable dramatic skill, she extended her arm towards an imaginary distant horizon and intoned, "Imagine you are on board a ship, far out at sea, and Ellen and I are two sailors. We are going to dance the sailors' dance. It is called the Hornpipe. This dance shows what the sailors do, like pulling on ropes, rowing, saluting and climbing up the... the..." she faltered and turned a worried face towards Mary.

"Rigging," helped Mary.

"Climbing up the rigging." Roseanna stepped back, happy now that her introduction was concluded satisfactorily. There had been many words to learn!

"Cousin Mary plays the music really, really fast!" added Ellen.

Mary assisted them in getting ready for this energetic dance, ensuring they were facing their parents and standing side by side with their arms rigidly folded and horizontal. She sat down to play the syncopated rhythm of William Vickers' manuscript entitled *College Hornpipe*.

It *was* fast! The children were breathless as they curtsied at the end of their entertainment while their parents laughed and clapped. The performance was perfect.

"Cousin Mary is going to help us finish our puppets tomorrow," Roseanna told her parents. "If they are ready, may we do a puppet show for you tomorrow?"

"Can we? Can we?" Ellen jumped up and down as she implored her parents.

"May we!" corrected Mary.

"May we? May we?"

"Yes, indeed you may!" Aunt Russell agreed, smiling.

Once the children had been taken off to bed by Elizabeth Braden, each cradling their new dolls, which would spend all night cuddled up beside them, Uncle Russell enjoyed a final glass of port.

"Mary, tomorrow will be your last day with us, but we shall eat and be merry, because we have much to discuss," he enigmatically pronounced. "However, I have estate management to attend to during the day, so you will have to wait until dinner to hear what I have to say."

Mary and Aunt Russell looked interrogatively at one another in an attempt to understand his meaning, but neither was any the wiser.

Then sighing loudly, he exclaimed, "Upon my word, I am dashed tired. The weary traveller longs for his rest! Come, my dear," he said, standing up and extending a hand towards his wife, "let us climb the wooden ladder together!"

Before they left the drawing room, Mary said, "I should like to stay for a while and practise a few pieces in the music room. Will this disturb you?"

"Not at all, my dear," Aunt Russell assured her. "If you need more candle power, ring for Mrs Brown. Goodnight, and thank you so much for the girls' delightful entertainment."

"Yes, delightful!" Uncle Russell heartily echoed.

"It was such a pity that Charles could not have been here too. He would have been so proud of them."

"Damned good show!" Uncle Russell agreed.

"It was a perfect homecoming, do you not think, John?"

"Now, my dear Ruby, let us go before sleep overtakes us!" On the point of departing he added, "We shall have words tomorrow, Mary, depend on it," and he escorted his wife out of the room, closing the door behind them.

Mary was intrigued. What could there be to discuss? Details of her return journey to Longbourn, most probably. Perhaps arranging a return visit to Willow Wood? It could not be unpleasant news, or her uncle would have informed her immediately; of this she was sure. She would have to satisfy herself that all would be revealed the next evening at dinner.

There was a peculiar, almost magical quality to the light in the music room. The candle flames flickered in the gently wafting warm air which filtered through the open windows, yet there in the darkening violet skies the full moon was shining. As Mary sat down to play the adagio movement of *Quasi una Fantasia*, she remembered the story of the blighted love affair between Countess Giulietta Guicciardi and the despairing Ludwig van Beethoven which Charles had told; she remembered the shimmering waters on the lake at which Charles and she had looked together in the moonlight; she remembered his gentle touch on her cheek when he had brushed away her tears. The music engulfed her. Her body swayed to the music as she remembered the warmth of Charles's body when they had sat together on the piano stool, as he played this very piece. Her breathing almost stopped. Her body and soul became one.

And then something strange and wonderful happened: through her fingertips the pianoforte keys gently responded to her touch, and, as she allowed the keys to push her fingers upwards, she knew with a deep certainty from the bottom of her heart that it was Charles whom she loved.

CHAPTER XXIII

THE PROPOSITION

Uncle Russell, seated at the head of the inlaid mahogany dining table, finished his glass of claret and looked in Mary's direction. Mary had been on tenterhooks during the whole four-course dinner, waiting for her uncle to divulge whatever he wanted to discuss. Aunt Russell had chatted amiably about the delightful puppet show which the children had presented before bedtime, and how grateful she was for all Mary had done during her time at Willow Wood, since poor Miss Kenyon had died. She offered a few pleasantries about the weather and the first leg of Mary's forthcoming journey the next day, but she grew unusually quiet during dessert and, as the end of their dinner approached, she seemed to be waiting nervously for some event. Yet her eyes were sparkling with delight, and she was obviously hugging some secret which she looked forward to sharing.

When dinner was over, Uncle Russell tapped the table with a silver dessert fork, as if he were about to make an important speech to a crowd of assembled guests. Mary and Aunt Russell looked towards him expectantly, Mary with a worried frown, Aunt Russell with an excited smile.

"Mary, this is your last evening with us. We shall be exceedingly sorry to see you go."

"As I said yesterday, I shall be very sorry to leave."

181

Uncle Russell put up his hand. He had the demeanour of a man who had much more to say. "Yet I warrant that you really will be exceedingly glad to leave, with all this unpleasant business. Your aunt and I had hoped that your time here in Ely would have been joyous and fulfilling."

Mary opened her mouth to speak, but what could she have truthfully replied? The opportunity was fortunately denied her as her uncle continued speaking.

"But instead it has been ruined by that blackguard."

"Not entirely, Uncle," Mary was honour-bound to say.

"When you leave, Mary, what do you intend to do?"

"Return to my normal life at home," Mary answered simply and assuredly, but with a defeated undertone.

"No further aspirations or hopes? You are a young woman with talent and a superior mind. You must have given some thought to how you might utilise these gifts."

Uncle Russell seemed to be prompting her to talk about her underlying hopes to be some use in the world, to have independence, and for people to respect her for her book learning. But to do that would be to admit that these were foolish hopes, as foolish as believing that Fitzroy had loved her, or that she loved him!

"I do hope you have no matrimonial hopes in the direction of your uncle's apprentice, Mr Bolton."

"I have neither hopes nor desires in that direction, Uncle," Mary quickly responded.

"I am relieved to hear that! He does not apply his mind or his abilities effectively. He is a rather shallow individual in my opinion, though I only conversed with him on a couple of occasions at the Philipses' house. Perhaps he improves with time."

"Indeed he does not, Uncle. He is of the opinion that women should not offer any comments of any sort on any important issues."

"A foolish fellow!" Uncle Russell said in agreement.

"To marry such a man, I should be shackled for the rest of my life, unable to share my thoughts and all the wonderful things I have learnt through my reading: about people and places, inventions and history, philosophy and morality. It would be worse than being in prison."

Uncle Russell's recent visit to Marshalsea Prison forbade him to agree with her; nothing could have been worse than that dreadful place. He shuddered at the memory.

Turning to her aunt at the other end of the table, Mary asked, "How would you fare, married to such a man?"

"I confess, it sounds like a life sentence, but I do not know the man, so am reluctant to pass judgement."

Uncle Russell gave his opinion. "With your abilities, Mary, as amply demonstrated last night and tonight by the entertainment provided by our two daughters, you are an excellent teacher. Roseanna has applied herself under your guidance to practise the pianoforte, with the result that she played excellently last evening, she performed her dances to perfection and she was so confident in her introduction. And dash me! Little Ellen, who was fearful of even speaking to me a few weeks ago, actually piped up and corrected me about dance 'positions'! The puppet show was extraordinarily good and comic, too. In this short time you have taught them well."

"Thank you, Uncle," replied Mary, gratified by his approbation.

"Now, this is what I have to discuss with you." Uncle Russell drank some more claret before continuing, savouring the delicious liquid as it rolled around his mouth. He was deliberating on how to frame his next thoughts. "It would be a pity to let all your natural talent go to waste. You should continue your good work."

"Surely you do not consider that I should be a governess?" Mary was shocked at the very idea. "I am a gentleman's daughter, sir!" she flared.

"You mistake your uncle, my dear," Aunt Russell hurriedly interjected, alarmed by Mary's reaction. "Pray let him continue!"

Uncle Russell swallowed hard. "What say you, Mary, to starting up a school for girls in Meryton?"

Mary's heart missed a beat. One of her dearest dreams, ever since she had espoused Mary Wollstonecraft's views on the education of women, was to follow in her footsteps and open up a school for girls. However, she had always known this could never move beyond a longed-for aspiration. She found herself almost laughing at the futility of such a suggestion.

"Like Mary Wollstonecraft, you mean?" she asked.

"Who is she?" asked Uncle Russell. Although unknowingly a clear supporter of women's rights in his own sphere, he was unaware of feminist literature.

"She had some very revolutionary ideas and her morality left much to be desired," Aunt Russell answered. To Mary she smiled as she commented, "You set such store by Mary Wollstonecraft, my dear. I hope you would not model yourself entirely on her."

"Not entirely, Aunt, but she had such spirit! I admired her starting up a school, and I should very much like to model myself on her in this respect. But she had financial backing. How can I model myself on her without that?"

"I shall give you backing!" Uncle Russell declared, pushing his shoulders proudly against the cushioned chair back. "It is all decided!"

"I do not understand, Uncle. What is all decided?"

"Everything is decided. Listen!" He sat forward, placing his hands firmly in front of him on the table. "Your aunt Ruby and I have talked about this all day." He looked towards Aunt Russell for some moral support.

"That is correct, my dear, and I am in total agreement."

"I wish to be your benefactor, to put at your disposal immediate funds to start up the school and refurbish

184

premises to your satisfaction and an annual trust fund to offset running costs and general expenditure, and to pay you a decent salary. Before long, money will come pouring in from the parents of your pupils, so you will be able to enlarge the premises and become self-supporting." Uncle Russell's face was aglow with excitement at this whole idea. "What say you, Mary?"

Mary was dubious. Her uncle, a genuinely generous and personable man, now appeared extravagant in his approval of this rash idea.

"You talk of premises, Uncle..." she begun.

"Ah, yes indeed," he answered in the next breath. "Your aunt and uncle Philips insist that you set up your school in the empty rooms in the return of their property. We were entertained at their house on two occasions, you know, and Mr Philips and I inspected the rooms with a view to converting them into a school. He is as excited as I am at the prospect, always disconcerted that the rooms had lain empty for so long. Mrs Philips cannot wait until she hears children's voices, something she says she has sadly missed all these years. She is gregariousness personified and is ecstatically anticipating meeting so many people every day as they bring their children to school, and she assures me that she will be in 'seventh heaven' with all the comings and goings. Her very words!"

Uncle Russell's speech had come out in a rush, and he now had to pause and inhale deeply to get over his breathlessness.

"I hear it is in the town with easy access for the families from roundabout, near and far!" Aunt Russell sensitively felt it necessary to fill the extended pause in her husband's discourse while he drank some more claret.

"That is true, Aunt," agreed Mary, thinking of the location. "It is on the main street, but set back a little in its own grounds."

The Philipses' sprawling seventeenth-century house, which had once been a hostelry with a thatched roof and apartments to accommodate up to ten paying guests, complete with stables and coach house to the rear, was in a most convenient position for a community school.

"Now hear this, Mary," Uncle Russell continued, fully recovered. "Your own parents have money for you kept in trust; did you know that?"

"My father kept money for each of us until we got married. Jane, Elizabeth and Lydia have already received their trust fund. Kitty will receive hers when she marries Reverend Doorish of Kympton parish."

"He believes that it would be to your advantage to release your trust fund to you now, so that you can buy equipment like desks, slates, paper and pens. He thinks that you will succeed magnificently in this venture, and says the money could not be better spent."

Although gratified that her father was so confident in her abilities that he should wish to release this money kept in trust for her, Mary was pained that, by doing so, he was tacitly acknowledging that she would never marry.

Aunt Russell, always quick to notice changes in Mary's mood, understood why she now had an expression of wry resignation on her face. "My dear Mary," she said, "you will be delighted when we tell you that Mr Bingley is donating many books from his library, books which he believes could be better used in the school."

"He admits he hates reading, and would far rather be in good company than sitting with his head in some great tome or other," added Uncle Russell. "I can heartily agree with him on that score."

Mary sat bewildered at the suddenness of this life-changing proposition. In a strange way, Mrs Sinclair had been almost right when she had said that "Sadness and Joy always ride together". Perhaps not quite together, but the one following close behind the other! Mary's own recent misery over Fitzroy, and her deep sadness that her love for Charles would have to remain hidden deep in her heart, were now relieved by a light at the end of a dark tunnel. A bright future had been offered to her. That her family collectively supported her gave her a warm feeling of joy. She felt even sadder for poor Lydia who sat on the outside of this cocoon of loving care, wilfully sacrificing it all for some whims to give her a laugh.

Mary sat so still and quiet, Uncle Russell feared she may have been offended again. He would be the last person to wish to occasion his dear niece any further hurt.

"The Meryton School for Girls!" Uncle Russell's generous bonhomie was tinged with uncertainty. "What do you say, Mary?"

"I do not know what to say. This is all so sudden."

"It is a fine opportunity," Aunt Russell stated, with her practical sense. "You would be a fool to let it pass you by!"

"It is a fine opportunity," agreed Mary, beginning to weigh up the possibilities; she was wary, and was not going to rush headlong into accepting the proposition for fear of making a foolish mistake again. "Indeed, my first reaction is to welcome this idea with open arms. After all, it was always what I wanted. But I must consider the implications. There will be money to be repaid over time. Uncle, your kind loan to start the school…"

He interjected, emphatically and simply stating, "It is not a loan. It is a gift."

"A gift?" Mary was genuinely taken aback by this generosity. Her hand flew to her heart. "I do not know how to thank you."

"No thanks are necessary. Consider it my investment in the future!" Uncle Russell was thinking of Roseanna and Ellen as he said, "There will be a new generation of fine young educated women to make their parents proud. If we lived closer to Meryton, our daughters would be the first pupils on your register!"

Mary's mind was now racing ahead of her. "So my father is in agreement?" she asked for confirmation.

"Your father tells me that, in your conversations with him, you have longed to start a school."

"That is true. We have discussed it in the past, but only as a pipe dream which could never come true."

"He knows you have read widely and says you 'will do admirably'."

Mary smiled at her uncle's attempt to imitate her father's speech. "But what about my mother?" she worried. "I can hardly believe that she would welcome this. Who will care for her?"

"Do not worry on that score!" Uncle Russell assured her. "Your mother is delighted that you will be close by, and not married to that scoundrel, Fitzroy, living far from civilisation in Wiltshire, aptly named in her opinion, a place where you would surely wilt! And then what help would you be to anybody? Her very words, or words to that effect!"

Mary smiled again. She could hear her mother's voice.

"And what was Charles's opinion?" Mary quietly asked, wanting his approval above all others'. No mention had been made of him, yet he must have been there when discussions were taking place. He must have also known about Fitzroy, and her foolishness. He would be censuring her, she felt sure.

"He sold his horse!"

Mary did not know whether to laugh or cry.

"Damned fool!" exclaimed Uncle Russell. "I told him so, but he insisted, so I bought it from him, paid him fifteen guineas there and then. He said you would understand. I am sure I do not!"

Mary was now overcome with so many emotions. Tears of joy and relief flowed down her face, but they were also tears of gratitude and amazement that so many people had come to her aid, tears of love for Charles as she cherished the hope that he perhaps cared for her. She laughed through her tears to think that Charles was now only one step away from losing the clothes off his back!

She pushed her chair back from the table and stood with unabated tears, not knowing which way to turn. Should she run to her uncle who was giving her this chance of a lifetime, or should she run to her aunt and embrace her with gratitude? Aunt Russell saved her any decision-making by rising and coming to her with her arms outstretched.

Aunt Russell gently repeated her husband's question. "So, Mary, what do you say?"

Mary threw her arms round her, sobbing. "I say yes. Thank you, thank you so much."

Together they walked arm in arm to where Uncle Russell still sat.

"The Meryton School for Girls!" Uncle Russell recited the words. "It has a good solid ring to it!"

"Oh, Uncle, how can I ever repay you?"

"For a start, you can stop crying, my girl," he ordered in mock severity. "It may be Friday the thirteenth, the harbinger of bad luck, but this is your lucky day. And, as one of the trustees of the new school, I suggest that we adjourn to the drawing room to get down to some proper planning. There is much to discuss before you leave in the morning."

Three hours later, Mary and her aunt and uncle finally retired to bed, having finished their discussions. Mary's mind was delightfully charged with financial matters, development of the premises, equipment required, heating, the construction of a new entrance with a cloakroom for the children's outdoor clothing, the paving of a new driveway and an enclosed play and exercise quadrangle, how many pupils she would be able to accommodate and how many teachers would be necessary, which subjects would be taught, how many hours would be in a school day. How many days' holiday would there be, what age groups should be catered for, who else should sit on the board of trustees, which religious denominations should be educated there, what uniforms should be worn?

However, despite the gratification of knowing that the people whose opinions she respected had confidence in her to be independent, and the fact that she would find satisfaction in this opportunity to start a school, she found it impossible to keep at bay her niggling thoughts: that she was being manipulated by others, and the ironical twist that her future independence would come from her dependency on those very people who supported her.

Mary willed sleep to overtake her, as she had a long journey the next day. Simon Braden was to take her as far as Cambridge in the Russells' barouche, and she knew this would be a long and slow journey, with frequent stops to allow the two horses to have adequate rest. She was to stay the night in the Eagle and Child, a post house appropriately positioned in Benet Street in Cambridge, where she was to pick up the fast mail coach to Hertford on the Sunday. The Bennets' barouche, with its familiar, distinctive maroon exterior, was to collect her in Hertford and take her on the last part of the way to Longbourn. However, no matter how hard she tried, lying first on one side and then on the other, tossing and turning, sleep would not come.

She longed for Charles. Her whole body yearned for his touch. She tingled all over at the thought of him lying close to her. She bit her lip as she imagined him there beside her now, holding her in his strong, manly arms. She looked into his grey-green eyes, she smiled with him as they sat together at the piano, she laughed as they perfected their line dance, she was safely cradled in his arms as he carried her back to Willow Wood on his bay hunter. Why had he sold his horse? As sleep finally claimed her, tears were wet on her pillow. The date, Friday the thirteenth, was surely significant; after all. Charles, the man she loved, would be far away in Cambridgeshire, while she must need stay in Meryton. Charles could not be part of her bright new future.

CHAPTER XXIV

HOME AGAIN

"Dear Jane and her Mr Bingley have only just left!" exclaimed Mrs Bennet, on greeting her daughter in the front room at Longbourn. "Less than two hours ago. They could wait no longer for your arrival, as they had to get to London before nightfall, and with Jane in her condition, and the roads in such an appalling state, all humps and bumps, they have to go slowly, you know. You must have passed their very carriage! You must have seen them!"

"Indeed, Mama," said Mary, seating herself beside her mother on the chaise-longue, "I did not see them, and I can assure you that I scrutinised every carriage and stage coach which I passed from Cambridge to here, and all the faces within."

"Upon my word, Mary!" retorted Mrs Bennet teasingly. "How could you do that? There must have been five and twenty vehicles at least and an hundred faces! I think the Cambridgeshire air has affected you! You have been away too long."

Mary's reply was the very truth. She had searched the faces through the small windows of each carriage as it passed, in the hope of seeing Charles. But it was to no avail. Charles must have taken a different route.

"No doubt she will be restored to her senses under your guidance, my dear," Mr Bennet suggested.

Ignoring this jibe, Mrs Bennet continued, "And you have missed Mr Tremayne as well. He left early this morning, even though we pressed him to stay until you had arrived, but he could not extend his leave of absence any longer and had to get back in time for his work tomorrow."

Putting aside her intense disappointment at Charles's decision to return to Cambridgeshire without even waiting to see her, she simply said, "I understand he will visit Willow Wood when he arrives back in Cambridgeshire. How Roseanna and Ellen long to see him again!"

"So now we have the house to ourselves," said Mrs Bennet, giving out a long sigh of relief.

"I shall be glad to get back to my study and a modicum of peace and quiet!" Mr Bennet remarked.

Mrs Bennet patted Mary's hand affectionately, genuinely pleased to see her daughter. "It is very good to have you home, dearest!"

Mary placed her other hand over her mother's. The superlative term of endearment used by her dear mama had not gone unnoticed. "And I am happy to be home. Six weeks away from Longbourn is a long time!"

It had been on the tip of her tongue to say that so much had happened in those six weeks that she was a different, wiser person. She had fallen victim to a foolish infatuation with an undeserving young dandy, but she was ready to hold her head high and rebuff any censure or mockery, and withstand any looks of scorn or pity.

In reality, the people of Meryton respected Mary's accomplishments; mothers wished their own daughters to be as able and educated as she. The few gossip-mongers in the town enjoyed the tale of Mary and Fitzroy – a seven-day wonder – but they felt no pity. They were of the opinion that it would have done Mary some good, livened her up, and given her a taste of real life and not just what was to be discovered through reading her books. There was no one in the environs who mocked, scorned or censured Mary. She was part of the community, accepted and well-liked for her quiet demeanour, her sense of propriety and her independence of character.

Mary's experience of real love for Charles, a deep and lasting love, unrequited though it might be, gave her strength to carry on. Her determination and spirit of independence, which she had developed through her reading, could now be utilised to the full, to make a success of her new life. The faith that everyone had put in her was stimulus to succeed, whatever the cost.

"Welcome home, dear Mary!" Mr Bennet greeted her. "I have quite missed your influence around the house. Jane and Mr Bingley are such pleasant souls, with plenty to say for themselves, but much of it is inconsequential tittle-tattle."

"What do you know of tittle-tattle, pray, Mr Bennet?" asked his wife, picking up on an expression he frequently used in criticism of her.

Mr Bennet averted the need to respond by adding, with some disapproval, "And they have eyes only for each other."

"Looks of endearment, Mr Bennet. Looks of endearment! Surely you have not forgot?" Mrs Bennet enquired peevishly, yet with some affection. A fortnight with the loving Bingleys had had an effect on her.

"Indeed I have not, Mrs Bennet," reciprocated Mr Bennet.

Mary thought it would be appropriate timing to broach the subject which she wanted to discuss. She would not let another moment pass; she needed to talk about the school.

"The Meryton School for Girls…" she began.

"Hah! Such foolishness!" exclaimed Mrs Bennet. "I knew you would think so too, with your sense. But no one would listen. Mr Bennet has already made arrangements for money to be at your immediate disposal, but I warned him not to be too precipitous, knowing that you would not entertain the idea of running a school as well as looking after Longbourn, as you do so admirably." She paused to take a breath.

"You are quite mistaken, Mama…" Mary began again, but her mother was in full vocal flight.

"Then your uncle Russell, always a silly man with absurd views…"

"My dear, that is most unjust; you always speak so disparagingly of him, yet he entertained us royally while we were at Willow Wood."

Ignoring her husband's interruption, Mrs Bennet enunciated, "…your uncle Russell pronounced that he would give money to set up the school, and your uncle Philips offered part of his house, and Mr Bingley wanted to donate books. I told them all it was wasted talk and that their time would be better spent playing whist."

"Mama, I simply do not know how to show my gratitude to everyone for their kindness."

"Kind it may be, but foolish too."

"No, Mama, not foolish. I shall be delighted to run a school for young girls."

"Well!" exclaimed Mrs Bennet, fanning herself in some agitation. This was not the reaction which she had anticipated.

"There you are, my dear," Mr Bennet triumphed. "I told you that Mary would be delighted. My very words, if you recall?"

"Tush! How can I remember all the words you say?"

Mary continued, giving an all-too-brief summary of her rationale. "I wish to educate today's young girls in order to make a better future for women, to help them towards a life of independence." Even to herself this sounded drab and drear, words out of a dull book and not from the heart. They were hardly words to inspire or convince anyone.

"I commend you, Mary!" Mr Bennet said, with some feeling, as the father of five daughters who were totally dependent on him. Turning to his wife, he commented with a wry smile, "You see, Mrs Bennet, all her reading has not gone to waste, after all."

This ironical observation was not wasted on Mary, always attuned to the nuances of language and how expressions could be moulded and manipulated.

"Do not fret, Mama. I shall be doing something worthwhile, and you, with your free spirit and independent views, surely would not deprive other young ladies of the opportunity to develop the same!"

"Well said, Mary!" Mr Bennet enjoyed this clever approach.

Mrs Bennet softened. "If this is what you really want, then I shall of course be happy for you. Anything is better than marrying that scoundrel, Fitzroy."

Mary had no wish to discuss Fitzroy Sinclair, now or at any time in the future. "All that is behind us. The school is before us." She stood up. "Now I should like to walk into Meryton, and offer my thanks to my aunt and uncle Philips for their kindness."

"Take the barouche, my dear," offered Mr Bennet. "The evenings are drawing in. You do not want to be returning at dusk."

"I shall walk, thank you, Papa. I do not intend to stay above an hour."

"Just the three of us now!" Mrs Bennet suddenly stood up and made her way to the door with Mary. "I must remind Cook that there will be only three for dinner. Otherwise she will present us with a banquet to gorge ourselves on, and my constitution would not stand up to it."

When Aunt Philips spied Mary walking down the main street in the direction of her house, she lifted her skirts and rushed down the pebble path towards the gate with her arms outstretched in welcome.

"I am so glad you are come, my dearest niece. It has been a long six weeks, with such a mixture of happenings. Your mother has told me all. I am so sorry, my dear, about your beau turning into such a rogue, and you with all your pretty gowns, too. And your mama said you had pretty ringlets. Where have they gone?"

Mary was relieved that her aunt did not question her about Fitzroy.

"Such excitement here too, I declare! Two farmers were brawling over land rights over at Bayston, and Mr Philips was called early this morning to settle the dispute. He is not yet returned. Come in, come in!" Aunt Philips led the way into the house.

Mary said, "Aunt, I have come particularly to thank you for your generosity. The Meryton School for Girls! I can hardly believe it even yet. To give over some of your house is more than anyone could ever ask. How can I thank you enough?"

"It will be good to hear the happy voices of children, something which we have sadly had to do without all these years. It will make up for Mr Philips and me not being able to have children of our own."

To diffuse the inherent sadness of unfulfilled hopes which Aunt Philips usually managed to conceal by her jolly and brash outer appearance, Mary said, "Dear aunt, I long to see the rooms. I have almost forgotten them."

"Indeed, they were shut up for years. Now they are aired and dusted. Mr Tremayne helped to get it spick and span. So very kind of him, do you not think?"

Mary listened to this with some amazement. "Yes, very kind!" she responded politely.

Oh! how she wished she could tell Charles how very kind and thoughtful he was, and how much she loved him.

"And he is a veritable handy-man too, mending and fixing, white-washing walls, all so that it would be ready for your return. He worked day and night, like a man possessed, and all this was in between helping Mr Philips with his legal work."

Aunt Philips collected a large, old key from a hook in the vestibule and held it up for Mary to inspect. "The key to your future!" she laughed. "Follow me!"

Aunt Philips unlocked the door at the end of the panelled hallway with its old oak beams, and led the way down five steps into the two-storey return. This part of the house had originally been the servants' quarters, where food was prepared for the owners and hostelry guests, and where servants lived, ate and slept, their keep acting as part of their wages.

There was a long corridor with a large bolted back door at the end. "That will be the entrance to the school," Aunt Philips explained, pointing towards the door.

There were four more doors: two to the left and two to the right, one of the latter located under a sloping wooden staircase, which in turn led to what had been four sleeping quarters above.

"These two rooms will be a cloakroom and a store room," Aunt Philips was saying as she opened each of the two doors to the right. "Charles put up these rows of pegs. He made these shelves, too!"

Mary was almost in a daze as she took in all of these new ideas. Her aunt led her through the first of the doors on the left, which opened up into a spacious apartment to be eventually converted into the main schoolroom. It had originally been used as the kitchen, with wooden tables, ovens, open cooking fires and bustling red-faced cooks. Now it was completely empty, except for a fireplace with a clean but blackened grate. It was a light, airy room, with the September afternoon sun, brighter than it had been for months, shining onto the walls which Charles had painted.

Aunt Philips walked briskly to the front corner of the room, between the fireplace and a window looking out onto the stable yard. "I can imagine your high, professorial desk positioned right here, and there in front of you will be three rows of desks, and twenty shining faces looking up at you expectantly."

Mary could imagine the desks, smelling of new polish, and the fire brightly burning in the grate. Looking out of the window, she asked, "And that is where the quadrangle will be?"

"Yes. Of course, it will need to be paved evenly to prevent the girls from tripping and falling."

"And for hopscotch!" Mary gleefully remembered the game she used to play with her sisters on the paved area at Longbourn.

"And skipping games! Do you remember *Old Lord Nelson*? How you girls just loved this one." Aunt Philips began to recite the skipping rhyme which had been written to commemorate the great Admiral Lord Nelson, who won the Battle of Trafalgar of 1805 but died in battle. As she recited the rhyme, she acted it out, except for the last two lines, which were beyond even her energies.

"Old Lord Nelson lost one eye,
"Old Lord Nelson lost the other eye,
"Old Lord Nelson lost one arm,
"Old Lord Nelson lost the other arm,
"Old Lord Nelson lost one leg,
"Old Lord Nelson lost the other leg;
"Old Lord Nelson fell down dead."

Mary watched her aunt with amusement and with happy memories of her own childhood. "Oh, Aunt! I could almost skip like a child! This is all so exciting."

When Aunt Philips had regained her breath, she led Mary across the corridor and up the stairs.

"Your uncle and I have enjoyed ourselves so much thinking about this whole project. It has given us a new lease of life! Two of these upper rooms will be for the older girls, do you not agree, to give them peace and quiet for individual study? One will be a store room, and this one," she said, opening the door and waving her arm in a wide arc, "will be the headmistress's study!"

Mary laughed. Never in her wildest dreams had she considered having her very own study! It sounded very grand!

"Now, come on downstairs to see the last room! It is the only one which has something other than four bare walls."

The last room had been the servants' parlour, where they could rest after a hard day's labour. It was not as large as the first school room, but what it contained completely transfixed Mary. She stood at the door, her eyes wide. There before her, like a beacon in the centre of the room, was an upright piano with a smooth walnut casing.

"A piano!" Mary hugged her aunt for joy. "This is indeed too much."

Mary opened the piano lid and ran her long, tapering fingers delicately along the white keys. She sat down and began to play the children's song which had been part of her very own childhood, *Come Lasses and Lads*. As the music echoed around the empty room, in her imagination she could hear the happy voices of children singing to her accompaniment.

Come lasses and lads, get leave of your dads
And away to the maypole hie,
For every fair has a sweetheart there
And the fiddler standing by,
For Willy shall dance with Jane
And Johnny has got his Joan
To trip it, trip it, trip it, trip it,
Trip it up and down,
To trip it...

When she had finished playing, she continued to sit at the piano in her imagined future scene. Her face was flushed with happiness.

"Thank you! Thank you!" she whispered, her emotions beginning to overcome her.

"This is not a gift from us, my dear. It is from Mr Tremayne."

"From Charles? But..."

"He sold his horse. Everyone said he was a fool, but nothing would do but he sold it to your uncle Russell, for fifteen guineas, and went straight out the next day and bought this piano with the money!"

Mary now was completely overcome and wept for joy. Charles had sold his horse, for her, to buy her this beautiful piano for her school!

"Oh, dear!" Aunt Philips came to her side and put her arm round her shoulders. "This will never do! You sit there and compose yourself, while I go and tell your uncle that you are arrived safe and well. I heard his carriage arrive while you were playing. Come into the drawing room when you are ready."

The jolly lovers' song continued to sound merrily in Mary's ears, but the words became distorted with a yearning in her heart:

For every fair has a sweetheart there
And the fiddler standing by,
For Mary shall dance with Charles
And Mary has got dear Charles
To trip it, trip it, trip it, trip it,
Trip it up and down... the aisle...

Mary's tears of joy and gratitude turned to tears of piteous heartache as she remembered Charles's voice, his touch, his very being. How she would give anything to be his sweetheart, to dance with him again, to capture his heart as he had captured hers!

But it was not to be.

With this stark realisation, and the philosophy that Sadness and Joy would always ride together, she straightened herself up, dried her eyes, and walked sedately through to the drawing room, with a smile on her face, to thank Uncle Philips for his generosity.

Uncle Philips was the kind of man who expected gratitude to comprise two words, "thank you", and to move on, so, no matter how effusive Mary would like to have been, he would hear no more and changed the subject.

"My dear," he asked his wife, "did you tell Mary of our meeting with Reverend Farnham today, after morning service?"

"No, it completely slipped my mind, what with Admiral Lord Nelson and lasses and lads!"

Uncle Philips looked nonplussed, but he refrained from asking what his frivolous wife meant by this unusual comment. "The vicar listened attentively to all we had to tell him about your school. He was surprised that it was the first he had heard of it, but we assured him that it had been decided between last Sunday and this Sunday, and there was nothing secretive about it. So he was satisfied on that score. He intends to go to Longbourn tomorrow to discuss the school. A good sort of fellow! I knew he would be impressed!"

"Mary, tell your Mrs Hill that he particularly likes scones, freshly baked and warm," Aunt Philips advised.

"Now, my dear aunt and uncle, two of the most generous souls in the world," said the smiling Mary, with polite regrets, "it is time for me to return home before it gets dark."

"Take my carriage, my dear," offered Uncle Philips.

"No, Uncle, I prefer to walk. I have so much to think about. So much to take in!"

CHAPTER XXV

OPPOSITION

"Excuse me, Miss Bennet," Mrs Hill said, as she entered the back parlour where Mary and her mother had been sitting for most of the morning.

Mary was positioned at the escritoire, pen and blank page before her. She was totally absorbed in the possible combinations of words which she needed in order to express her thoughts and feelings clearly, so that there would be no misunderstanding or foolishness.

Mrs Bennet was proudly sewing the first of her planned total of twenty seat cushions for the children to sit on in her daughter's school, "to protect their little posteriors", as she had announced gaily when Mr Bennet had first questioned her about this activity.

"Yes, Hill?" Mary looked up abstractedly from the still-unwritten page.

"Your father desires your presence in his study."

"Does he know that we are extremely busy at present?" grumbled Mrs Bennet, but with a smile and a giggle. Such a comment had rarely, if ever, been uttered by Mrs Bennet in all her married life. She now was imbued with a mission, and her invigoration suited her. "Mary and I are hard at work!"

"I am sorry, ma'am, but Mr Bennet requires Miss Bennet's assistance immediately." For Mary's ears only, as they left the parlour, she whispered, "He mentioned moral support. Reverend Farlowe is in there with him. There have been raised, angry voices these past twenty minutes, ma'am."

When Mary entered the study, both men stood up and Reverend Farlowe stiffly bowed while Mary politely dropped a neat curtsy.

Reverend Farlowe was the Church of England vicar of Meryton, accountable to the Suffragan Bishop of Hertford, who acted on behalf of the bishop in the Diocese of St Albans, that old cathedral city of Verulamium. He was sitting with his back to the window, silhouetted against the morning sun. He was aging badly, with deep furrows in his forehead. His completely bald pate reflected the sunlight around the curvature of his cranium, resembling the corona surrounding the sun in eclipse. His face was as dark and thunderous as the blacked-out sun.

Mr Bennet looked grim. Mary had rarely seen her father so serious, with such fiery eyes. What could have passed between these two men within the confines of her father's quiet haven?

Without any of the pleasantries usually afforded by way of greeting, Reverend Farlowe aggressively asked as a statement, "I hear you have plans to start up a school for girls in Meryton?"

Mary disregarded his frowning countenance. He was relatively new to the district, and, not knowing all the families intimately, he rarely smiled even when praising the Lord or offering congratulations after wedding ceremonies. This had been amply illustrated three years before, shortly after his taking up the incumbency in Meryton parish church, at the joint marriage of her sister Jane to the affable Mr Bingley and of her radiantly happy sister Elizabeth to Mr Darcy.

"Yes, indeed, Reverend Farlowe. It is a most exciting venture."

"And one which will go no further!" Reverend Farlowe clasped his hands together in pious objection.

"Our vicar objects," Mr Bennet offered, clenching his teeth in an attempt to stem his anger for politeness's sake. "I have been trying this past hour to convince him otherwise."

"It is as absurd as it is unfeasible. For a young woman who is reputed to be intelligent and learned, you show a complete want of intellect. A school for girls is preposterous, and to suggest that a woman could possibly teach is laughable. Have you no sense, girl?" The reverend's voice rose in pitch with every sentence.

"Sir, I protest!" Mr Bennet objected to this verbal barrage on his daughter in his own peaceful and secure inner sanctum.

Mary listened in astonishment as Reverend Farlowe heaped insult upon insult, wondering which peculiar Christian values he espoused, but it was his insolent term of address which cut her to the quick. Lately her confidence had risen with the support of family, and now she might be in danger of losing it all, faced with this tirade. However, in true spirit, with absolute propriety against his incivility, she held her head high and responded calmly and coolly.

"I must confess that I am surprised by your opinion, sir. I should have thought that you, as a man of the world and a devout Christian, would have welcomed the education of your flock, so that they may understand the scriptures more fully."

"The scriptures need to be taught by those who know how to do it, and not some self-appointed instructress!"

"I had assumed that you would wish to present the school with weekly useful religious tracts to edify the minds of young girls. These would, as a matter of course, be followed assiduously."

"I do not doubt that you can follow ideas, but you are but a young miss, barely old enough to be out on your own, let alone to be in charge of educating our children, whether you follow religious tracts or not."

"But, you see, I had hoped that you, yourself, would come once a week to give Bible instruction and to offer moral guidance to the women of tomorrow. That would make for a better community, do you not think?"

Reverend Farlowe could not disagree. "Moral guidance will always be of benefit to any community."

"Exactly so!" Mary smiled politely, knowing that on one count she had won a victory, though whether it had been morally won was debatable. "You suggest that as a woman I could not possibly teach. What about governesses? These are exclusively women, who are admirable in their sphere as educators of our gentry."

"That is a different matter! They teach in the pupils' homes."

"Have you considered the numerous 'dame schools' in our towns and villages?"

"You can hardly compare a few old women teaching a handful of boys reading, writing and arithmetic to proper instructors."

"There are many dame schools in your bishop's diocese of St Albans. I believe there is even one in Verulam Road, the street where the Diocesan House is located, under the very nose of the bishop!"

Changing tack, Reverend Farlowe persisted, "You have no experience!"

"But you have just said that I am reputed to be intelligent and learned. Where did these opinions originate? Did you dream them up? Are they mere fabrications?"

"Indeed, ma'am, they are not. I never deal with untruths."

"So they are truths, which you have discovered from conversations with your parishioners?" Mary posed the question and waited. "Is that so?"

Reverend Farlowe nodded. He had no option but to assent. "There are those who have commented on your accomplishments."

"Would these same people change their opinion if I were to set up a school and teach their children to help them become accomplished? Would they be resentful of my intrusion into their children's lives? Would they actively block the gates to my school like some ignorant, vengeful Luddites?"

Mary knew she had the winning card, because she had discovered, quite by accident through reading a political pamphlet, that Reverend Farlowe had been a vicar in a small parish on the moors on the outskirts of Nottingham in 1811, and a number of his parishioners had been Luddites, who were involved in machine breaking in the factories as a protest against bad working conditions. This was a capital offence, and two of his flock had been executed, despite pleas from Reverend Farlowe himself. He had even gone so far as to suggest that these men had been falsely accused by magistrates, who were seeking to use them as scapegoats and act as an example to other law breakers. He had been branded a Luddite supporter and, fearing he risked imprisonment, hurriedly left his parish in search of another living.

Mary had touched a raw nerve.

Reverend Farlowe loosened his neck ties. He was beginning to perspire unaccountably in the presence of the composed and assured young woman before him. Runnels of sweat trickled down the fissures between his scant eyebrows. He blinked them away.

"I see you know much about gossip-mongering," a cheap attack, "but how little you know about facts. Do you not know that schools for girls are unheard of?"

"You are misinformed, sir," argued Mary stoutly. "You, with your own radical views, must surely have heard of

Newington Green, the home of so-called dissenters and revolutionaries!"

Reverend Farlowe was beginning to look flustered.

Mary continued, "It was also where Mary Wollstonecraft had her school for girls. A fact!"

"Mary Wollstonecraft!" He sniffed in scorn. "Known at the time for her immorality, and her children outside marriage!"

"Best remembered for all time for her passionate belief in the rights of women!" Mary countered.

"Rights of women!" The vicar shook his head disparagingly.

"In your time in Nottinghamshire, you were a staunch supporter of workers' human rights, were you not?

Reverend Farlowe would rather not be drawn on that best-forgotten period of his life, so he remained motionless and unspeaking.

Mary continued, "Many of those workers were women, were they not?"

There was no answer to what was becoming a relentless opposition to the views he had started with.

"As a Christian, do you oppose human rights? As a Christian, can you honestly wish to deny girls the right to be educated?" Mary asked, but she did not expect an answer. "Mary Wollstonecraft wrote about human rights in her books, and in her very first one, *Thoughts on the Education of Women*, she tells the reader about the school she started in Newington Green, a school to educate girls, as their human right. Her church supported her."

Reverend Farlowe now spoke. "My dear Miss Bennet, that was in London! And the church you speak of was the breakaway Unitarian Church. Meryton is a small community and my church is the Orthodox Church of England. The bishop would take a dim view, if I were to support this school which you propose."

"Then perhaps I should approach the Methodists?" Mary formed this question with a smile. With staunch conviction she stated unequivocally, "I can assure you, sir, that one way or another this school for girls will come into being, and before the year is out." She added sweetly, "However, I had hoped that you, as the minister of my own church, would be sitting on the board of trustees, and officiate at the inauguration. It would be a blow to so many parents if you appeared to be cast out."

This biblical allusion upset Reverend Farlowe. He had been cast out of his last parish for his unorthodox leanings; he did not wish to be cast out of Meryton, like Lucifer from the Kingdom of God.

"Very well," he sighed. He knew he had lost his argument, but now made it seem as if he had not been presenting his own views. "Perhaps I could persuade the Bishop of Hertford."

"You might remind him that it is only five years since the Church of England formed the National Society for Promoting the Education of the Poor, and he might wish to apply to the Bishop in St Albans to make Church of England funds available, to assist the more needy families in our community by giving their children an education."

It was evident that Reverend Farlowe was storing up as much ammunition to convince the bishop as possible, so that his own status in Meryton was not compromised. As a vicar, his tenure was far from secure, and, however much he might wish to contribute to needy families himself, his income was based on the impropriation of tithes, a tenth part of goods levied or equivalent taxes, solely based on agricultural output of the parish. In this year without a summer, such output had been scant and consequently his living had been adversely affected. He would have to apply to the bishop for funds.

Mr Bennet, who, after a lifetime of sparring with his wife, was a master at knowing when a battle was on the brink of being won, now made the final decisive assault. "Sir, the Bennets are well-respected in the area, and my wife's family, the Gardiners, are a long-standing family of means in the town, going back for five generations. I believe I can speak for the rest of the people of Meryton and surrounding district when I say that they would welcome you as chairman of the board of trustees of Meryton School, as a mark of the esteem in which the people hold you in your office as Church of England minister."

"Very well," Reverend Farlowe repeated, now recovering some equanimity as he imagined himself as chairman. "If I am to approve this school and convince the bishop, what about the legalities? Miss Bennet, have you considered them?"

Mary was aware that his mode of address to her was now respectful. "My uncle, Mr Philips, is one of the benefactors. He has most charitably offered part of his dwelling, the Gardiners' family home, no less, to be converted into appropriate premises. He is an attorney, as you know, and presently he is investigating all aspects of the law surrounding the opening of a new school."

Mr Bennet added, "You can have no doubt on his capabilities in all matters legal. He is renowned and revered throughout the community, dealing with the Inclosure Acts and land disputes, rights of access, theft, common assault and all types of criminal activity. He defended some of the Littleport rioters..."

"Yes, yes!" interrupted the minister impatiently. In his support of many of the poor people of Littleport and the surrounding district, who had been impoverished when their land had been taken over by the Inclosure Acts, he had had many dealings with Mr Philips. He knew him to be a good and fair man whose first priority was to bargain for a secure future for the victims. "And who are the other benefactors?"

Mary spent the final quarter-hour of this interview with Reverend Farlowe expressing her gratitude to Uncle Russell and Mr Tremayne, extolling their capabilities and what an excellent contribution they each would make to the effective running of the school. Uncle Russell's annual philanthropic patronage would ensure that the school would be secure financially for years to come, until such time as the school would become self-supporting. His charity would be a moral lodestar to promote the Christian values of the school. Mr Tremayne's donation of the piano would bring music and joy to the pupils, as well as facilitating praise of the Lord through accompaniment to hymns in the Church of England hymnal.

She concluded with an assurance that their school would be a success and that she and Reverend Farlowe must now work together, with a common goal, to spread the good word round the town and its environs at every opportunity, beginning with the next Sunday's morning service.

When Reverend Farlowe was gone, Mr Bennet and Mary enjoyed a happy half-hour before luncheon discussing his weaknesses, and how clever Mary had been in using these against him.

"My dear Mary," Mr Bennet said, "you have triumphed where I failed. He stolidly refused to listen to my opinions, yet you were able to convince him."

"Papa, there is no defence against logical argument."

"Now, Mary, it was not all logical argument," Mr Bennet said, raising his eyebrows in amusement. "You know that you deliberately cast some barbed remarks in his direction. These were cunning, if not underhand, manoeuvres to outwit him."

"One cannot deny that where logic fails, emotions may succeed in winning an argument." Mary smiled demurely. "However, I suspect that you too were using a similar strategy when you forced him to succumb to the seventh deadly sin, the most serious of all."

"Pride!"

"For which Lucifer was cast out of heaven!" Mary began to laugh quietly at the pincer movement perpetrated by her father and her on the poor, unsuspecting, departed vicar.

"I cannot decide into which category Reverend Farlowe should be placed. Is he simply a stupid man and easily led? Or is he a genuine champion of human rights, male and female? Or does he fear adverse reactions from his parishioners if he refuses to give you support, which would result in his losing his tenuous living? Or is he mainly lured by pride when he imagines himself sitting at the head of the table as chairman of the board?"

"All of those in equal amounts, Papa. However, let us accept that, without the support of the church, there would have been no school. We were all naïve to have thought otherwise."

CHAPTER XXVI

TIDES OF CHANGE

Luncheon was over, Mrs Bennet wished to continue with her new hobby of cushion construction, Mr Bennet had just retired to his study to mull over the interview with Reverend Farlowe, and Mary was about to sit down to finish the letter she wanted to write to Charles, when Aunt Philips was admitted to Longbourn and entered the back parlour in a state of agitation and breathlessness.

"Sister, Sister!" she panted, taking a breath after each word.

"Pray, sit down, Aunt," advised Mary.

"Mary! Mary!" Aunt Philips greeted her niece, as she took heed and flopped down into the comfortable armchair which Mr Bennet favoured when he spent time in the parlour.

"Good heavens! Anyone would think you had run all the way from Meryton, Sister!"

"I have! I have!" Aunt Philips was speaking in doubles. "All the way! All the way!"

"Calm yourself, Aunt. Let me get you some sal volatile to assist you."

"No! No!"

"Whatever is the matter, Sister? Pray tell us before we two become as breathless as you are, in anticipation!"

"It is Mr Bolton! Mr Philips is almost out of his mind and doubts if he will be able to carry on, what with riots and arguments and legal wrangling!"

"What has happened, Aunt, to occasion this? And what has Mr Bolton done to cause my uncle such worry?"

"He has upped and left, that is what has happened. Mr Bolton has gone!"

"Gone where?" Mary and her mother asked simultaneously.

"Gone to Bath!" Aunt Philips almost squeaked the response in her dismay and disgust. However, her breath was now almost fully restored and she explained the circumstances. "He received a letter yesterday from Mrs Maria Tamworth, who has found a position for him as an attorney in Bath. Her father has connections, and she has the money, so between the two of them they have persuaded him to go to Bath, leaving Mr Philips in the lurch."

Mary was inwardly delighted that she would not have to suffer the company of Mr Bolton ever again, or to put up with the looks and glances of her aunt Philips who might still entertain the hope that Mary would marry him.

"Do we understand that all is forgiven and that Mrs Tamworth will now marry Mr Bolton?" Mary asked.

"I am given to understand that she stated so categorically in her letter. When he arrived at Mr Philips's rooms in town, he announced that he had already left his lodgings, paying the rest of his month's rent to his landlady, with a few extra shillings to boot. He informed Mr Philips that he was resigning his position as apprentice attorney, thanked him for his time in Meryton and left in a hired cart which was to take him to London, where he would join the fast mail coach to Bristol, where Mrs Tamworth's high phaeton would meet him."

"We must wish him well, Aunt, do you not think, because he is certainly assured of a comfortable future."

"No, Mary. I find it difficult to wish him well. Had he given Mr Philips more advance warning of this precipitous decision, then I should have felt more disposed to wish him well."

Mary smiled at this nonsensical combination of words.

Mrs Bennet put down her sewing and gravely commented, "I always said he would be a bad choice of husband for you, Mary, and I was right!"

Mary thought that this had been her mother's opinion at the time when the unmentionable Fitzroy was a most likely suitor for her hand in marriage. She was glad that at least her mother's and her own opinion concurred now. Mr Bolton would have been a disastrous choice in every way.

"Mr Philips and I have long entertained the hope that Mary and Mr Bolton would wed..."

"A silly notion, Sister!" interrupted Mrs Bennet with conviction.

Ignoring her sister, Aunt Philips continued, "...and we would have welcomed him into the family."

Mrs Bennet tutted.

"With this being a leap year, we went as far as to think that Mary should ask him to marry her."

"Really, Aunt!" exclaimed Mary in some alarm.

"If he refused he would have to pay a fine of one pound or two silk dresses, so you would win either way!"

Mary shook her head. Marrying Mr Bolton could never be construed as a victory!

"Do not shake your head, Mary. That is what we thought. However, after this... this betrayal, I am heartily glad that no such matrimonial ideas were promoted." Then remembering her own husband, she cried, "Oh! Oh! Poor Mr Philips! He came home in such a state and refuses to go back to his work until his head settles."

"Surely he must go back to work, Aunt! There is much to see to, including legal requirements for the school." This was paramount in Mary's thoughts at present, after the

215

assurances which had been made by her father to Reverend Farlowe less than two hours before.

"He has taken to his bed!" Aunt Philips moaned. "Oh! What shall we do?"

Before the afternoon had given way to evening, Mary had accompanied Aunt Philips back to Meryton to offer remedial help to Uncle Philips in his distraught state. She had encouraged him to come downstairs to discuss urgent school business. By the time the evening sky had turned a deep purple, Uncle Philips was back to his usual energetic and practical self. Mary had worked with him as they examined numerous legalities regarding the new school, and indeed she had helped him pore over some legal precedents regarding land rights. Much work had been completed.

"Upon my word, Mary," he affably said, as she stepped into the barouche which he had offered to take her home, "I think that if the school fails I shall employ you as one of the first female apprentice attorneys at law, and be damned to public opinion!"

It was only after dinner that Mary eventually was able to find time to write her letter to Charles, ready for collection by the messenger in the morning. She deliberated long and hard over the greeting, before she put pen to paper. Should it be *Dear Charles* or *My dear Charles*? How she longed to put her heart's feelings into this letter with no inhibitions! How correct *Dearest Charles* sounded to her, yet it overstepped the boundaries of convention!

My dear Charles, she wrote, *I hardly know where to begin to thank you for your support of the Meryton School for Girls.*

You will smile at my foolishness to learn that I cried when I heard from Aunt Philips that the walnut piano was from you. This generous gift exceeds all bounds, especially as I have heard that you sold your beautiful bay hunter, which was your last possession before you lose the clothes

216

off your back! But how saddened I am that now you have not the means of transport to be a frequent visitor to Meryton, where we could spend time together, on school matters if that was solely what you wished, and I could persuade you to give piano lessons once a week in the school music room.

I must also thank you for all the hard work which you put into making the school rooms habitable and whitewashed in readiness for lessons to begin. I am gratified that you should wish to have spent so much of your valuable time on this work. But I was unhappy that you did not return to Willow Wood with our uncle Russell, because, before I left, I longed to hear you play Quasi una Fantasia again like you did before, even though there was only a half moon. I wanted to see you again, if only to say goodbye!

Today has been exceedingly busy. Indeed, I have hardly had time to draw breath since my return yesterday. Reverend Farlowe, our vicar, came to visit Longbourn to voice his serious objections to a school for girls being opened in his parish, reservations about the ability of a woman to teach in a school, and worries about legalities and how he would be perceived in the community and by the bishop. If you had been able to stay at Longbourn longer, you would have been of invaluable assistance to Papa and me in our arguments. Papa and I did sterling work, however, in convincing the dull man that it was in everyone's best interests if he were to agree to support the school. It was to our advantage that he was particularly anxious to outdo the Methodists by giving the support of the Church of England. What would your landlady think of that, I wonder? What would poor Miss Kenyon have thought? He was finally convinced by Papa's master stroke that none other than the vicar himself should be chairman of the board of trustees. It cannot be to our disadvantage to have his support and that which he represents, so we must learn to get on with him as best we can, in the interests of the school's success.

Aunt Philips was here at Longbourn this afternoon, and she was in such considerable distress that I was almost on the verge of giving her some smelling salts to aid her. I do not know if she was more agitated by the fact that Mr Bolton had left, or that Uncle Philips had taken to his bed. You described Mr Bolton as "shallow". It is surprising how deep Mrs Tamworth must deem him to be, because she has retrieved him, lured him back with the bait of a lucrative living as an attorney at law and the promise of a comfortable existence as Mr Maria Tamworth! I wonder if ever the day will dawn when women's rights progress so far that men will take their wives' names?

Aunt Philips reminded me today that 1816 is a leap year, and that old traditions die hard. I so much want to take advantage of the fact. I hesitate to do so, for fear of disappointment, or that you would think I was being foolish. My recent foolishness in matters of love is for all to see and to censure. But, above all others, I most desire your good opinion.

I left Mr Philips in good spirits, once we had managed to sort through impending school business and immediate community affairs which needed attending to. He almost offered me employment. But he is in urgent need of an apprentice attorney to fill the vacancy which Mr Bolton's sudden departure has left, and I feel sure that he would be in search of someone whose capabilities have already been proven to him.

We shall meet at the inauguration of Meryton School for Girls, as a matter of course, though when the full moon shines bright through my window, I shall be thinking of you.

With affection, Mary.

Mary reread the letter once, blushing at times when she knew she had been forward, but she also knew that, if her sentiments were to go unheard now, they would be forever silent and she would have lost Charles irrevocably. She sealed the letter without further ado and gently brushed it with her lips before placing it on the silver salver on the hall table, in readiness for the messenger on the morrow.

Mary rang for Mrs Hill and then wrapped herself in her Paisley shawl.

"If my parents ask for me, Mrs Hill, pray tell them I am walking in the shrubbery. A breath of fresh air will do me some good."

"Yes, ma'am. It has been a busy day, somewhat fraught, one might say." Not much escaped the notice of Mrs Hill, especially when voices were raised and emotions ran high!

In the stillness of the ephemeral evening light, Mary dandered along the paths which meandered between the rhododendron and azalea bushes, now green and lush, with next year's buds beginning to form. There would be a magnificent display next year, thought Mary: bright and colourful.

Charles was everywhere. At every turn, wherever she looked, Charles was there. Where, oh where, would he be next year? Would he be here with her in reality and not just in her heart and soul?

She wandered aimlessly to the hexagonal gazebo, the one which her father called "Mary's hermitage", and sat down in this familiar and erstwhile comforting place. Now, as she looked out at the evening star, Venus, she was consumed by a deep longing for Charles's touch, his voice, his very presence. The star, that ancient symbol of sexual love, provided her with no comforting rays of hope, as it moved relentlessly and imperceptibly across the sky. It would soon be out of sight, reappearing at dawn as the morning star, Lucifer, that bringer of light to show up the austere reality and the hopelessness. Yet Venus, as both the evening and the morning star, was also the symbol of togetherness. Would Charles and she ever be together?

Or were Charles and she two star-crossed lovers, thwarted by circumstance? Images of such lovers as Romeo and Juliet, Pyramus and Thisbe, Hero and Leander, and Lancelot and Guinevere swung out centrifugally, round and round like revolving puppets on a fairground carousel. Mary desperately tried to put these images to the back of her mind, because they were all tragic tales. Her hope that the letter to Charles could overcome the huge forces stacked against them was waning. Even the moon in its last quarter was waning, dying. Was this too a symbol? Mary was so sad. This yearning, this deep longing was gnawing away at her heart.

Footsteps were approaching, and Mary was attempting to brush away her tears when her father appeared before her, blocking out the moon and the evening star.

"I thought I would find you in your favourite place."

"My hermitage!" Mary said, feebly attempting to choke back her tears.

"It is time to go inside, do you not think, my dear? The evenings are drawing in, and you will catch your death if you stay out much longer. Your mother insists that you come indoors."

Mary leaned forward and gave him a hug around his middle, sobbing into his waistcoat, desiring his comforting arms around her.

Unused to such treatment, he simply patted her head, saying, "There, there," as if she were a little girl again. "What is it that troubles you, child?" he asked kindly.

"Everything!" she cried from the heart.

"But you have everything you could possibly want."

Mary looked up at him. "No, dearest Papa. I lack the one thing in life I most desire. The man whom I love."

"Do not fret, Mary! Some pleasant fellow with much book lore will come along and you will find love. Even I found it all those years ago, and, with Mrs Bennet's new lease of life, I may well be tempted to find it again."

Mary could not help but smile at this. "I *have* found the man I love."

"Will he not have you?"

"I do not know. I have written him a letter."

"Is this the letter which I spied in the hall?" Mr Bennet had noticed it on the silver salver on his way through the hall from his study. "Is Charles Tremayne the man?"

Mary nodded.

"Well, who would have thought it? Well done, Mary! He is a fine gentleman. Now let us go into the warmth of the house."

For all of her father's congratulatory words, Mary knew that, during her times with Charles Tremayne, little had been "well done". There had been many occasions when Charles had had every right to censure her and to be hurt by her insensitivity. What, oh what! would Charles think of her now when he read her letter? Would he scorn her? Could he love her? Would he marry her? She so wished that she could see him again.

As Mr Bennet escorted Mary back to the security of their Totternhoe stone house, bats flittered around them, their shrill squeaks just audible in the gathering darkness. Suddenly, a bright shooting star streaked across the deep azure of the northern sky. Mary cast aside all rational, logical thought, in favour of the superstitious belief that a wish made on a shooting star will be granted. She made her wish.

CHAPTER XXVII

REALITY

Each day of the following week, Mary waited for a reply from Charles, but none came. She received a brief letter, delivered by special messenger, from Uncle Russell, in which he enclosed a banker's draft for her to make some initial purchases for the school. With this she secured the services of Thomas Ridley, a highly respected carpenter, to construct desks and chairs for the main school room, two forms and thirty chairs for the music room, a bureau and studded leather chair for her headmistress's study, and four desks and chairs for the upstairs study rooms. He was also making four cabinets for storage, and six glass-fronted bookcases. This would keep Thomas Ridley and his two sons busy for a couple of months.

Mary's reply to her aunt and uncle in Willow Wood was to convey her thanks, to apprise them of all the items of school furniture which she had commissioned, to inform them of Reverend Farlowe's increasing support and enthusiasm now that the bishop had given the school his approbation, and to tell them of the bishop's gift of a one-horse chaise, as "she could not be seen walking to and from school in her position as headmistress", and how her mother already had made a total of ten cushions for the school chairs.

The following Wednesday, Mrs Hill knocked and entered the back parlour where Mary and her mother were usually to be found in the afternoon.

"Here is a letter for you, ma'am," she said, handing it to Mary. Mary's hands were actually trembling as she took it.

"Thank you, Hill," she murmured composedly.

When Mrs Hill had left the room, Mrs Bennet could keep back her curiosity no longer. "Is it from Mr Tremayne, Mary? Is it?" Mr Bennet had informed her that Mary had found someone else to attach herself to: first Mr Bolton, then Mr Sinclair and now Mr Tremayne. He had also stated that Mary was improving in her choice with each successive suitor!

Mary's heart rose and sank within the space of two beats. This letter was not from Charles, but from Aunt Russell.

My dear Mary,

Thank you so much for your letter about the progress made so far regarding the Meryton School for Girls. It is of considerable interest to your uncle and me, and we are pleased to hear that the money is being spent so sensibly.

Miss Potter, the new governess, is proving to be a most capable young woman, who possesses many skills which will ensure that Roseanna and Ellen will be welcomed into the society of gentlefolk. However, our dear children miss you every day, and your interesting and innovative ideas. They have told me about their volcano lesson and Cook using pink icing! And they are busy at present making two new puppets, to represent their favourite cousins, Charles and Mary. Miss Potter is particularly proficient at music tuition, which is a blessing now that Charles has left us. We hope that he will visit as often as his new employment will allow. Indeed, we hope that you will both visit.

Your uncle has already begun his fight for prison reform, first attending a humanitarian meeting by Mr

Wilberforce in Cambridge, and distributing pamphlets around the district. Now that Elizabeth Fry, the famous Quaker, has announced her intention to continue her fight for women prisoners in Newgate by starting up a school for the prison children, both your uncle and I are committed to help by donating money to the school funds. You see what you have started, my dear? Education has gone to our heads!

We look forward to seeing you at the inauguration, and trust that the weather will be kind to us so late in the year to allow us to travel to Meryton for that purpose, with no heavy rain to turn the roads to impassable mud, nor high winds to bowl the carriage over.

We hope for more of your news, and news of our dear nephew, Charles. Did you know that your uncle refused point blank to take his bay hunter, even though he had paid him fifteen guineas for it! I find your uncle quite an enigma at times!

Please write soon.

Your loving aunt, Ruby Russell.

Mary rushed from the room. So Charles had left, had ridden off somewhere on his bay hunter, and she knew now with a certainty that she would never see him again. Neither she nor Aunt Russell knew anything of Charles's news. He had disappeared without trace, no forwarding address, nothing. The two puppets would be another fairground mockery of the two of them, Charles and Mary, as they enacted silly plays, written by Miss Potter, to entertain languid drawing-room ladies, who would fan themselves and sip their Malmsey wine!

Mary would keep herself busy. No crying, no sentimentality for her now, There was work to attend to. She ordered Leonard, one of the stable lads, to hitch up the black mare to her new one-horse chaise, and set off to Thomas Ridley's home to see at first hand how the school furniture was progressing. Next she visited Mr Clegg's stationery store in Meryton and ordered fifty exercise books, thirty slates, ten boxes of chalk pieces, a ream of paper, one hundred pencils, thirty quill pens and a box of one hundred pen nibs, ten bottles of ink, thirty India rubbers, compasses, dividers and wooden rulers.

Then she spent an hour with Reverend Farlowe considering the texts and hymns which should be the cornerstones of the new school, and which particular readings and hymns would be most appropriate for the inauguration ceremony, which was to take place on Friday, November the first.

"It would be most pleasing if we could include the twenty-third psalm," suggested Mary. For all the correctness in the phrasing, her tone was one of assurance that her request would be met. "For me it has a special significance, and I am certain that the words will be appropriate reminders to parents and pupils about our Christian values."

"This shall be as you wish," Reverend Farlowe agreed. In fact, now he rarely, if ever, thought it advantageous to disagree with such a sweetly-smiling, formidable young woman.

"Thank you, vicar!" Mary nodded her head in recognition of his easy agreement to her wishes.

"I consider it most auspicious that the school should be officially opened on All Saints' Day," he pontificated.

"Let us hope that the pupils will behave like little saints," said Mary with a smile.

"They will, I am sure, under your watchful eye. It would be a most foolhardy child to get on the wrong side of you, my dear Miss Bennet. I can vouch for that!" he said, smiling back.

She and the Reverend understood one another now, and she had quite grown to like him for his ability to listen to reason and at the same time be ruled by his emotions.

Perhaps this was a useful mixture in a profession such as his.

When she returned to Longbourn, Leonard the stable lad took control of her black mare as she stepped out of her chaise. He looked hot, with sweat running down his cheeks.

"It's a busy day, ma'am!" he complained. "First your black mare, then the bay hunter, now the black mare again! I'll be done in by the time I gets home to my mother!"

When Mary entered the hallway, both Mrs Hill and Mrs Bennet were standing immobile by the study door. Both simultaneously put their forefinger to their lips and mouthed, "Shush!"

When Mary handed her cloak out for Mrs Hill to take, Mrs Hill tiptoed across the hall to where Mary stood stock still. Voices could be heard.

All of a sudden the study door opened. Mrs Bennet and Mrs Hill both jumped back to pretend they were simply passing through the hall, but Mary continued to stand still. She knew whose hunter was in the stable; she knew whose voice she had heard in the study; she knew who was there on the other side of the door. Her heart was pounding in her bosom, and her breathing was coming fast.

"Ah, there you are, Mary!" Mr Bennet exclaimed crossly. "We have been in here these last ten minutes waiting for you. There is a difficult matter to settle, and only you can do it. Mrs Hill, you would be better employed preparing an afternoon tea with buttered scones and butterfly cakes in order to fortify us." He held the door for Mary to enter.

"Mama, please come with me," Mary implored, taking her mother's arm, for moral support to settle this difficult matter, "if Papa will have no objection."

"No objection. Enter!" Mr Bennet invited ceremoniously. It was a rare occurrence for Mrs Bennet to come into his study, but somehow he really did not object. She had a pert and jaunty air about her these days.

Charles stood there, tall and strong, a smile spreading across his handsome face, his grey-green eyes almost glistening with emotion.

"My dearest Mary!" he whispered. He, who was so manly and strong, was quite overcome. Mary ran to him and took his hands in hers.

Mr Bennet was not going to suffer any more displays of emotion in his study. He brusquely interrupted the silence which prevailed in the electrically charged atmosphere. Even Mrs Bennet was speechless, waiting for something, though she knew not what!

"Now, Mary, I have this to say." Mr Bennet spoke in awesome tones. "Mr Tremayne has come here with a most peculiar request."

"Request, Papa?" Mary tentatively asked, hardly daring to hope what it might be.

"He has come to ask me," Mr Bennet frowned as he drew out his explanation, "if I will give him permission to accept *your* very kind offer of marriage."

"Mary!" cried her mother, scandalised out of her silence.

"Now, I have told him that this is most irregular!" Mr Bennet's smile belied his heavy words. He was enjoying this scenario immensely. "It is I who should be giving him permission to ask you to marry him, but it seems you have jumped the proverbial gun."

"It is 1816, Papa!"

"I think your recent success over the school is affecting you, Mary. You will be sitting in parliament next!"

"It is a leap year."

"Leap year or no leap year, what answer am I to give this poor fellow who stands before us? Did you ask for his hand in marriage?"

"I did, Papa."

"And do you wish to marry him."

"I do."

"And Mr Tremayne, Charles if I may, is it your intention to accept this proposal?"

"It is, sir."

"And will you make my dearest daughter very happy?"

"I will." Charles enveloped Mary in his arms. "I shall try my utmost."

"Oh, Mr Bennet, this calls for more than a buttered scone!" cried Mrs Bennet, rushing to the door. "A bottle of finest champagne at the very least."

"But, my dear, it is only four o'clock. What will Mrs Hill think?"

"Mrs Hill can go swing a cat!"

Never had Mr Bennet had occasion to quit his own study and leave it to others to enjoy, but now it seemed propitious that he should leave Mary and Charles alone together. They had eyes only for one another in any case, so he was superfluous and felt awkward.

"Pull up a chair and sit down!" he invited to cover his embarrassment. "Pull up two seats! Champagne in the drawing room in five minutes!" he said as he left his study.

When Mr Bennet had shut the door behind him, Mary was filled with indignation. She sat in the leather armchair, with her back straight. "I thought I would never see you again. You did not write."

"I could not be sure of your sentiments. Whichever way I read your words, there was always a double meaning, always a play on words which gave you an escape route."

"I feared you would think I was foolish. I could not endure your censure. It is too, too terrible!"

"You make me sound like an ogre! Are you sure you want to marry an ogre?"

Mary laughed.

"Beauty and the Beast!" he said, looking admiringly at her. He added softly, "I like your hair much better like this, Mary."

Mary smiled. She had never liked the ringlets! Then she remembered the practicalities of his being here in Hertfordshire. "But what about your work?"

"Your uncle Philips has offered me a position of apprentice attorney in his law business, and full partnership in the new year!"

"A partnership?"

"A full partnership, with a view to taking over from him when he wishes to retire. My dear Mary, how cunning of you to suggest that I apply to him! You must have delivered him some words in my praise."

"I assure you I did not."

Charles looked disappointed.

"I would have done, you know," Mary said, biting her lip and trying to retract her words, "but he had a good opinion of you anyway. What more could I have added? I know nothing of the law and its workings."

"Now, Mary, Mr Philips has given me to believe the exact opposite!"

"Where will you live?"

"With you, my dearest Mary. Mr Philips has found a detached property for sale, for immediate occupancy, suitable for you, as the headmistress of Meryton School for Girls, and for her husband, the attorney at law! Let us go tomorrow and inspect it!"

"And what about your music?"

"I have secured employment as a piano tutor," Charles said, a twinkle in his eye, "every Friday, I am given to understand, in a local girls' school."

Mary looked up into his handsome face. "Oh, Charles, I am so happy. I do not know whether I should laugh or cry."

"Laughing is better, for, if you cried, I could not wipe away your tears."

Mary looked at him quizzically.

"I have lost my handkerchief. I gave it to a lovely woman in the moonlight, and she never returned it!"

Mary untied her reticule and handed him his silk, monogrammed handkerchief. "I kept it to remind me of you."

"And I shall keep it close to my heart, to remind me of you in the hours when we are apart." Charles took her left hand in his. "Will you wear this ring for me? It was my mother's."

As Charles slipped a beautiful diamond and ruby ring onto her finger, Mary said, "I think I shall need your handkerchief again!"

Her eyes were brimming with tears of joy.

Her cup now truly overflowed.

POSTSCRIPT

Mary and Charles were married almost immediately, allowing just enough time for invitations to be sent out, the banns to be read, and a wedding dress to be made in Summerton by the tiny yet indomitable Mrs Snell, who insisted that the Lady of Distinction would approve of the delicate voile gown which was proposed, especially with the addition of cream rosebuds around the neck. Mary was radiant as she and her new husband walked proudly down the aisle of Meryton parish church, where Reverend Farlowe had officiated at the wedding ceremony. He had actually given way to a smile when he pronounced them "man and wife"!

Mrs Bennet was beside herself with joy when Kitty too was married at the end of November to Mr Doorish, the vicar of Kympton church on the Pemberley estate. Now that all her daughters were married, her nerves and attacks of the vapours grew less frequent, and she would sometimes, girlishly, ask Mr Bennet into her dressing room for a nightcap. And sometimes, just sometimes, he would follow her into her bed-chamber. Mrs Bennet kept herself busy during the day with her sewing activities: cushions for the school seats, aprons for the girls to wear during cookery lessons, tabards to be used to protect their clothing during art lessons, and she became expert in making infants' clothes.

There was much celebration when Jane produced a boy child at Michaelmas. Mr Bingley had two sisters and Jane four, so a male heir was a novelty. The child was christened Geoffrey Charles Bingley: Geoffrey after his maternal grandfather, and Charles after his father. Mr Bennet was as proud as a peacock to have a male descendant and to have the child named after him. He became as frequent a visitor to the Bingleys' estate as to Pemberley to visit Elizabeth and her Mr Darcy. The allure of coarse fishing on the Pemberley estate was almost overtaken by his desire to watch little Geoffrey grow into a sturdy, handsome boy, who would one day inherit the Bingley fortune.

The Philips hosted their usual lively soirées throughout the year, with Charles and Mary taking it in turns to entertain the guests with light music and more weighty pieces. Even Mr Walker and Mrs Adams, who would often fall into a doze during the entertainment after overeating at dinner, would become alert when Charles took out his half-hunter fob watch, with the express purpose of timing Mary as she played the fast rondo *Alla Turca*. The guests even went as far as to indulge in some gentle betting, attempting to predict the exact time to the nearest second, and money was heard to change hands! Mrs Bennet declared that she now much preferred Mozart to any Scottish airs, but Mr Philips, who enjoyed dancing with Mrs Philips, would ask Mary to indulge him and play a lively piece from north of the border which would be suitable for a square dance!

Lydia and George Wickham continued to move from place to place with the army, never settling down to a normal social life, and remaining childless. Hers was a sad existence, punctuated less and less by "larks" which would make her laugh. Understandably, Mary was not particularly disposed to keep in contact with Lydia, but for her mother's sake she would write each Michaelmas and send her five pounds to buy new dresses and ribbons for her bonnet, in the knowledge that George Wickham still spent more money than he could afford on gambling with his captain friends.

It may be assumed that Fitzroy and Matilda enjoyed their honeyed life in Wiltshire on his Blandon Estate, despite Mrs Bennet's humorous prediction that they would probably wilt in Wiltshire. She never tired of this saying, and, although Mary and Charles initially did not desire ever to talk about the Sinclairs again, they grew to laugh with Mrs Bennet, thereby reducing Mary's embarrassment about her affair with Fitzroy, and Charles's censure of the dandy upstart.

The Meryton School for Girls became an established institution before the academic year was out. The inauguration ceremony was a triumph. Girls from all walks of life sat on the forms and front seats in the music room, all wearing cobalt blue school dresses with white collars, while their parents sat proudly behind on the new chairs expertly crafted by Thomas Ridley and his sons. A rostrum had been hurriedly erected as a platform for the trustees. Reverend Farlowe, who officiated as chairman of the board of trustees, was filled with the satisfaction of knowing that he had persuaded the bishop to sanction this school and to release church funds to enable two deserving, poor children of the parish to be educated there. The newly appointed assistant teacher, Miss Shirley Bodkin, sat at the piano and played the opening and closing hymns. One can only surmise what nickname this lady would be given in time by these pupils, who sat all scrubbed and innocent on this first day. The most senior pupil, Mr Walker's granddaughter, read the twenty-third psalm with beautifully modulated tones. Surely all the trustees, parents and girls could not doubt that these pastures were indeed green and verdant, with assurance of a better future for the women of tomorrow! And, if Mary Wollstonecraft were alive, she would surely applaud.

Aunt Russell kept up a regular correspondence with Mary, informing her of her children's exploits, Miss Potter's abilities, Uncle Russell's growing involvement in measures to effect prison reform, and her own visits to

Newgate prison to help Elizabeth Fry set up her school for the children of prisoners. Uncle Russell never accompanied her on any of these visits; in his opinion, one visit to a prison was enough for any man in a lifetime.

What of Roseanna and Ellen, without whom Mary might never have discovered her penchant for teaching? On her visits to Willow Wood twice a year, the children would always have an entertainment prepared, under the guidance of their governess, Miss Potter. On the first of these visits, the African footman carried a miniature proscenium stage into the drawing room, and the two stringed puppets, Charles and Mary, dressed in wedding attire, acted out a wedding ceremony, speaking the words of the short play which Miss Potter had written specially for the occasion.

And when it grew dark, and the Willow Wood entertainments were over, Charles would take Mary by the hand, and together they would walk out into the moonlight, the music of Mr Beethoven's *Quasi una Fantasia* lingering in the stillness of the evening air, and look towards the shimmering waters of the lake. Charles would take Mary in his arms, and they would kiss one another softly, with Venus twinkling in the clear night sky.

FINIS